THE THRONE OF SHADOWS

EVANGELINE ANDERSON

The Throne of Shadows, **1st Edition,**
Copyright © 2023 by Evangeline Anderson
All rights reserved.
Cover Art Design © 2023 by Reese Dante

This book is a work of fiction. The names, characters, places and incidents are products of the writers' imagination or have been used factiously and are not to be construed as real. Any resemblance to persons, living or dead, actual events, locale or organizations is entirely coincidental.

All rights are reserved. No part of this book may be used or reproduced in any manner whatsoever without written permission except in the case of brief quotations embodied in critical articles and reviews.

This ebook is licensed for your personal enjoyment only. This ebook may not be re-sold or given away to other people. If you would like to share this book with another person, please purchase an additional copy for each person you share it with. If you're reading this book and did not purchase it, or it was not purchased for your use only, then you should return to a retailer of your choice or evangelineanderson.com and purchase your own copy. Thank you for respecting the author's work.

**Cover content is for illustrative purposes only.
Any person depicted on the cover is a model.**

Dedicated to:
Jen Moderson
for naming the hero of this book Liath.
Thanks for helping out my muse, Jen!
Hugs, Evangeline

PROLOGUE

One does not often hear of an ugly fairy princess, but we do exist.

I am ugly—by the standards of my court.

I am Princess Alira of the Seelie Court—some call it the Summer Court, for it is always fair and bright in my father's kingdom. And so are the inhabitants—High Fae all of them—with the palest skin, hair like spun gold, and eyes like jewels.

I am pale, all right, but I miss the mark in all other respects and thus I am ugly—at least according to my cousins, Asfaloth and Calista and my father, King Euberon, to whom I am a great disappointment.

I do not have the fair, golden hair or the jewel-toned eyes, so prized in the Seelie Court, that the other High Fae possess. Nor am I slender as a sapling, with tiny breasts no bigger than Spring buds.

This boyish beauty has eluded me all my life. I swear I came from the womb a chubby infant—so big in fact, that my passage took my mother's life, for her hips were too narrow and her body too delicate to bear me. For this, my father has never forgiven me—for my ugliness killed her beauty and deprived the Seelie Court of its Shining Star.

As I grew, I never "leaned out" as my old nurse kept hopefully predicting I would. Instead, I developed unsightly curves—broad hips and a large behind. And worst of all, full, heavy breasts tipped with large nipples and wide areolas, obscenely dark against my pale skin.

I am a throw-back, they say. A mutation, with my long, midnight blue hair and dark gray eyes like a storm on the ocean, about which there is nothing jewel-like at all. My seamstress tries to hide my over-full curves in voluminous dresses—but such garments only makes me look bigger and even more unlovely.

Of course, even an ugly fairy princess is still a princess and might be tolerated if she has strong magic. But here again, I am caught out—for I have none. I cannot do the simplest thing for myself—I cannot heal a wound if I get cut, or clean a spot from my dress. I cannot bless or curse anyone—I cannot even turn cream into butter to spread on my toast.

Not that I am supposed to be eating toast. My maid is always trying to tempt me with thistle-down tea and rose petal stew. Such delicate fare is what most of the Court enjoys and also what is considered proper for a princess of royal blood. I think my father believes that if I subsist on nothing but moonbeams and stardust, I may in time grow slender and willowy as a Fae maiden is supposed to be.

Or that was his hope for many years. But now, it seems he has given up. For today I am leaving the Seelie Court forever and he will never have to see me again.

Today I am to be married.

"Here you are, my Lady." My maid, Tansy, bustles into my room, a long white dress draped carefully over her twig-like arms. "Your wedding dress—just finished and fresh from the seamstress this moment," she tells me.

Tansy is a Brownie, sometimes also known as a 'hobgoblin' by the ruder denizens of the Seelie Court. She has a small, thin body with rough, brown, bark-like skin and a large, round head that seems too big to be supported by her skinny neck. Her nose is long and crooked but her eyes are kind.

She is considered quite shockingly ugly in a Court obsessed with beauty and symmetry, but I don't care. I chose her to be my maid because, of all those who applied for the position, she was the only one who didn't sneer when she saw me.

I chose her from among a lot of fairies, their shimmering, gossamer wings flapping idly as they gossiped among themselves in their high, flute-like voices. Some creatures may straddle the line between the Seelie and Unseelie Courts, but the fairies belong firmly in the Summer Realm. They are utter perfection with their tiny, symmetrical features and slender, androgynous bodies—my exact opposite. Maybe you can see why I didn't want one for a maid.

"My wedding dress," I say, echoing her words, but the thought brings me no joy. The man my father has agreed to give me to is from the Dark Realm—the Unseelie Court or the Winter Court, some call it—for it is always cold and barren there. Or so I have heard—I have never been to visit.

The Courts do not mix, as a general rule, except in battle, for there is a long-standing feud between the Seelie and Unseelie Realms. This is something my marriage is meant to fix—I am a peace offering—a sacrificial lamb being sent to the slaughter. The hope is that by marrying a princess of the Summer Court to a prince of the Winter Court, peace may be achieved.

But no one asked me if I wanted to be married to the Unseelie Prince. The decision was made for me and I have been given no say in the matter.

If the issue was simply my father—the King of the Summer Court—trading me away to a warrior from the Dark Realm, it would have been bad enough. But it is so much worse than just an arranged marriage to a man I do not know.

For you see, the Unseelie warrior I will be marrying today—Prince Liath Blackthorn of the Shadow Throne—is the man who killed my older brother.

And for that, I will have my revenge.

I

"How can you *do* this to me?" I demanded of my father, when he first informed me of his decision and the impending nuptials. "How can you give me away to the one who killed Quillian?"

"It is true, Quillian is gone while *you* remain."

My Father's voice was bitter and he looked at me with resentful eyes. He was tall and kingly and the Sun Crown made him look even more regal, casting its golden glow upon his royal person which was always draped in the finest of silks and satins.

Behind him on a high dais was the Shining Throne, a wide chair which was actually more of a couch, carved in mystic and magical symbols upon which only those of the royal blood of the Summer Court may sit. My father had sat there alone since the death of my mother—for which I knew he still blamed me.

"But you're giving me to his killer!" I protested again. "How can you, Father? How can you reward such treachery—such *evil*—by giving Liath Blackthorn your only daughter? By giving him *me*?"

"You will serve as a bridge between the Courts," my Father

informed me coldly. "Perhaps no more of our warriors will need to lose their lives as Quillian did, if your marriage can make peace."

"How can you wish to make peace with the killer of your son?" I could feel the tears pricking my eyes but my grief and longing for my older brother did not move my Father in the least.

"Enough of this mewling," he snapped. "Liath Blackthorn has agreed to take your hand in marriage and he shall have it, no matter how you mope and moan. You will go to the Winter Court and I will never have to see you again."

Then he dismissed me from his presence and I knew there was no more to be said—I would be married whether I liked it or not. But I still couldn't cool the burning anger in my heart against my soon-to-be husband. Especially when I thought of my big brother and how much I missed him.

Quill was my best friend and my only ally in the Summer Court—before my husband-to-be stabbed him through the heart. He was six years older than me and had long, fair hair and eyes like sapphires. He had grace and poise and he was a fearless warrior on the battlefield. In short, he was everything a prince ought to be. But he was also a kind big brother.

It didn't matter to him that I looked different than the other Fae maidens or that I had no magic. He treated me with kindness and respect and he wouldn't let our cousins, Asfaloth and Calista, bully me if he was there to stop them.

The problem was, Quill couldn't be by my side all of the time—he was often out with our father, learning how to rule, since he was the one and only legitimate heir. A woman could sit the Shining Throne of course, as long as she was a High Fae with the proper bloodlines—but not one like me, not one with no magic. And so Quillian was the one my father doted on, the one who was to rule after he stepped down.

As a consequence, I was often left to the tender mercies of my cousins—and they had no mercy—none at all. Often, Quill came upon me crying, because of the cruel things they had done to me.

I remember one incident in particular—I was around ten at the time. I had wandered into a shaded grove on the edges of the Fae lands, which were spelled to keep mortals and anyone not of the Summer Court out.

I had always preferred the shadows to the sunshine that pervaded most of the wild lands around the Seelie territory. My fair skin did not glow with golden warmth when it was kissed by the sun—instead I burned and peeled as no Fae maiden should. So I kept to the wooded glades when I was out seeking solitude.

I had gone to the grove for some privacy but then I had seen Asfaloth and Calista together doing…things I did not understand at the time.

I thought nothing of seeing them together at first. They often went off, just the two of them. Sometimes they caught squirrels or rabbits to torture and test their magic on. I often found the little furry bodies mangled and bloody when my cousins were done with them.

I wept bitter tears and dug them little graves, covering them as best I could with dirt and twigs and leaves. I had no power in me to heal them or to bring them back to life, as some of the very greatest of the royal Fae were able to do. So there was nothing I could do but bury them and weep.

On that day, I tried to stay clear when I saw my cousins in the glade below the shaded grove I was in. I did not wish to see them perform their cruel tricks on another unsuspecting animal and I knew from experience that I couldn't stop them. They would only turn on me and make my life hell for as long as it pleased them.

So I was about to move through the shadows as quietly as I could and go to another part of the wild lands, when I saw what they were doing. It seemed strange to me…so I stayed a moment to watch.

Calista had the top of her lavender gossamer dress open to show the tiny buds of her breasts. As with most Fae maidens, they were no larger than wild strawberries and her nipples were tiny pink pinpricks in the centers. They were not big, but they seemed to be extremely sensitive because Asfaloth was touching them and Calista was sighing and moaning in a way that made me think she was either in pleasure or pain—or maybe both.

Fascinated by this strange display between my cousins, I crept a little closer. As I said, I was completely innocent, for my nurse had not seen fit to tell me where babies come from or the pleasure and pain of making one. So I had no idea what my cousins were doing together. I only knew that at least they were not torturing another rabbit or squirrel or some other hapless creature.

"You like that, sister?" Asfaloth was saying as he touched her.

"Ah...yes, brother. It feels *good!*" Calista moaned and stuck out her chest, as though inviting him to do it even more.

I shifted my position and it was at that moment that my clumsy foot found a dry branch and a loud *crack* alerted them to my position.

They jumped up at once, Asfaloth scanning the forest for intruders and Calista quickly fastening her top to hide her breasts.

I tried to run—of course I did—but as I have said earlier, I was only ten and my cousins were five or six years older than me. They had me in an instant and were dragging me back to the Summer Palace between them, twisting my arms behind my back fiercely and threatening to do much worse if I cried out.

Once they got me to the privacy of my rooms, Calista cast a summoning to cause a swarm of nimble-bugs to roost in my long midnight-blue hair. Then Asfaloth put a binding on me to keep me frozen in my chair with my hands behind my back so I couldn't get them out.

The bugs were as big as my thumb and had long spotted legs—red with yellow splotches. They made a *chrr-ep!chrr-ep!* sound as they crawled through my hair and nibbled the ends of my pointed ears with their sharp mandibles.

I have never liked bugs—I know few maidens who do—and I was nearly mad with the horror of having a whole swarm of them crawling on me. I remember I wanted to scream but I was afraid one would crawl in my mouth—so I simply sat where I was, bound in place, crying silent tears and hating my cousins so much I felt like I was dying inside.

"Alira?" My older brother Quill had a shocked expression on his face when he came to find me for the evening banquet and saw my predicament. "By the Shining Throne—what happened?"

I was unable to answer—afraid to open my mouth. But my big brother waved a hand and did a quick banishment to get rid of the bugs. And then—because I was still frozen in place—an unbinding.

I fell into his arms, crying and scrabbling at my hair, as soon as the nimble-bugs were gone. Asfaloth and Calista had left me that way for *hours* in the darkest corner of my room and the feeling of those creatures crawling through my hair and all over my skin was still with me even though Quill had banished them.

"Who did this? Who would dare!" he demanded, but I didn't need to answer—he knew who, of course. Only those who also had royal blood in their veins would dare to treat a princess so. Only *they* would suffer no reprimands or reprisals. Their mother—my Aunt Lyrah—would never punish them for anything. She simply laughed and said that "children would be children" and then went back to ignoring them for the most part.

But Quill wouldn't stand for it. I saw him confronting our cousins later as I hid in the shadows—they were all about the same age, though Quill was always the tallest.

"I know what you did to my sister," he growled, glaring at the two of them. "How dare you treat a princess of the royal blood that way? How dare you treat *anyone* that way!"

Calista and Asfaloth looked at each other. They were twins—they had the same shimmering, golden blonde hair and large amethyst eyes that shone like stars. To look at them, you'd think they could never do wrong—so innocent and beautiful were their perfect faces.

But I knew the truth about them—there was darkness behind their perfection—an ugly kind of evil that never showed in their physical appearance.

"You think *we* hurt Alira in some way, cousin?" Calista asked, opening her amethyst eyes wide to give him her most innocent look. "Pray, whatever would make you think so?"

"Yes, what can you mean by such accusations?" Asfaloth demanded.

Quill glared fiercely at them both.

"Don't play the innocent babes with me—I know how you love to torment Alira!"

"Why do you care so much for her, anyway?" Asfaloth asked, making a face.

"Yes, she's such a *nasty* little thing," Calista sniffed. "And she doesn't even have any magic to make up for her ugliness."

"She's as fat as a troll's wife!" Asfaloth added. "Really, your father should have sent her to the Unseelie court as soon as she killed your mother coming out. *That's* where such ugliness belongs."

"That is *enough!*" Quill's blue eyes had been snapping with rage by this time. "How dare you speak about my sister that way? I'm telling you now, you're going to pay for the way you tormented her. You—" he pointed at Calista and made a motion with one hand, squeezing his fist hard and bringing it down in a rapid motion, "Will feel like you're walking on hot coals. Every step will be agony! And you—" he made another motion and pointed at Asfaloth, "You're going to feel like you're constantly shitting fire, cousin. Your ass is going to burn both inside and out!"

Both my cruel cousins were already dancing in pain as my big brother finished his curses, crying that they didn't deserve such harsh punishments and that he was being horrible and unfair.

"How can you do this to your own blood?" Calista whined. "Our mother is your late mother's sister!"

"How dare you? Remove the curse at once!" Asfaloth was clutching at his bottom, clad elegantly in silken breeches woven by a fairy seamstress.

Quill crossed his arms over his chest. "Not until you admit what you did to Alira."

"So we let a few bugs crawl on her—so what?" Calista exclaimed, dancing from foot to dainty foot. "She deserves it! The nasty little thing was *spying* on us!"

Of course, this was a lie. I had never meant to see them doing... whatever it was they had been doing. But I had certainly paid the price for it. That was why Quill had found me in my rooms, alone and covered in nimble-bugs.

But of course Calista and Asfaloth weren't about to admit their misdeeds. They only danced and cried in outraged pain when he cursed them with his much stronger magic.

"How long is this curse going to last?" Calista exclaimed, her pretty purple eyes filling with tears. "We only left her there a little while and my feet feel like they're on *fire!*"

"And my arsehole's burning!" Asfaloth snarled. "This is uncalled for!"

Quill gave them both a cool smile.

"My curses will last for *exactly* as long as you left Alira sitting there in the shadows, bound, with bugs crawling on her," he told them. "So if you really only left her there a 'little while' you have nothing to fear."

Then he left them, dancing and howling their outrage and pain. As you may imagine, following that incident it was quite some time before they bothered me again.

I did my part—I did my best to stay out of their way. I kept in the shadows and avoided them in Court for years. And Asfaloth and Calista ignored me—or at least they left me alone and basically pretended I didn't exist—which was fine with me. I would much rather be beneath their notice than the focus of their attention.

No doubt my cousins left me alone because they feared my brother's retribution. But after Quillian was killed, they seemed to remember me—to remember how much they loved focusing their cruelty on their younger cousin. And so it started again. My cousins had been tormenting me of late—so much so that I was almost glad to be leaving the Summer Court.

Almost.

2

I studied my wedding gown—a huge white mound of white fabric. Tansy bustled over with the crown of white flowers which would complete the outfit. I did not like any of it, but I knew I had no choice but to put it on.

"Come, my Princess," Tansy said coaxingly. "Let's get you dressed. The ceremony starts in less than an hour."

Sighing, I agreed. I reminded myself that I had a plan—a reason I was entering into this wedding without complaint instead of doing my best to run away. I had considered escape, you know—of course I had. I thought I might be able to pass in the mortal realm if I dyed my hair with witch hazel and black oak bark and concealed the pointed tips of my ears. But I had chosen not to.

I had a plan for Liath Blackthorn, my husband-to-be and murderer of my beloved older brother. A plan I meant to carry out at the earliest opportunity.

Once we were married and he had taken me away to his palace in the Unseelie Court, I would wait until he was off his guard and then I would kill him. I might die myself in the process but I had decided that I didn't care.

I would have my revenge for Quill's death, one way or another.

"Come on, let's get you into this." Tansy's soft, coaxing voice brought me back from my murderous thoughts to the present—my wedding day.

"Yes, all right," I agreed. I had bathed earlier in water scented with primroses and lilies and Tansy had brushed my hair until it shimmered like midnight blue silk. Now I allowed her to unwind the drying sheet I was wearing and help me into the virginal white undergarments which would go under the wedding dress.

First the lacy underpants, made specially for me from the gossamer of the giant albino spiders which spun only for the fairy seamstress who kept them. They barely hid the tiny patch of midnight blue curls on my mound and did nothing at all to make me feel thinner for they were cut low and the tiny strings at the sides seemed to emphasize rather than hide my wide hips.

Then a special garment which Tansy had commissioned just for me.

"It is a kind of under-halter for your breasts, my Princess," she had explained when she first showed it to me. It was made of a sturdier silk with whalebone stays that lifted my large, full breasts proudly as though they were resting on a shelf. It did not, however, cover my too-large nipples.

"Never mind," said Tansy, when I pointed this out. "You still have the underslip and then the dress itself to cover everything."

As she spoke, she pulled the long, silky underslip over my head. It was a kind of sheath made of close-fitting silk which started at my shoulders and ended at my ankles. The silky white material clung to my curves almost as though to show them off and clearly showed my nipples, poking against the thin fabric. It had long, flowing sleeves that came down to brush the backs of my hands and a slit up the center of its skirt, presumably to allow me freedom of movement.

The top of it was cut in a low V-neckline so that jewelry could be worn with it. A special necklace that a mother might pass down to her daughter, for instance. I had no such pendant to wear, however. If my mother had set aside anything for me, my father had never given it to me. He probably thought I didn't deserve any part of her, since my birth had killed her.

I wished now that I had a living mother to help me get dressed on my wedding day—to love and care for me and possibly to cry because she was losing her little girl. I wished also for Quillian who had always been so kind and supportive. But I had no one but Tansy and though she was an excellent maid and I considered her a friend, she was not family.

"And now for the dress itself," Tansy said brightly. "Let's see what the seamstress has done, shall we?"

She lifted the mountain of frothy white fabric over my head and helped me find the armholes to get into it. Then she pulled it down and straightened the long train and pointed me towards the tall mirror in the corner of my room.

I generally avoided the mirror—I did not like to be reminded of my ugliness—but now I supposed I had better look to make sure the dress was straight. And so I looked bravely into the shiny, reflective surface.

The dress was hideous.

"Oh my," Tansy said weakly as we stared at the mirror together.

I have said before that my seamstress, who was accustomed to making sylph-like dresses for the other High Born Fae maidens of the Seelie Court, often tried to make my clothing larger to hide my unsightly curves. But in this instance, she had gone far overboard.

The dress was a monstrous confection—almost smock-like in its volume. It strove to hide the fact that I had any curves at all by covering me completely in yards and yards of white fabric worked with delicate lace and frilly bows. It was the ugliest thing I had ever seen and it made my own deficiencies even more glaring even as it sought to hide them.

"Well, that's…nice," Tansy said at last, though she couldn't put any conviction into her voice.

"Nice? It's *horrid*," I said flatly. "I look like a wedding cake with too much frosting!" I moved a few steps, dragging the mound of loose fabric with me. "It's huge on me! I know my curves are unsightly, but this dress only makes me look even bigger and uglier than I am!"

"You're *not* ugly, my Princess!" Tansy said stoutly. "You just don't look like the rest of the maidens here. Except for your face," she added. "All your features are so *delicate*." Here, she stroked her own long, crooked nose. Brownies set great store by the length of that particular feature. "Your hair is lovely, too," she added.

"I *am* ugly," I said, lifting my chin. "I have curves when I should not. I will never be thin—I faced that long ago, Tansy—but I do *not* care to look like I am wearing a huge white *sack* to my own wedding!"

"Well, well—it *does* look like a sack, Cousin!"

I froze where I was at the voice coming from the doorway. Turning, I saw Asfaloth and Calista standing there.

My cousins were dressed, as usual, to match. Both wore pale lilac, though Asfaloth had on breeches and a long coat with lace at his wrists and throat and Calista was wearing a pale, shimmering gown. The color complimented their amethyst eyes and their sleek, platinum blonde hair, which both of them wore long to frame their perfect features.

My heart went cold when I saw them standing in my doorway. There was so much they could do to me—their magic had grown considerably since that day when Quill had punished them for tormenting me. And I still had none—not a drop of magic in my veins to protect myself.

"What's the matter, dear Cousin? Aren't you happy to see us?" Asfaloth sneered as he and Calista stepped into my room. "We've come to wish you joy on your special day."

"I know exactly how much joy you wish me," I said steadily. "Which is exactly as much as I wish for you."

"Oh, we *will* have joy—plenty of it—as soon as you are gone," Asfaloth told me. "And twice as much joy as soon as your tired old father finally steps down and *we* ascend the throne."

I frowned at them.

"You were made his heir when Quillian was killed, Asfaloth, but you *cannot* ascend the throne with your sister. I am certain my father means for you to choose a bride from among the Court ladies, to rule with you, as he and my mother ruled together."

"Before you *killed* her, you mean," Calista snapped. "Who says my brother cannot choose me to rule with him? There is no law against it!"

I was pretty sure there was, but I was also fairly certain they were looking for a reason to be nasty to me, so I held my tongue.

"Indeed, sweet sister, you *shall* rule by my side." Asfaloth looped an arm around her slender waist and pulled her closer. Leaning down, he placed a kiss on the corner of her perfect mouth. Only Calista turned her head at the last moment and his lips landed exactly on hers. Nor did she pull away for quite a long moment.

"Mmm, indeed I *shall*, brother," she murmured, when at last their kiss ended. They locked eyes and I was almost certain she was going to kiss him back.

For a moment I hoped that the two of them would become too engrossed in each other to bother me, but then Asfaloth pulled reluctantly away and looked down his perfectly straight nose at me.

"So, as I said earlier—we have come to wish you joy. And to give you an idea of what you can expect—since you have never seen your groom-to-be, dear Cousin."

"And *you* have?" I shot back. "He is prince of the Unseelie Court—you can't tell me you've ever been there—either of you."

"As if we'd want to visit such a horrid place!" Calista shivered delicately in apparent horror. She didn't seem to care that the place that made her wince in disgust was to be my home for the rest of my life.

"Of *course* we've never been to the Winter Court. I have seen him on the battlefield, you little fool," Asfaloth snapped. "And let me tell you, you're in for a *treat* on your wedding night!"

"Liath Blackthorn is *huge!*" Calista's eyes widened. "I saw him through my brother's eyes," she added. "Perfectly *enormous* with dirty gray skin and an ugly, twisted scar right across his face. And he has horns on his head! *Rams* horns!" she motioned to either side of her own sleek blonde head, as though to make her point.

"It's well known that the Unseelie are so twisted they'll fuck anything," Asfaloth scoffed. "Perhaps the Unseelie Royal line includes a bit of sheep somewhere in the lineage. Or maybe something even *worse*."

"I wonder if he'll put a horned baby in you when he *fucks* you tonight," Calista speculated, giving me a nasty smile. "If he can bear to *touch* you, that is."

"Oh, he'll touch her all right—he *asked* for her hand," Asfaloth sneered. "Can you imagine? *Wanting* such a fat cow for a wife?"

Since I'd been hearing their insults all my life, they barely fazed me. But knowing that Liath Blackthorn had asked for my hand was disquieting news. My father had said he'd *agreed* to take me as a wife—not that he'd *asked* for me. What could it mean? Why would he ask to wed the sister of the warrior he'd killed? And was Calista telling the truth about my husband-to-be's beastly appearance?

I knew that the Unseelie Court welcomed beings that were not conventionally beautiful—creatures the Seelie Court shunned. Goblins and Trolls and Redcaps and Sprites were among its denizens, just to name a few. It is also a fact that the Fae have the ability to breed with anything—it is part of our magic. That was the origin of the Satyrs and Minotaurs and Centaurs and various other crossbreeds. But I didn't know how I felt about marrying a crossbreed or a half-blood myself.

Don't be foolish, a little voice whispered in my head. *You're going to kill him—remember? It doesn't matter what he looks like—he's going to die!*

How, exactly, I would kill my soon-to-be-husband, I hadn't quite worked out yet. But I knew I would find a way. My hatred of my brother's killer would lead me in the right direction.

"I wonder if the baby's horns will poke you from the inside," Calista said, drawing me back to the dismal present. "Once Liath Blackthorn swells your belly with his seed." She giggled unkindly. "He's so *big* you know—I bet he'll rip you in two when he fucks you! At least if he's anything like what I saw through Asfaloth's eyes!"

I glared at her, angry enough to throw caution to the wind.

"I thought that Sight-Sharing was something only *lovers* could do, Calista. Maybe the Unseelie line isn't the only Royal lineage that has something *twisted* about it."

Her amethyst eyes narrowed as she understood my implication.

"How dare you, you nasty little slut? So what if my brother and I are close enough to Sight-Share with each other—that doesn't *mean* anything!"

"I'm fairly certain it means you've been to his bed," I snapped. "So who's the slut now?"

I had gone too far and I knew it. Calista's hand shot out and I gasped as her palm connected with my cheek. The stinging pain made my eyes water and my temper got the better of me. With a cry, I lifted my hand to slap her back—only to feel my wrist caught in Asfaloth's iron grip.

"You *dare* to try to strike my sister?" he demanded, glaring down at me. Though his fingers were long and artistically tapered, he was a trained warrior and much stronger than me.

I winced and tried not to show the pain I felt as his grip tightened and the small bones in my wrist ground against each other.

"She…hit me…first," I got out at last. I could feel my pale flesh bruising and I wondered if he would actually break my wrist. Here I had been so worried about the two of them using magic on me when actually I should have been worried about my cousin's superior strength. But I was damned if I'd beg for mercy—I wouldn't give either of them the satisfaction!

To my surprise, it was Calista who ended the stalemate.

"Now, now, Asfaloth," she chided sweetly. "Have you forgotten why we came? We must give out dear sweet cousin the bouquet we picked for her."

She did a swift summoning and, reaching up, pulled a large bunch of wilting flowers out of the air. The blooms were all withered, their petals falling off and they smelled like they were rotting. There were still roots attached, which dripped muddy water on my wooden floor.

"Here!" she said and thrust them at me.

"No!" I took a half step back—as far as I could go with Asfaloth still holding me—refusing her filthy offering. It was a mockery of our tradition, that the female relative closest to the bride should go out into the wild lands and gather her wedding bouquet. That was supposed to be a gesture of love and good wishes for a happy marriage—Calista had turned it into a malicious act.

"Take them, Cousin—with our very best wishes for happiness in your marriage," Asfaloth sneered.

"Yes, take them!" Calista said. Shoving the bouquet at me, she smeared the smelly, wilted mess against the pristine white lace of my sack-like wedding gown, leaving a muddy stain right in the center.

I gasped—I couldn't help it—and looked down at myself in horror.

"Oops!" Calista dropped the wilted flowers at my feet and her eyes went wide. "Oh *dear*—only see, sweet brother, what I have done to our cousin's *lovely* gown."

Asfaloth was laughing so hard he could barely reply. At least he finally released my wrist, which felt bruised if not broken.

"That's not a problem, darling sister," he finally managed to say. "The gown was already ugly—I think you've *improved* on it."

"I think I have, at that." Calista did a quick cleaning spell on her own hands but of course she left my dress the way it was. "Don't look so upset, Cousin," she told me. "Just do a cleaning spell. Oh wait—I forgot—you *can't*." She laughed cruelly. "I suppose you'll just have to get married in a dirty sack."

"It doesn't matter—I'm sure Liath Blackthorn will tear it off her as soon as he gets her back to the Winter Court so he can fuck her," Asfaloth remarked, also laughing. "Come sister—we must be seated at the front. I'm anxious to see if he'll even *have* her once he sees her in person."

"By the Shining Throne—if he doesn't, we'll be stuck with her *forever*." Calista rolled her eyes expressively. "For I'm sure no one else will have such a fat sow for their wife!"

Laughing at their own wit, my cousins turned and exited my rooms, leaving me fuming. But as usual, there was nothing I could do to retaliate—they had magic and I had none. I could not even clean my own dress or heal my wrist.

I could do nothing but hate them…and wonder uneasily if they were right about my husband-to-be.

3

"Oh, my Princess…" Tansy crept out of the corner where she'd been staying out of the way of Asfaloth and Calista. Brownies are very good at becoming, if not invisible, then extremely unnoticeable during times of conflict or danger.

I didn't blame my maid for making herself scarce during the confrontation with my cousins. There was only so much that they could do to me—I had royal blood in my veins. But the servants were another matter.

I had seen Asfaloth turn a butler who displeased him inside out—*literally*—his organs were on the outside of his body when my cousin was done with him. I'll never forget the muffled screams of terror and agony or the sight of his beating heart clearly visible on the outside of his chest.

He didn't live for long.

Tansy swept away the mass of ugly, wilted flowers and set about trying to clean my wedding dress. But though her cleaning skills were second to none—Brownies are excellent at household magic—the damp, putrid spot wouldn't come off. I wondered if Calista had put a staying charm on the dirt as she ground it into my gown. It would be like her to add that extra little bit of malfeasance to her magic.

"Stop," I said at last. "The ceremony is in fifteen minutes and this isn't working."

"Please, my Princess—let me try once more," Tansy pleaded. "You can't go out there with a great huge spot on your gown."

"Then I won't," I said. Reaching down, I grabbed handfuls of the frothy white fabric and began pulling it up and over my head.

"Oh, Princess—what are you doing?" Tansy exclaimed.

"Taking this damn thing off. Come on—help me!" I demanded, my voice coming out muffled because of the yards and yards of white fabric and lace and bows.

Reluctantly, Tansy helped me pull the sack-like dress off and I promptly discarded it, leaving it in a heap on the floor. Then I looked in the mirror again. As I had hoped, the stain didn't extend to the silky underslip, which was still a pure, pristine white.

I hated white. White made me look twice as big—made my wide hips even wider, my large behind *enormous*. Not to mention that the underslip was thin enough that you could see the obscenely dark rings of my areolas and my too-large nipples poking at the silky fabric.

"Tansy," I said. "I need this to be a different color."

"The underslip? Whyever for, my Princess?" she asked, clearly confused. Then a look of understanding came over her face. "Oh no—no! You're not thinking of just wearing the underslip as a wedding dress, are you?"

"Of course I am," I said stoutly. "I have no other garments that will work for the ceremony and no time to change into them even if I did. But we *do* have time for you to change the color of the underslip." I gave her a pleading look. "Please, Tansy—you know I can't do it myself."

"But my Princess, it's so...so *revealing!*" she protested.

"It's no more revealing than anything the other Fae maidens wear at Court and you know it," I told her. "It's just that they have less to reveal." I looked again at the way the thin silk sheath clung to my curves. "Liath Blackthorn ought to know what he's getting. Don't you think?"

In the back of my mind, I was thinking that if he saw how different I was from the other maidens—how thick and un-sylph-like—he might leave me alone on our wedding night. But also, I was tired of hiding my curves.

All my life I'd been told how fat and ugly I was and the seamstress was always trying to hide my body away, as though it was a shameful thing which must not be seen in polite company.

At that moment, I didn't care anymore. They all thought I was ugly? Fine—I was finished hiding it. Finished swathing myself in voluminous clothes to keep from disgusting them. Let the whole Summer Court see me as I really was on this, the last day I would ever spend among them. Let them choke on their own tongues when they saw me flaunt my curves!

"My Princess," Tansy said in a low voice. "Are you...sure about this?"

"Quite sure," I told her. "Turn it a different color—turn it black!"

"Oh not black, surely! It will seem to your new husband as though you are mourning your marriage!" she objected. "Why can it not remain white? What if he thinks...thinks you are not a virgin?" she whispered, her eyes wide.

"I don't care what he thinks," I said recklessly. "I will not wear a white gown—you can see all my bits through it," I added, appealing to her sense of modesty as I pointed to my breasts.

This seemed to change Tansy's mind.

"Well..." She sighed deeply. "All right. But I *won't* make it black. The best I can do is to have it match your eyes. Here..."

She waved her hands and said some words under her breath—a Brownie cantrip that went something like:

"Change it now,
Change it how
The Princess wants
Not how she shan'ts
White isn't right
It's such a fright
Make it gray
To match the sea
To match her eyes
To make her free."

I felt the familiar tingle of her magic against my skin—rather like a coarse bristled scrubbing brush rubbing me everywhere, if that makes sense. The sensation was uncomfortable, though not unbearable. It wasn't nearly as bad as when Calista or Asfaloth worked a spell on me. *Their* magic felt like stinging insects biting me all over.

The momentary discomfort passed and I looked down to see that the underslip had been turned a smoky gray, the exact color of my eyes, just as Tansy had promised.

The color went well with my pale skin and long, midnight blue hair. It almost matched the bracelet of bruises which were forming on my wrist where Asfaloth had gripped it, I thought grimly. I drew the right sleeve down lower, to hide the injury. I wasn't going to be able to lift anything heavy with my right hand for some time, but I would heal eventually. I always did.

As for my cheek where Calista had slapped me, it was a bit pinker than the other, but I didn't think anyone but Tansy and I would notice.

"You look lovely, my Princess," Tansy said. She spoke in a hushed and reverent voice. I looked in the mirror again and was surprised at what I saw.

For years my seamstress had been dressing me in pastels, for such were the fashions of the Summer Court. I looked dismal in pink and baby blue, lavender caused my skin to look yellow, and mint green just made me look sick. But this deep, smoky gray…it suited me somehow. It showed my curves but slenderized me a bit at the same time, because the dark color was slimming.

I looked at the girl in the mirror and wondered why I hadn't asked for darker colors years ago. Probably because I was too busy trying to fit in with those who had never wanted me in the first place.

"It's perfect," I said decisively. "And if Liath Blackthorn doesn't like it, too bad. Too bad for the rest of them too—I'm never going to see them again, anyway," I added.

"Oh, my Princess…" Tansy's large brown eyes filled with tears. "Are you *never* coming back then? Not even for a visit?"

"Why would I?" I asked. "My father hates me for killing my mother and my cousins are tyrants—you saw them." I shook my head. "No—there's no one here I'll miss but you, Tansy. And you can come and visit me in the Winter Court if you like. You know the Brownies are some of the few Fae who are welcome in both Courts."

"Thank you, my Princess." She sniffed and swiped at her eyes. "All right—we must get the flower crown settled on your head. The ceremony is almost starting."

"Make it gray too," I said, looking at the crown of pure white lilies which was meant to adorn my hair.

"No," Tansy said firmly and this time I knew there would be no changing her mind. "No, for your husband-to-be must have *some* indication that you are a virgin."

She set great store by my virtue—more than I did myself. I would have been rid of it, if I could—but no noble of the Summer Court would have wanted to help me with that particular task. None of them wished to call down the king's wrath by sleeping with his daughter—or risk having a baby as chubby as its mother as his offspring, if I should fall pregnant.

So, though I had not meant to save myself for marriage, I somehow had after all. I allowed Tansy to place the flower crown upon my head and then straightened up and looked in the mirror one more time. I readjusted my sleeves—the better to be certain my bruised wrist was hidden—and nodded my head.

"All right," I said. "I'm ready."

And by the Shining Throne, Liath Blackthorn had better be ready too. Ready to die, as soon as I married him…and then found a way to kill him.

4

There was a muted gasp when I stepped out into the courtyard, where the ceremony was being held. All of the High Fae were assembled there, waiting to see me married off to the enemy.

As I walked out into the golden sunlight, I saw their eyes widen. I had the pleasure of seeing Calista and Asfaloth look at each other in puzzlement. Where was the dowdy little cousin they had tormented so often and who was this princess who held her head high?

My Aunt Lyrah was sitting to one side of her children and she gave me a shocked and disapproving look. As for my Father, who was standing to one side of the Joining Arch, his sapphire eyes went wide for a moment and a frown spread across his face.

The Druid Priestess who was to perform the ceremony said nothing but only kept her thoughts to herself and her eyes cast down. She could barely be seen behind the roughly woven hood and cloak she wore. This was one of the only times when a mortal was invited into the Realm of the Fae and she doubtless wanted to keep from offending anyone, lest she be kept forever in the Summer Court to serve at the pleasure of the Fae King.

She probably had an iron amulet around her neck, hidden under her homespun cloak, I speculated. Iron is deadly to Fae of all kinds. It kills lesser Fae and saps the strength of the High Fae almost to the point of death. It would be powerful protection against my kind and knowing how unpredictable my people are, I wouldn't have blamed the Druid Priestess for thus protecting herself while she was among us.

Holding my head high, I stepped up to the Joining Arch, which had been woven with flowering honey-musk vines. The tiny white blossoms filled the air with a thick, almost cloying scent. I ignored my father's glare and looked around. Where was Liath Blackthorn? Had he decided he didn't want me after all?

The thought filled me with a mixture of relief and humiliation. I would never live this down—to think that a denizen of the Unseelie Court would reject me, a Princess of the Seelie Court and leave me at the altar—it was a shame that would follow me all my days.

And yet, if he failed to show, at least I didn't have to fear my wedding night. Though I was hoping to be able to find a way to kill him *before* he took me, I couldn't be sure the opportunity would present itself...

My mind was still racing when suddenly a black rip appeared in the fabric of reality. My mouth opened in a silent O as it grew taller and wider, turning into a vast black oval about seven feet by four feet. And then, out of it stepped the strangest male I had ever seen.

Liath Blackthorn was as my cousins has described him to me... only their descriptions fell far short of the mark. He was immense for one thing—both extremely tall and muscular in a way I had not seen before. All the Fae of the Seelie Court are slender—even the males. But Liath's biceps bulged and his broad chest flexed with muscle as he stepped out of the portal he must have created.

It was easy enough to see these details, since he wore no shirt. He had on black trousers and a rich black cape clasped around his broad shoulders and joined at the front with a delicate silver leaf. His skin was gray, as Calista had described it, but again, her description could not do him credit. It was the gray of shadows and smoke with a faint, opalescent gleam—in fact, not too far from the color of the underslip I was wearing as my wedding gown.

The vast expanse of smoke-gray skin was decorated in golden tattoos—markings the like of which I had never seen before. They seemed to shift patterns as he moved, gleaming in the dimness. For somehow the sun didn't shine on him—it was almost as though he had brought a patch of shadow with him from the Winter Court.

"Have you looked your fill, wife-to-be?" His deep rumbling voice startled me and I jerked my head up to stare at his face.

He did, indeed, have curling ram's horns protruding from either side of his head. They curved from his temples, framing a face that was handsome but scarred—a white ridge ran from his forehead all the way down to his right cheek, narrowly missing his eye.

And speaking of eyes—he had eyes like I had never seen before. A glowing bronze which seemed to shine from his dark features. They were even more brilliant than the golden tattoos. In fact, the only thing brighter was his long mane of white hair. It was thick and wavy and he had the top pulled back—the better to show his horns, perhaps.

I had the sudden urge to plunge my fingers into those moonlight waves...and then pulled myself up short. Where had such a thought come from? This was the male who had killed my brother—the one I was going to kill as soon as ever I could.

Only...how was I to manage it? It had seemed an easy thing when I lay in my bed at night, crying for Quill's loss and plotting my revenge. But now that I saw my husband-to-be, I wondered if the thing could be done. He was so *huge*—his shoulders were fully twice as broad as my own and I judged that the top of my head would only come halfway up his muscular arm—I would not even reach his shoulder.

Then I realized that he had spoken to me again and I had missed whatever he had said in that deep, rumbling voice because I was too busy staring at him like an idiot.

"I...what?" I asked, forcing myself to speak.

"I said, are you ready for our marriage? The Joining of the two great Courts?" he asked, lifting his eyebrows at me, which I noted were black instead of white like his hair.

"Oh...oh, yes. Of course." I nodded, feeling the fool. I *had* to regain my composure—where had all my courage gone to? I'd been brimming with it when I'd walked into the courtyard, but it had all fled when I saw the enormous Unseelie warrior who was to be my husband.

"Come, both of you, if you are willing to be Joined," the Druid Priestess said, speaking for the first time in a sweet, low voice. "Come to the Arch of Joining that you may take your vows."

I was already standing under the arch and I watched as Liath Blackthorn stepped forward to stand beside me. He seemed to loom over me in a threatening way which made my heart skitter nervously in my chest. I noticed for the first time that he wore a jeweled dagger at his side—the silver hilt set with moonstones. Who came armed to their own Joining?

Was he sorry he had asked for me, I wondered? Now that he saw me—saw that I was far too curvy to be considered in any way beautiful—did he wish he had not made this bargain with my father?

But he said nothing, only looked down at me silently with those burning bronze eyes of his, catching and holding my gaze as though he was waiting for me to speak. I, however, had nothing to say. I turned to look at the Druid Priestess, anxious to break the staring contest we had somehow fallen into.

"The ceremony is about to begin," the Priestess murmured, speaking to both of us. "Do either of you have someone you wish to stand at your side as you pledge your troth?"

It was tradition for a maiden to have her closest female relation stand by her during the Joining ceremony—and for the groom to have a friend or relative stand by him as well. But Liath and I both shook our heads.

"I have no one I want with me," I said, casting a quick look over my shoulder at my cousin Calista and my Aunt Lyrah. I would rather die than have either of them stand with me. I would have asked Tansy, perhaps—but I knew it would not have been allowed—she was a Brownie without a drop of High Fae blood in her veins.

"I had one I wished to stand with me, but he is dead," Liath said shortly.

This surprised me and I looked up at him briefly but his burning bronze gaze was too intense and I quickly dropped my eyes.

"Very well," the Priestess said, nodding. "Then we will proceed."

No doubt you have read of the way a Fairy wedding *ought* to be. A ceremony which lasts for hours and a merry celebration which continues for days afterwards. But I wanted none of that.

At my request, the ceremony of Joining would be nothing but a simple hand-fasting ritual. I did not wish to draw out this moment in the least. And to my relief, Liath didn't seem to want to either. Or at least, he made no remark or objection when the Druid Priestess pulled out a tasseled cord to bind the two of us together.

The cord was woven of two strands—one gold and one silver—to signify the Summer and the Winter Courts, I supposed. The Priestess held it up, as though asking for a silent blessing and the Court murmured as the sunlight made the gold and silver fibers glow.

"Would each of you clasp the other's right wrist so that the hand fasting may begin?" she said to us.

Liath put out his hand at once—it was nearly twice as large as my own with long fingers and short, clean nails. There were calluses on his palm—no doubt where he gripped his sword. I do not know why I noticed such details—I was nervous and my mind was grasping for something to think of other than the fact that I was getting Joined to my beloved big brother's killer.

Biting my lip, I held out my own right hand. I grasped Liath's thick wrist...and winced as he grasped mine. It was my right wrist that Asfaloth had gripped so hard before the ceremony and it was still painfully bruised. I wished I would have had time to go to the Palace healer or possibly asked Tansy to help. But though she was excellent at household magic, my maid had never been much good at the art of healing.

Liath seemed to notice my wince for he frowned and turned my hand over. He pulled up the long sleeve of my underslip, exposing the cruel bruises left by my cousin's fingers. They had been red earlier but they were turning an ugly purple now.

He looked first at the bruises and then at me, his face like a thundercloud. My heart skittered in my chest like a frightened animal—would he think I was used goods? Decide to call off the match? If he did, I would be free of him, but I would never get my revenge.

Hastily, I pulled my sleeve back down, making sure to cover the finger marks on my pale flesh. Then I gripped his thick wrist as firmly as I could and gave him a defiant look. He gave me a surprised one in return, his eyebrows lifting almost to his hairline. Then I nodded at the Priestess, letting her know we should proceed.

This silent exchange took but a moment but it seemed much longer. I didn't think anyone in the audience had noticed and the Priestess went on smoothly, as though nothing had happened.

I felt the warmth of Liath's palm and long fingers wrapped around against my wounded wrist but it seemed he was being careful, holding me loosely instead of squeezing. This surprised me somewhat—I had expected nothing but cruelty from the one who had killed my brother. I did not know what to make of gentleness instead. I looked up at him, searching for an answer but his bronze eyes were unreadable.

"High Fae of the Summer Realm and the Seelie Court, we are here today to join Princess Alira Starheart of the Seelie Court to Prince Liath Blackthorn of the Unseelie Court," the Priestess began.

As she spoke, she started wrapping the gold and silver cord around our joined arms and hands, symbolically tying us together.

"Princess Alira of the Summer Court," she said to me. "Have you come today to be joined to this male, Prince Liath—to plight your troth and join your path to his?"

My throat was suddenly so dry I couldn't speak. I opened and closed my mouth, feeling like a fish out of water. At last I managed to squeak out,

"I have," in a tiny voice that could barely be heard.

"Good." The Priestess nodded and turned to Liath. "And Prince Liath of the Winter Court, have you come today to claim this Fae maiden as your own and join your path to hers?"

Liath didn't hesitate.

"I have," he rumbled in a voice I could feel as well as hear since the vibrations seemed to travel down his arm and up mine.

"Very good." The Priestess nodded. "Then I ask that the two of you would place a hand on the other's heart and repeat my words."

I was nervous all over again. I wished now that I had on the enormous sack-like wedding dress the seamstress had made me. The thin underslip I was wearing showed far too much cleavage and my breasts felt naked beneath the silky, thin material. I did not know when I had felt so vulnerable before.

I half expected the huge warrior across from me to grab one of my breasts—they were certainly accessible, pushed up as they were by the wale bone contraption Tansy had made for me. His hands were big enough that one of my overlarge breasts would probably fit just right in his palm.

But again Liath surprised me—he placed his large, warm hand on my chest instead, above the swells of my breasts, and just over my heart. Then he leaned closer so that I might do the same for him.

Maybe my breasts disgust him, I thought, though I couldn't help feeling relief that he hadn't grabbed me. *Maybe he thinks them ugly and far too large.*

That was what I had heard all my life from everyone around me, anyway. I had thought they might have different standards of beauty at the Unseelie Court, but maybe they were not so dissimilar to the Seelie Court after all.

I put my hand tentatively on the hard wall of muscle that was Liath's chest. His skin was warm and smooth—not rough at all, as I had half-expected. Beneath my palm I felt the steady beat of his heart, a deep rhythm that seemed to call to me somehow.

"Very good," the Priestess said approvingly. "Now please repeat after me, Prince Liath: Wife, to thee I pledge my troth. My loyalty, honesty, and love shall all be yours for as long as we two shall live and the sun and moon shall endure."

Liath said the words but he didn't just repeat them—he spoke them directly to me, looking into my eyes. For somehow he had caught me with his bronze gaze again and I found I couldn't look away.

"Good." The Priestess nodded. "To continue—As my Wife, I offer you the protection of my Court, my house, and my body. None shall harm you when I am near and if any offend you, I shall punish them with my strong right arm."

All these words, Liath spoke in his deep, rumbling voice as I stared into his eyes, mesmerized and unable to look away.

I hate him, I reminded myself. *He killed Quill—he deserves to die!* And yet I still couldn't keep from staring into the huge warrior's eyes.

Then it was my turn for vows.

"Princess, please repeat after me," the Druid Priestess said. "Husband, to thee I pledge my troth. My loyalty, honesty, and love shall all be yours for as long as we two shall live and the sun and moon shall endure."

This time I managed a little better, speaking my vows in a voice that didn't sound quite so high and frightened. Then the Priestess continued.

"As my Husband, I offer you my complete obedience, the abundance of my womb—which you will fill with your seed—and the comfort of my body to ease your needs. I shall withhold nothing but give myself to you freely and completely."

I opened my mouth and then shut it again. *What?* Who had made up these vows? I was certain this wasn't how a regular hand fasting went.

"Well?" Liath rumbled, arching an eyebrow at me.

"I...uh..." I cleared my throat.

"Princess?" The Druid looked at me uneasily, concerned that the ritual wasn't proceeding as it ought to.

"Perhaps my new wife objects to the promise that she will obey me," Liath growled softly. "You may leave that part out if you wish, little bird," he added, looking down at me.

Little bird? I wondered where he had heard that. It was Quill's nickname for me, mostly because my name—Alira—means "songbird" in the Elder language, but also because I tend to sing or hum to myself when I'm busy with a task—it's a habit I can't seem to break. But how would my husband-to-be know any of that?

"You may proceed with the vows and leave the 'obey' part out, Princess," the Priestess urged me quietly.

As it happened, it wasn't the "obey" part that was tripping me up —it was the promise to offer Liath my body without reservation. *That* was scary—more frightening than any oath to obey him. But the audience was getting restless and it became clear the ceremony couldn't proceed until I said the vows.

My heart was pounding like a rabbit's as I looked up at Liath again.

"As my Husband, I offer you the...the abundance of my womb, which..." I cleared my throat, which was suddenly dry as dust again. "Which you will fill with your seed. And the...the comfort of my body to ease your needs."

"I shall withhold nothing but give myself to you freely and completely," the Druid murmured, reminding me I had forgotten a bit of the vow.

I found myself looking into those bronze eyes again. The worst thing was that these were no ordinary Joining Vows—this hand fasting was being made in the presence of the Goddess and in the center of the Summer Court—the seat of power for the entire Seelie Realm. They *would* bind me, just as Liath's vows bound him.

But again, I had no choice.

"I...I shall withhold nothing but give myself to you freely and...and completely," I said quickly, trying to get it over with.

A slow smile spread over his dark face.

"I shall hold you to that vow, little bird," he murmured.

To my horror, I found my face was growing hot with a blush. By the Shining Throne, when he looked at me like that...why did it make my heart beat so much harder under his large palm?

He killed Quill, I reminded myself again. *And you don't even know why he asked Father for your hand. In all likelihood, he wants to take you back to the Winter Court and torture you the same way Asfaloth and Calista torture small animals.*

And I would be caught in his trap—unable to free myself or to fight back since I had no magic.

None of that matters, I told myself grimly. *Just get this ceremony over so you can get back to the Winter Court with him and find a way to kill him!*

Luckily I hadn't vowed not to slit his thick throat and I swore to myself that it *would* be done. Though I still didn't know how I was to accomplish it, I would take vengeance for my beloved brother.

"And now with the vows complete, may I give you this blessing," the Priestess said, interrupting my murderous thoughts. "In this Joining of hands and the fashioning of this knot, so are your lives now bound, one to another. By this cord you are thus bound to your vows—may it draw your hands together in love and never in anger. May this knot remain tied for as long as love shall last and the sun and the moon shall endure."

Then she raised the golden chalice filled with Joining wine over her head and tipped it first for me, that I might take a sip and then for Liath—though she had to almost stand on her tiptoes in order to get the cup to his lips.

As the sour tang of the wine flowed over my tongue, the realization of what I had done swept over me—I had married my brother's killer.

How was I ever going to get out of this?

5

There was polite applause from those assembled—all from the Summer Court since my new husband had not brought anyone to stand with him or even to witness the ceremony. I wondered who the mysterious person he wanted to have with him could have been and how he had died. They were probably questions I was destined never to learn the answer to, since I was going to kill my new spouse as soon as I could.

The Druid Priestess untied the gold and silver cord and folded it away. Then she nodded to both of us, indicating that we might leave the Joining Arch and join in the festivities that were beginning in the courtyard and the gardens beyond.

We stepped out from under the arch of flowering honey-musk vines—Liath was so tall the tiny flowers brushed the top of his head. But I hadn't gone a single step before I felt his hand on my shoulder.

"What—" I began but he was already turning me to face him. His strength was frightening—I could feel it in his big hand, even though he was clearly being careful.

"What...what is it?" I asked again, looking up at him. By the

Shining Throne—I was going to get a crick in my neck if I stayed married to him for too long! He was too damn *tall*.

Liath took me firmly by my right hand and pushed up the long sleeve of the underslip, exposing the angry bruises that marred my wrist.

"What are you doing?" I tried to push the sleeve back down but he wouldn't let me.

"Who did this to you?" he rumbled, frowning down at me.

"I...I don't know what you mean! I...I hurt myself running into a door."

I could feel my cheeks getting hot with a blush—we hadn't been married five minutes and already I was lying to him. But I didn't want to admit to him that I had no magic to defend or heal myself—on the off-chance that he didn't know already.

Liath's bronze eyes narrowed.

"I know you're lying, little bird—those are finger marks on your arm. Now let me ask you again—and remember you vowed your honesty to me—*who did this to you?*"

I bit my lip and cast a glance over my shoulder. Asfaloth was standing near Calista—of course, the two were always together—laughing and drinking wine from a golden goblet. Clearly he was enjoying himself but I had a feeling that was about to change.

Liath's eyes followed mine and his scowl deepened.

"Of course—the little shit," he muttered.

It was my turn to frown—did he know my cousin? If so, how? It seemed to me that the only time the two could possibly meet would be on the battlefield, where there isn't much time for social niceties—at least as I understand it.

Then, to my horror, Liath drew the moonstone dagger from its sheath on his belt. I had thought it must be a ceremonial piece, but the silver edge gleamed with deadly light as he pulled it out.

"Wait!" I exclaimed, putting a hand on his arm. "This is a wedding—*our* wedding! You can't just—"

He silenced me by turning the long, silver blade and drawing it down his own palm—the left one.

Blood as dark as rubies welled from the cut as Liath sheathed the dagger with his other hand. Then he gripped me—gently but firmly—by my wounded wrist with his bleeding palm pressed to my bruised flesh.

It was then that I felt his magic for the first time.

Just because I have no magic of my own, does not mean that I am insensible to the magic of others. As I have said, the magic of my cousins is like biting or stinging insects and Tansy's magic feels like a coarse bristled brush scratching my skin. My father's magic was like stinging nettles—laced heavily with his disapproval and the Palace healer's magic had less of a feel and more of a smell—the sharp scent of alcohol which is used to cleanse wounds. Quill's magic—back when he used to heal me of my little scrapes and cuts—was like the sunshine warming my face.

But Liath's magic was different from any I had ever felt. It was like the softest fur imaginable touching and rubbing me everywhere—and I do mean *everywhere*. I felt it sliding between my legs and slipping sensuously over the tips of my nipples, which went instantly tight.

Around my wounded wrist, it felt warm and soothing but I was—I think understandably—more focused on the other sensations. I never touched myself in the areas Liath's magic was touching me—they were forbidden places, my old nurse had told me, when she once caught me exploring. She had bound my hands at my sides for a week to teach me a lesson. If you're wondering, her magic felt like coarse rope wrapping around my limbs—I had disliked her intensely.

Finally, I found my voice.

"What...what are you doing?" I gasped at last, looking up at my new husband in alarm and confusion.

"Healing you," he said shortly. "Since you cannot heal yourself—yet," he added, which was almost as confusing as the way his magic was touching me all over.

"By...by using your blood?" I asked, grasping onto another aspect of this strange healing to avoid talking about the physical sensations it was causing in me.

Blood magic was strictly forbidden at the Summer Court but it wasn't an issue that came up often. Usually when a Fae of any kind did magic, they drew power from the bounty of Nature. There was no need to bleed when any amount of power was available all around us, simply for the taking.

It was yet another reason the Seelie Court was located in the heart of a forest, where natural power was abundant and easy to access. Had we lived in villages, like the mortals, our powers would have been much diminished.

I say "we" meaning my people of course—it didn't matter where I lived, since I had no magic and so, no way to draw on the power around me and shape it to my will.

"Blood magic is true magic," Liath growled. "It's *earned* magic—not stolen."

"What?" I shook my head, uncertain of what he was talking about.

But he didn't answer—only withdrew his hand and bent to examine my wrist.

The sensation of ultra-soft fur brushing my skin and all my sensitive areas ceased when his magic stopped flowing, which should have been a relief. Instead, I found I still felt achy and somehow unfulfilled in a way I never had before.

Liath turned my wrist this way and that—his dark gray skin a sharp contrast to my own milky paleness. At last he nodded, as though satisfied.

"You're healed," he pronounced. Then he looked at me sharply. "Do you have any other injuries I need to tend to?"

"What?" My hand went involuntarily to the cheek Calista had slapped earlier. It didn't really hurt anymore—she wasn't nearly as strong as her brother—but I could still feel a faint tingle.

"Ah—they both went at you, did they?" Liath shot a glare at my cousins, who were completely oblivious. "I won't hurt a female, though the Goddess knows that little bitch deserves it!"

Again, it seemed as though he *knew* my cousins somehow, which should not have been possible. I had no idea what was going on but Liath didn't give me time to ask. He turned his left hand—the one he'd cut—upward and I saw that the slice he'd made across his palm with the dagger was almost closed.

So he'd been healing both me and himself at the same time—no easy feat. In fact, even the Palace healer would struggle with a double healing, but Liath hadn't even broken a sweat.

There was still a drop of blood left in his mostly-healed palm. He dabbed his fingertip in it and pressed it to my cheek.

At once, I felt the soft fur of his magic brushing against my skin again—it felt like I was naked and someone was rubbing a mink blanket all over my bare body. The intimacy and pleasure of it seemed obscene—it made me blush and gasp as my nipples tingled and the place between my legs came to life in a way it never had before I'd felt his magic.

Liath studied my flushed face with a knowing look.

"Hmm...you feel that do you, little bird?" he murmured.

"I...I don't know what you mean," I stammered. "Feel what?"

He frowned again.

"Don't pretend and don't lie to me. I'll remind you again that you vowed me your honesty."

He removed his hand abruptly and the feeling of his magic cut off at once.

I didn't know what to say. Should I apologize? Then I felt myself harden inside. By the Shining Throne, I would apologize for *nothing*. It didn't matter how good his magic felt or that he had healed me—he was still Quill's murderer and I didn't intend to forget that, just because we'd taken a lot of vows together.

"Stay here," Liath told me.

I frowned at him.

"Why? Where are you going?"

He raised an eyebrow.

"To fulfill the pledge I made to you. Unlike you, little bird, I honor *my* vows."

Then he strode across the grassy courtyard, straight up to Asfaloth.

My cousin stopped what he was doing and looked up at the grim specter of the horned Unseelie menace looming over him. Never could one see the difference between the two Courts so clearly as now, I thought numbly.

To the naked eye, Asfaloth was all that a Fae warrior ought to be —tall and straight and slim with shining blond hair and eyes like amethysts. And then there was my new husband, who looked like darkness itself beside my cousin's golden form.

With his gray skin gleaming with golden tattoos and the burning bronze eyes glaring out from his dark face—not to mention the curling ram's horns—Liath looked like the devil himself beside my cousin. And yet, Asfaloth had only ever wounded me, while my new husband had healed me.

I pushed the disloyal thought from my head. I hated Asfaloth and Liath equally, I told myself. They were both worthy of my animosity. But the scene unfolding between my cousin and my new husband soon hushed the yammering thoughts in my head.

"What do you want, Unseelie?" Asfaloth somehow managed to sneer down his nose even while looking up at Liath.

"I want to honor the vows I made to your cousin—my wife," Liath growled.

"Honor your vows then." Liath shrugged his slim shoulders elegantly. "What do I care? How do you even mean to honor them?"

"Like this."

Suddenly, Liath had him by the throat and was lifting him high into the air.

Asfaloth kicked and struggled, his amethyst eyes bulging from their sockets in surprise as much as pain.

"Here now—what are you about? What are you doing?" my Aunt Lyrah exclaimed, going pale.

Calista was more to the point.

"Put him down, you great Unseelie beast! Put my brother down!" she cried. Jumping up, she grasped one of Asfaloth's hands and yanked on it, trying to get him down, but of course it didn't work. Liath just stood there, holding my cousin by the throat as he kicked feebly in the air.

"You've hurt my wife for the last time," he growled at Asfaloth. "The next time you touch her, you *die*. Do you understand?"

Asfaloth just gurgled. His face was turning beet red by now as his limbs flailed—well, all but the arm Calista was hanging on.

"I said, do you fucking *understand*?" Liath demanded, and shook him like a rag doll.

My cousin seemed to be trying to nod his head but the only word that came from his mouth was a strangled sound like, "Ysggg!"

"Here, now—what is the meaning of this?" My father came striding over, his face set in a righteous rage. The Sun crown gleamed on his brow, casting a golden glow all around him.

"The *meaning* is me teaching this little shit a lesson about hurting my wife," Liath growled, still not releasing Asfaloth. "He damn near broke her wrist—left bruises all over her flesh!"

"How dare you act in this manner?" my Father blustered,

completely ignoring the part about Asfaloth hurting me. "These are not the actions of one who wishes to make peace between our Courts!"

"I never said I wanted to make peace with you." Liath abruptly loosened his grip and dropped Asfaloth to the ground. My cousin went sprawling and his mother and sister gasped. Their hands fluttered like wounded doves as they knelt to attend him. The marks of Liath's big hand were already appearing as a necklace of red marks around his elegant throat—just as the marks of Asfaloth's own fingers had so recently decorated my wrist.

My father looked up at Liath, perplexed.

"You...if you do not wish to make peace, then why did you ask for my daughter's hand in marriage?" he asked, looking genuinely confused.

"Because I fucking *wanted* her," Liath growled. "And because she's spent long enough in the wrong Court. She needs to come *home*, with me."

With a final glare at Asfaloth, who was still sprawled on the ground, he turned and came back to me.

I had been frozen on the spot, watching the whole scene unfold with mixed emotions. On one hand, this was *certainly* not the proper way to behave at a wedding—especially one's own wedding. But on the other hand, I couldn't quite ignore the surge of pure joy I felt at being vindicated. No one in my life had stood up to my cruel cousin since my brother had died. No one had defended or protected me or avenged the malicious and vicious acts he and his sister had worked on me until now.

But I had to remind myself that this vengeance was being taken by my brother's killer and tamp down my joy at finally being avenged.

Before I could say anything to him—though I don't know what I would have said—Liath took me by the hand and drew his dagger again. He stabbed it into the air above his head and pulled downward with the same motion one might make if they wanted to rip a curtain in two with a blade.

Immediately, the fabric of reality parted and the black rip began to form. Even before it expanded fully to an oval, Liath was dragging me through it.

I gasped as I went from a sunlit glade to a dark courtyard swathed in shadows. It looked very like the courtyard we had just left, except the trees around it were barren of leaves and a cold wind blew through their branches.

Behind me, the golden oval which led to the Summer Court was already closing. I looked over my shoulder and watched it shrink to a line and then disappear altogether.

I turned back to Liath, not sure what to say.

"You...you didn't have to do that," I finally got out.

"Yes, I fucking did," he growled.

Then he surprised me by sinking to one knee in front of me and taking both my hands in his.

"Alira," he said, using my true name for the first time. "I know how often he—they—have hurt and tormented you. I vow to you now—they'll never touch you again! Not while I draw breath."

I stared at him, uncomprehending. Was he talking about my cousins—about Asfaloth and Calista? And if so, how did he know of their long animosity against me and the many times they had wounded and tormented me? There was so *much* I didn't understand.

"I...all right," I said at last, feeling breathless.

"Good. I'm glad we understand each other." Liath rose abruptly to tower over me once more. "Come—I'll show you to our rooms."

6

I followed him through the palace, still in a daze. I did manage to notice that the grounds of the Winter Palace—and indeed, the Palace itself—looked almost identical to the Summer Palace. The only difference appeared to be that all the plants were bare of leaves and the temperature was much, *much* colder. I shivered in my thin underslip, putting my arms around myself to try and keep warm.

Liath must have noticed because he halted his long stride for a moment and unhooked his cloak.

"Here." He put the heavy black cloak around my shoulders, fastening it under my chin with the delicate silver leaf clasp. This left him completely bare from the waist up and I couldn't help watching the play of muscles on his broad back as I followed him through the silent, seemingly empty palace.

Where was everyone, I wondered? Where were the High Fae and the servants who looked after them? The couriers and cooks and pageboys and maids and all the other staff necessary to keep an enormous palace running?

"Where are all your people?" I asked at last, plucking up the courage to speak after he had led me through a dozen richly furnished but empty rooms.

Liath turned his head to glance at me, the dim light gleaming on his curving horns and in his bronze eyes.

"They've been told to keep out of the way—at least for tonight," he growled. "I thought you'd be frightened enough without confronting a bunch of Unseelie Fae. Believe it or not, I'm not the strangest of the lot."

I didn't know what to say to that. So everyone was hiding from us? Somehow that seemed even more ominous than if the Palace was empty. I imagined many glowing, curious eyes peering at us from the shadows and a shiver ran through me. I gathered the heavy black cloak closer around my body, wrapping myself in it fully. It had the scent of Liath's skin—warm and masculine with a note of some wild, dark spice I could not name. It felt dangerous but it drew me nonetheless.

I liked the scent, though I told myself I didn't. I tried not to notice how good it smelled as I huddled in the garment my new husband had given me to wear.

The way he took led us through the Throne Room—which looked exactly like my father's throne room back in the Summer Court... except for the throne.

"Oh..." I whispered, halting before the broad dais to stare.

The Shining Throne in the Summer Court is, as I have said, more of a broad couch—big enough for two. The throne I saw on the dais in the Winter Court was clearly built for just one.

It was a tall, narrow chair made entirely of some black metal. There was a fist-sized ruby embedded in its top and it had a blood-red cushion. There were carvings in red too—only they didn't *look* like normal carvings. It was more like someone had carved ridges in the throne and all of them were filled with rivulets of blood.

I wondered how the craftsmen who had made it had managed that effect. It almost looked like the blood was moving—flowing sluggishly through the etchings on the throne as though it was a living creature and these were its veins, located on the outside of its body for some bizarre reason.

"Ah—the Shadow Throne," Liath rumbled, coming to a halt beside me. "Does it call to you, little bird?"

"Call to me?" I frowned up at him in puzzlement. "Why would it call to me?"

He shook his head.

"Never mind—later perhaps when you reach your full potential. For now, the Shadow Throne sits empty."

"Why is that?" I asked curiously.

"Because my mother, Queen Mab, abdicated some time ago," Liath told me. "I have not seen her in years. It's just as well," he added. "She was going mad and it was beginning to show. The Shadow Throne extracts a heavy toll."

"Why don't you take it for yourself?" I asked bluntly. "You're the Prince—the next in the line of succession, aren't you?"

"I am." He nodded. "But the Shadow Throne will accept only a female ruler. Did you know that?"

Wide-eyed, I shook my head.

"It's true," Liath told me. "And it doesn't sit empty because no one wants the power it bestows. Many have tried to take it since my mother left."

"What happened?" I asked. "They tried to sit the throne and failed?"

"They tried and died," Liath said grimly. "The Shadow Throne will accept only a worthy candidate. If it doesn't think you're worthy—or maybe just doesn't fucking like you—it will strike you down when you sit on it."

I sucked in a breath.

"That's...not the way it is with the Shining Throne."

"I know," he said simply. "And I also know that the Summer Palace and the Winter Palace are mirror images of each other—but you need to remember, little bird—even if they look alike, they are *not*. They couldn't be more fucking different. Come."

He took me by the wrist—the one he had healed—and led me out of the Throne Room. I went with him but I couldn't help turning my head to stare back at the Shadow Throne.

Liath had asked if it called to me—it did not. But I felt a kind of dark fascination as I watched the blood-filled carvings in the black chair. It sat in shadows and seemed to brood to itself, like a monster that was sleeping but waiting for the right person to waken it.

I was sure that person wasn't me...but I wondered who it might be. By rights, Liath—as his mother's heir—should have found a woman to marry who could sit the throne so that he could rule through her. But that would take pure High Fae bloodlines and an immense amount of personal magic. I had the one—at least on paper—but I was completely bereft of the other.

Why *had* he married me? I could be no help to him in taking the Shadow Throne—it would probably sense my lack of magic and kill me if I even dared to come near it. Also, he had told my father he had no interest in making peace between the two Courts. And I was *certain* he hadn't picked me for my beauty any more than he'd picked me for my magic—it was the same in both cases—I had none to offer.

So why had the Prince of the Winter Court chosen me as his bride?

I had no idea and there didn't seem to be any way to find out unless he chose to tell me.

7

After walking through what felt like the entire Palace, we at last came to a suite of rooms which Liath told me was "ours." Which meant, I guessed, that we would be living together—not a comfortable proposition at all.

In most royal households, the King and Queen have their own quarters—often at opposite ends of the palace from each other. The idea of actually living in the same set of rooms with my intimidating new husband hadn't occurred to me and I found myself dismayed by it now.

Never mind, I tried to comfort myself as I walked into the dark but opulent living area. *This gives me that many more chances and ways to kill him.*

Which was true, of course. I needed to start looking around my new rooms, scouting for weapons. I would have to take him off guard, of course—there was no way to face him directly. He was so huge he could doubtless break me over his knee like a stick of kindling. So, subtlety would have to be my game. It was too bad I hadn't been able to get my hands on any poison before my wedding, but it had been quite impossible.

The rooms were, as I said, grandly appointed. The carpet on the floor had clearly been woven by many clever hands and the chandeliers hovered near the arching ceiling, shedding remote golden light from their myriad of fairy crystals which not only shone but also sang with faint, high voices in a language too ancient to understand.

Half the walls were mirrored and I could see myself as well as Liath —his reflection was twice as large as my own. He strode through the room to a smaller sitting area where a round table had been laid for two.

"Are you hungry?" he asked, nodding at the table.

I started to shake my head...and then my stomach growled. I had been too nervous to eat that morning and of course, I hadn't had any of the delicate refreshments being served at our ceremony. Most of them were simply candied flower petals and the like, anyway.

No one at the Summer Court but me seemed to crave food with any substance. I'd spent half my life feeling like I was starving, even as I failed to even approach the Seelie standard of slender beauty.

"I beg your pardon, my Lord Blackthorn," I said, putting a hand to my traitorous stomach.

"Call me Liath," he said shortly. "And don't apologize, you're *hungry*—and for real food. Not that fucking cobweb stew and rosewater tonic stuff they serve in the Summer Court."

I was surprised that he knew the details of what we ate—how did he know so much about the Summer Court and its denizens when we never mixed? But I took a seat at the table, after Liath pulled out my chair. He might look beastly but he had the manners of a gentleman, at least in this instance, I decided.

He sat across from me and drew his dagger again. I watched uneasily as he pricked a fingertip and made a gesture with one hand while rumbling something under his breath.

At once, the round table was filled with serving platters, all of them full of steaming, savory-smelling food.

My stomach grumbled again but I sat frozen in place. A lady didn't serve herself when dining with a gentleman and there were no servers here to help. Also, though the food smelled amazing, not much of it was familiar.

My dilemma came to an end when Liath reached easily across the table with one long arm and began serving me some of everything.

"Here," he said, putting a piece of rare meat on my plate, followed by a scoop of something gooey and cheesy, followed by some hearty looking root vegetables which were crispy and brown on one side. "Well—go on," he urged as he started filling his own plate.

I looked at my plate, unsure what to try first. It all smelled amazing and completely unlike the kind of food I was given in the Summer Court. It seemed real—substantial. This was no wispy and delicate fare that would melt away, leaving me hungry again an hour later.

I tried the meat which was juicy and tender with a delicious salt crust on one side. It fairly melted in my mouth—I couldn't believe how good it was. I tried the cheesy dish next—salty and creamy with a hint of spice. The root vegetables were crispy on the outside and fluffy on the inside. After a moment, I found that they tasted even better when I paired them with a bite of the meat.

Before I knew it I had finished everything on the plate. How had that happened? I shouldn't have eaten so much, I scolded myself. This one meal was more food than I was used to having in a whole day back home.

*No—**this** is home now,* whispered a little voice in my head. *At least until you kill Liath Blackthorn—then you'll have to hide in the mortal world. If you can find it.*

I had a vague idea that the Mortal Realm began somewhere at the boundaries of the forest that surrounded the Palace, but I had never been there. Still, I would have to run *somewhere* if my plan to murder my new husband worked.

At that point, just as I was thinking again about killing him, Liath looked up and asked if I wanted seconds.

"Seconds?" I asked, frowning.

"A second helping—more food," he clarified. "Do you want some more?"

"But...all this food is really heavy," I pointed out. "Aren't you afraid if I eat too much of it I'll get even bigger than I already am?" There was no point in dancing around the issue, I thought, since our marriage wasn't going to last very long, once I found a way to kill him.

"What?" He frowned as though I was speaking a different language. "What do you mean 'bigger than you already are?' You're just the right size. Besides, a female has to eat to maintain her curves."

"She *what?*" I could hardly believe what I was hearing. "But...a female shouldn't *have* curves at all," I said.

"Yes, she fucking should," Liath growled. "Or were you hoping to starve yourself down to the size of one of those skin-and-bones Fae maidens who live in the Summer Court?"

"That's what I've been trying to do all my life," I admitted. "I'm too big—I always have been."

"Horse shit," Liath said crudely. "You're fucking perfect. If you don't want any more dinner, would you like some dessert?"

I stared at him blankly. Had he just dismissed a lifetime of body image issues in one sentence? Surely he didn't really believe what he was saying. A maiden should be "slim as a sapling"—that was the acknowledged wisdom of the Seelie Court. Could it really be that different in the Unseelie world?

"Dessert?" Liath asked once more and when I nodded hesitantly, he pricked his finger again. The savory dishes disappeared and several new ones took their place.

"Oh—what is it?" I asked, as Liath scooped out a portion for me.

"I believe it's called 'chocolate lava cake,'" he informed me. "It's from the Mortal Realm. And here—you have to have it with a scoop of this." He added a white ball of some icy substance to my plate and handed it to me.

I took a bit of the chocolate stuff first. I'd had chocolate once or twice—Tansy had smuggled it in to me though it was forbidden at the Summer Court, because it was so fattening. But the few dry, crumbling morsels she'd given me were nothing like this.

The smooth, velvety texture and the bitter-sweet taste made my eyes roll back in my head and I couldn't hold back a little moan of delight. It was absolutely the *best* thing I'd ever put in my mouth and I wanted more of it immediately.

I took another bite—pairing it with the cold, creamy white stuff this time. The mixture was even more delicious, making me close my eyes to savor the perfect combination. By the Shining Throne—this was the best food I'd ever had and my father had employed only the finest fairy chefs back home! But their food couldn't compare to what Liath had put on my plate.

Speaking of Liath, I opened my eyes and saw—to my consternation—that he was watching me eat. He seemed to be enjoying himself too—he had his chin propped on one huge fist and a little smile was playing around the corners of his sensuous mouth.

Seeing him staring at me like that gave me a start. I put down my spoon at once and swallowed what I had in my mouth. I felt as though he'd caught me doing something forbidden—something almost sexual—and my cheeks heated with a blush.

"What's wrong? Why did you stop?" he rumbled, lifting his eyebrows as I blotted the corners of my mouth carefully with my white linen napkin.

"Why are you staring at me?" I asked, returning his question with a question.

He shrugged, his broad shoulders lifting with the movement.

"I like to see you enjoying yourself. Is the lava cake to your liking?"

"It's...the best thing I've ever eaten," I confessed, wondering why I was telling him this. "But isn't it terribly fattening?"

"Does it matter if it is?" he asked. "It strikes me, little bird, that you haven't had many pleasures in your life so far. Why not take this one as it is and just enjoy it?"

"What do you know about my life?" I demanded. "And how did you know my nickname is 'little bird?'"

He frowned and shook his head.

"I'm not ready to tell you that yet. You'll have to wait until we get to know each other better."

This was a strange answer and I didn't know what to say to it.

"Your ice cream is melting," Liath said, pointing to the scoop of white stuff on my plate—which was, indeed, transforming into a white puddle. "Better eat it before it's too late."

I picked up my spoon again but though I loved the rich flavor of the dessert, I was almost too preoccupied to taste it. What did he mean he'd tell me when we got to know each other?

It doesn't matter, I told myself. *Because we're not going to have time to know each other—I'm killing him tonight!*

I didn't know how I was going to manage to murder my huge new husband but I knew I had to take revenge. If I waited too long, I might lose my nerve.

It was tonight or never.

8

The dining area led into a vast bed chamber with an enormous bed draped in dark blue satin at its center. The furniture was carved from heavy, dark wood and there were actual living trees and other plants growing in the corners, spreading their leafy foliage in the shady gloom.

Despite the greenery, it was a very masculine space. Clearly we weren't just moving in together—I was invading his room. I wondered why he wanted me there—why not just give me my own space?

Why do you think? It's your wedding night, whispered a sardonic little voice in my head. *Why else would he want you in his room—and in his bed—tonight?*

The thought made me shiver with fear and I looked around for something to distract myself. I was surprised to see floor to ceiling windows on most of the walls which let in a dim gray light.

"What time is it?" I asked Liath, peering out one of the panes, which only showed an abundance of branches and snow on the ground.

"It's evening but time doesn't really matter in the Winter Court. It's always dusk here—the same way it's always Summer afternoon back at the Summer Court," he explained. "You'll get used to it—though if you miss the sunshine, I can arrange for a trip to the Mortal Realm."

"I've always preferred the shadows," I admitted. "But…you go to the Mortal Realm?"

He shrugged. "Sometimes. It's getting late—would you like a bath?"

"A bath?" I was suddenly on edge again. Bathing meant taking off my clothes and getting naked. Unconsciously, I pulled his cloak—which I was still wearing—more tightly around myself.

Liath seemed to see my gesture.

"You've nothing to fear from me, little bird—I won't hurt you or take what you're unwilling to give," he rumbled.

I lifted my chin defiantly.

"I'm *not* afraid of you."

He arched an eyebrow at me.

"You're a terrible liar—do you know that? Should I show you the bathing and necessary room or not?"

"I can find my own way," I said stiffly.

"Through those doors." He nodded his chin at the far end of the room. "You'll find a dressing area with clothing which should fit you as well."

"Thank you." I didn't know why I was thanking him—he wasn't just my husband, he was my captor in this situation. And no matter what he said, I knew what he was going to expect once I got out of the bath and came back into the bedroom.

Accordingly, I took an extra long bath, putting off the inevitable. The tub was delightfully big—almost big enough to swim in.

Big enough for someone Liath's size, a little voice whispered in my head. I turned my head and looked fearfully at the door, which I had locked securely behind me. It didn't matter that I was locked in, however—Liath had demonstrated exactly how easily he manipulated matter with his blood magic. If he wanted to unlock the door and come in to catch me naked in the tub, he would.

He didn't though and after a time, I began to relax. Just like the bedroom, the bathing area had high ceilings and tall windows that showed the Winter twilight world outside. It was warm inside, though—none of the cold leached through the glass windowpanes, for which I was grateful, not being used to the harsh weather.

There were living plants and vines growing in the corners of this room too, though none of them seemed to shed their leaves or make a mess on the thickly carpeted floor. I wondered who tended to them or if Liath simply tended them by magic. It was rather nice to have so much greenery indoors, I decided. It made me feel as though I was living in a jungle—in a good way.

After at least an hour of soaking in the scented water—there was an array of little pots and jars and bottles all filled with hair and bath products on the edge of the tub which I had made liberal use of—I decided it was time to get out. Not that I *wanted* to, but Liath might get angry if I spent too much more time in here. Also, I wanted to search the area and see if I could find a weapon I might use later.

Lifting a little metal lever, I drained the tub and stepped out to wrap myself in a drying sheet. It was warm and fluffy and it felt good against my bare skin.

There was a small necessary closet set into one side of the bathing chamber and a much larger, walk-in closet at the other end. I had already made use of the former, now I decided to explore the latter.

I saw at once that the closet was divided in half. The left side was filled with Liath's clothing—neatly folded stacks of breeches, some shirts so huge they would have been dresses on me, extra pairs of enormous boots, and a brown cloak like the black one he had given me to wear.

I hung the black one up beside the brown one, though I didn't know why I was bothering. Was I trying to get into the good graces of my new husband whom I intended to kill tonight? But my old nurse had taught me to be tidy and old habits die hard.

The other side of the closet had clothing for me—clothing I stared at in wonder. Not a single piece of it was pastel! There was no pale pink or baby blue or mint green or buttercup yellow to be seen anywhere. Instead, I saw jewel tones—ruby red and deep emerald and forest greens, cerulean blue which would compliment my hair color, which always seemed to clash with the lighter clothes of the Summer Court.

There were silver and gold accented gowns as well, which looked like they were meant for banquets or feasts—more formal occasions. I wondered which of them I was required to wear for daily Court life and indeed, what daily Court life here included.

Well, I would never find out, since I was killing my husband tonight, I reminded myself. And right now I needed to find something to sleep in. Something that wasn't too revealing or tempting.

Not that it mattered—I was quite certain that I could wear a burlap sack and he would still have me, as was his right as my husband. He had said he wouldn't 'take what I wasn't willing to give' but I didn't believe it for a moment. I was going to have to endure his big body on top of mine, spreading my thighs, penetrating me, filling me up...

I shoved the thought aside. Why had my mind showed me all that in such graphic detail? I wished I could forget it but the images were burned into my brain. There was nothing to do but get dressed and go out into the bed chamber and take my medicine, as my old nurse used to say. It would hurt and I would feel violated, but afterwards I would kill him—in that way I would have revenge for both myself and my brother.

Blindly, I searched through the drawers, looking for something to wear. All the night gowns were made of soft, silky, thin material not unlike the underslip I had worn as my wedding dress.

At last I decided on one the exact color of my hair and slipped it over my head. It had a deep V-neck but it was no worse than what I had worn to the wedding. The outlines of my nipples could be seen through the thin material—they were tight with fear.

The gown fell to my ankles and had sleeves that came down to my elbows. I wished for some kind of slippers but didn't see any—my bare feet were cold despite the thick carpet. But then, I always had cold feet.

Telling myself there was no point in waiting any longer, I took a deep breath and left the closet. Then I unlocked the bathing chamber door, expecting that Liath would probably grab me the moment I came out. This was *not* going to be pleasant.

Bracing myself, I pushed open the chamber door only to find...

My new husband asleep in the middle of the huge bed.

9

I couldn't believe it—was Liath *really* asleep? His deep, steady breathing seemed to indicate it was so.

I tiptoed into the room, closing the bathing chamber door quietly behind me. The glowing chandeliers which floated magically near the ceiling had dimmed their lights and the fairy crystals were singing a soft, sweet lullaby so high it was almost inaudible.

I crept to the huge bed, which was two steps up on a raised dais. Sure enough, Liath was sprawled in the center of the mattress, taking up most of it with his long limbs. His eyes were closed and he was breathing in a deep, regular rhythm that wasn't quite a snore.

Then my eye caught on something else.

I hadn't found any weapons I could use in the bathing chamber, but on the night table to his right, Liath had left the dagger he had worn to our ceremony. It was still in its sheath but the moonstones in the silver hilt gleamed in the dim light, almost as though they were calling to me.

I couldn't believe my luck! Here was the perfect opportunity to take my revenge and I didn't even have to endure the indignity and pain of a wedding night coupling first.

Stealthily, I crept around the bed, taking my time and walking as quietly as a cat. When I reached the right side of the bed, I stepped up onto the dais, my bare feet making no noise at all on the wooden steps. Once there, I reached for the hilt of the dagger. Keeping my eyes on my sleeping husband the whole time, I drew it silently from its sheath. It came out without a noise—a heavy, lethal weight in my hand.

I would have liked to simply lean over the bed and slit his thick throat, but alas, the bed was too big and I was too small. If I wanted to kill him, I would have to get up onto the mattress with him—there was no other way.

I had no idea how light or heavy a sleeper he was so I told myself I had to be prepared to move fast. Slowly, carefully, I climbed up beside him, expecting every moment that my movements would wake him.

And yet, he slept on.

He even continued to sleep as I leaned over him and put the shining blade to his throat. I knew I should kill him at once—slit his throat and leave him choking on his own blood. But I had never done any violence before. So instead, I took a moment to study him—my husband...my brother's killer—as I tried to screw my courage to the sticking place.

His hair spilled like a mane of moonlight over the dark blue pillow almost obscuring his curving horns. His lashes were thick and dark—surprisingly long for a male's, I thought. They lay like fans against his high cheekbones. He had a straight nose and full lips. It was a handsome face, except for the long, white scar that marred his deep gray skin. I wondered why he didn't use his magic to heal himself and erase it.

His golden tattoos were mesmerizing. They seemed to move and change in the dim light, swirling first in one direction and then in the other in patterns that ought to make sense but didn't. His shoulders were so broad and his chest so muscular—so different from any other male I had ever seen and yet so striking.

All Fae value symmetry—it is part of beauty—and aside from the white scar on the side of his face, Liath Blackthorn was perfectly symmetrical. He was a powerful and yes—a beautiful physical specimen in every way.

Then I realized what I was doing—I was hesitating, wasting the perfect opportunity to kill my brother's murderer. And why was I doing it? Because I was admiring the perfect symmetry of his muscular body and chiseled features.

I wanted to slap myself—what was *wrong* with me? Resolutely, I lowered the blade until it was just a hairsbreadth above his strongly corded throat. I would do it, I told myself. I was actually going to do it...

And then his bronze eyes opened and he stared up at me.

"Do it, why don't you?" he rumbled, in that deep voice that seemed to shake the whole bed. "Slit my throat with my own dagger—isn't that your plan, little bird?"

I felt frozen to the spot. I wanted to strike the killing blow, but somehow I couldn't move.

Do it! I screamed at myself in my head. *Do it—you'll never get another chance like this! What are you waiting for—do it, Alira!*

But still, I couldn't move.

Suddenly, Liath exploded into action.

His arm came up, catching my wrist and squeezing until I gasped and dropped the moonstone dagger. Without missing a beat, he caught it by the hilt and put it back on the nightstand. Then he rolled, taking me with him, and pinning me under him.

"Let me go! *Let me go!*" I gasped, squirming against him. I was caught—trapped between his big, muscular body and the mattress—

but my top half was still free. I beat against his broad chest, but I might as well have been beating against a brick wall.

"So you were going to kill me in my sleep, were you?" Liath arched an eyebrow at me, completely unperturbed.

"Of course I was—I *am!*" I snarled fiercely. "You killed my brother—you took the only person I ever loved from me! You *deserve* to die!"

"Is *that* what you think?" He frowned, his face going dark. "You think *I* killed Quill?"

His use of my big brother's nickname surprised me, but I wasn't about to let it show on my face.

"I saw his body when they brought him from the battlefield!" I snapped. "You stabbed him through the heart—and you didn't even attack from the front! You stabbed him from behind, you craven bastard!"

His face went as dark as a thundercloud.

"You would accuse me of such a fucking cowardly act? What proof do you have?"

"What proof do I need? There were witnesses that saw what you did!" I spat. And then I was so angry I *literally* spat at him, spraying his face with my spittle to show my rage and contempt.

To my surprise, this didn't seem to make him angry. He was leaning on his elbows, pinning me to the bed and he simply grimaced and lifted one hand to wipe his cheeks.

"And what witnesses were these?" he asked, his voice low and steady. "Who saw me stab your brother in the back?"

"Well...my cousin, Asfaloth," I said, feeling uncertain for the first time. "He was at the battle that day—he saw what you did."

"And is he *known* for being truthful, your cousin?" Liath raised an eyebrow at me. "I'd say he's about as truthful as he is kind and compassionate. Which is to say *not fucking very.*"

"Are you saying he lied?" I demanded. "If you didn't kill my brother, who did?"

"How should I know?" Liath growled, frowning. "But I can tell you now—it *wasn't* me."

"Why should I believe you?" I demanded.

"You shouldn't," he said simply. "You don't know me well enough to trust me yet."

"I don't *want* to get to know you!" I snapped recklessly. "Why did you even ask for my hand? You told my father you didn't want to make peace between the two Courts and you *know* I can't help you take the Shadow Throne because I have no magic. And of course you didn't marry me for my beauty, for I have none! So why—why did you ask for me? Why did you take me?"

"Stop. Be still, little bird." I had been struggling furiously as I shouted my questions at him and now Liath took both my wrists in one big hand and pinned them above my head. He looked down at me, a stern expression on his face. "You're working yourself up—calm down."

"No, I *won't!*" I panted. "Let me go. Let…me…*go!*"

I fishtailed wildly under him, but again I might as well have been fighting a wall made of iron. He was simply so much bigger and stronger than me, there was nothing I could do to move him.

"There's too much here—let's take the things you said one at a time." Still, he was maddeningly calm, speaking to me as though I was a child having a tantrum. "First—no, I don't want peace between the Courts—not yet, anyway." he frowned. "Second, yes you *can* help me take the Shadow Throne because you *do* have magic—it's just buried," he went on.

This statement surprised me so much that I stopped struggling and just stared at him. He thought I had *magic?* That was impossible—I'd been trying all my life to do something—*anything*—magical. The wisest mages in the land had come to tutor me and…nothing. But somehow Liath thought he saw something in me that everyone else had missed. It made no sense.

But he hadn't even paused—he was still talking.

"Third," he said, frowning down at me. "Who says you're not beautiful?"

I looked away, feeling abruptly ashamed.

"Everyone," I mumbled. "I don't look like a Fae maiden should. I'm too big—all over."

"You're fucking *perfect*," Liath growled, frowning. "But I can see that no matter how many times I tell you that, you won't believe me. I'm going to have to *show* you."

"Show me?" I looked up at him in alarm. There was something hot and hard pressed against my thigh and, inexperienced though I was, it suddenly occurred to me what that rigid lump must be. I shrank away from him as much as I could—which wasn't very much, since he was still lying on top of me, pinning my hands above my head.

"No, not like that," Liath growled impatiently. "I'm no fucking rapist—I told you I won't take what you're not ready to give."

"But you…your, uh…it's *hard*," I whispered, nodding downward.

"How can I help getting hard when I have a beautiful maiden wiggling and squirming under me?" he demanded, raising his eyebrows. "My shaft doesn't just get hard when I'm going to fuck, you know—it gets hard when I'm fucking aroused and you're the most arousing thing I've seen in a very long time."

I shook my head.

"I don't believe you. Asfaloth always says—" I stopped abruptly, embarrassed to admit what my cruel cousin said of me.

But Liath wouldn't let me get away with it.

"No, go on. What does that ass say?" he demanded.

I looked away.

"He says looking at me would make any male sick—that the sight of my curves would turn his stomach."

Liath growled—a sound of pure frustration.

"All right—after a lifetime of that kind of bullshit, no *wonder* you think you're ugly. As I said before, I'm going to have to show you."

"What are you talking about?" I asked but he was already rolling off me. I sat up in the bed and watched in confusion as he walked across the room.

There was a large oval mirror in a golden frame which was taller than me. It was mounted in a heavy marble stand which I was sure wasn't meant to be moved. But Liath picked it up with one hand and carried it back. He set it up beside the bed and then beckoned to me.

"Come down here."

"What if I don't want to?" I asked in a low voice.

Liath gave me a stern look.

"Then I'll come and get you. Is that what you want, little bird?"

"I'll run and hide," I threatened. "Somewhere you'll never find me. Somewhere outside the palace."

"Then you'll freeze," he said shortly. "You're used to the eternal Summer of the Seelie Court. You won't make it an hour outside in the snow."

He was probably right, I thought. But I didn't want to just do whatever he said—I was too stubborn to want to be an obedient wife. However, I had to confess I was intrigued. How was he going to "show" me I was beautiful?

Reluctantly, I came down off the bed and went to him—though I didn't stand too close.

"All right, good." Liath nodded. "Now take off your gown."

"What?" I took a step back, clutching the long blue gown to me nervously. "I don't think so!"

He blew out a breath and ran a hand through his long hair.

"Do you really still think I'm going to rape you?"

"It...wouldn't really be rape," I pointed out faintly. "Not...not by the laws of our people."

Which was true. But the laws of Fae marriage, he was my husband now, so he owned me.

But Liath was shaking his head again.

"Little bird, I'd never force myself on you. For one thing, I'm not a fucking rapist, as I said before. For another, you'll soon have more power than anyone in either realm. I'd be a fool to provoke you."

I shook my head.

"What are you talking about? I don't have even a tiny *spark* of magic in my whole body! How could I be more powerful than anyone in either realm?"

"That's a lesson for another day. For now, take off your gown and come to me." Liath frowned at me. "And if we have to do it this way, we will—as your husband, I *order* you to do as I say."

"I thought you said I could leave the 'obey' part out of my vows," I whispered, but I was already walking towards him.

"Not in this case. Good—stand here—right in front of the mirror," Liath directed. "Now take off your gown. I need you naked for this to work."

I didn't want to do it. But he was my husband. All my life it had been drilled into me that I would obey my husband—whoever he turned out to be. I might put on a show of rebelliousness, but in truth, I felt compelled to do as he said—even though my stomach was twisted in knots at the idea of letting him see me naked.

Slowly, I pulled the dark blue gown over my head. I clutched it to my bare breasts for a moment but Liath frowned and shook his head.

"No, Alira—drop it."

I dropped the gown to the floor and stood there with nothing but my long midnight blue hair to hide me.

"Good." Liath came around behind me. I tensed up at once but he only rested his big hands very lightly on my bare shoulders. "Now look at yourself in the mirror," he murmured, leaning down to speak in my ear.

"Please, don't make me," I whispered. I had hated the sight of myself naked ever since Asfaloth and Calista had caught me swimming nude in a quiet pool in a forest glen one afternoon.

They had stolen my clothes and taunted me—saying I would have to go back to the Palace naked if I didn't do as they said. They refused to give my clothing back until I got out and stood with them, looking at my reflection in the pool. And all the while they were on either side of me, laughing and mocking me—saying how ugly and fat I was and how it should be illegal for me to ever take my clothes off again.

The memory was a painful one—it brought tears to my eyes.

"Hey...hey..." Liath was suddenly on one knee in front of me—it was the only way he could get down to my level, since he was so tall. He lifted my chin with one finger and looked into my eyes. "What is it? What's wrong?"

"I...don't like the way I look—*especially* naked," I whispered, blinking as the tears burned my eyes.

His bronze gaze softened.

"That's why I'm going to show how you *really* look, little bird. Trust me just for a moment—please?"

I still had no idea why he was doing this but he was my husband. I hadn't managed to kill him, so he basically owned me. I nodded dutifully and whispered,

"All right."

"Good." He rose to tower over me and then came to stand behind me again. He was still wearing just a pair of black breeches and I could feel the heat of his broad, bare chest radiating against my spine.

"Now look at yourself in the mirror," he commanded, putting his hands on my shoulders again. "Look and see yourself as *I* see you. See yourself as you really *are*."

I made myself look, though I didn't want to. I generally avoided my own reflection—especially when I was naked, as I was now. But I forced myself to examine my image anyway.

At first I saw what I always saw—the girl in the mirror was short and too curvy. Her breasts were too big and heavy, tipped with obscenely dark nipples. Her hips were too wide and her thighs were too thick. Her legs were too short and...

And suddenly things began to change.

Somehow, my eyes were drawn back up to my face in the mirror and I heard a voice whisper in my head,

"Such beautiful hair—so long and soft, like blue silk."

The voice was deep and growling. Was it Liath? Was he speaking inside my mind somehow? It must be magic—once again I had the sensation of soft fur brushing my naked body. The light, sensuous touch sent a shiver through me. By the Shining Throne, it felt so good! How was he doing this?

I wanted to ask, but I felt unable to talk—all I could do was look at what the voice was talking about. And sure enough, my hair *was* beautiful and long and thick and silky.

"Such a gorgeous face—cute little nose...big gray eyes like quiet pools...a mouth any male would want to kiss," the voice in my head went on.

To my surprise, I suddenly saw myself that way. I had never thought much of my face—it was agreeable, but not nearly pretty enough to make up for my unsightly curves. But now I looked at myself in the mirror and saw a girl with a gorgeous face looking back at me. I wondered breathlessly what else the voice would show me.

"Look at these lush, full breasts," the voice growled in my head and suddenly Liath was reaching around to cup my breasts. They filled his big hands, just as I had thought they might earlier, during our ceremony. I felt a shiver run through my body as he held me in his big, warm hands.

"Gods, I love how big they are! And such juicy nipples—a male could spend all night sucking them."

His long fingers pinched my tight peaks, making me moan. No

one had ever touched me this way before! And of course, it was forbidden to touch myself.

"Oh!" I gasped as he tugged my tender points, sending sparks of pleasure through my whole body.

"Love how they fill my hands," the voice growled. *"And they're so sensitive, aren't they, little bird? I bet you feel it all the way down in your pussy when I do this..."*

I shivered with the unfamiliar sensations of desire and pleasure as I watched in the mirror while Liath teased and tugged my nipples. All my life I'd been told my breasts were too big—too crude. That only the tiny, barely there bumps of the other Fae maidens were desirable. I had never dreamed that a male might *like* how big and sensitive my breasts were.

*"I like **everything** about you,"* the voice assured me and I wondered if he was somehow reading my mind. Then his big hands left my breasts and slid down my sides, framing my broad hips.

I had always hated the fact that I had such wide hips and thick thighs—they were the very opposite of the Fae standard of beauty which dictated that only straight, boyish hips and long, slender legs were attractive. But now I began to see myself as Liath saw me.

"Love how ripe you are everywhere, little bird," his voice murmured. *"A male needs something to hold onto when he's loving his female."* His hands caressed the wide curves of my hips and then slid around to cup my bottom.

I gasped as he grasped both cheeks and squeezed, a low growl of approval rising in his throat.

"I want these gorgeous thick thighs wrapped around my waist... around my head," he added, his big hands running down over my thighs. *"Want to feel you squeezing me and moaning my name!"*

I was panting by now—my bare breasts heaving as I tried to catch my breath. No one had ever spoken to me this way before or touched me or told me I was beautiful...desirable. I felt hot and flushed all over—as though my entire body was blushing and yet I didn't want him to stop.

"You look like a fucking goddess," Liath murmured—speaking aloud this time. "And I haven't even talked about *this* yet..."

His large right hand came back around and slid between my legs to cup my sex. He didn't try to penetrate me, but I could feel his long middle finger pressing against my slit—pressing against the little pleasure button there that I had known all my life to be my most forbidden spot.

"Look at this sweet little pussy," he growled softly in my ear. "Gods, how I'd love to taste it!"

"Wh-what?" I met his eyes in the mirror uncertainly. This was something new—something I had never heard before. Was he serious? He wanted to taste me *there?*

"You really are innocent, aren't you little bird?" Liath murmured. "You've never had a male's hands on you, have you? Or his mouth between your legs."

"N-never!" I stammered.

"Well then, perhaps this is enough for now."

Reluctantly, I thought, he withdrew his hands, placing them back on my shoulders.

"Look at yourself again," he commanded.

I looked...and saw a full-figured, curvy goddess. She had long, silky hair, big gray eyes that shone like stars, and sweet, kissable lips. Her full breasts were tipped with ripe nipples just begging to be sucked and her wide hips and thick thighs made her look both gorgeous and fertile. The tiny patch of dark blue curls between her thighs was the gateway to paradise for the lucky male who was privileged to be invited in.

"Tell me," Liath murmured in my ear. "What do you see?"

"Oh," I whispered with wonder and delight. "I...I'm *beautiful.*"

"Yes, you fucking are," he growled. "And don't forget it—if you do, I'll show you again." He turned me to face him, cupping my face in his big hands. "I'm going to kiss you now—since we didn't get to kiss at our Joining ceremony," he told me. "But not here..."

He led me up the steps of the dais to the bed again and sat on the edge of it, which put us more or less on the same level.

"Now, come here," he growled and pulled me to stand between his thighs.

I gasped as my bare breasts pressed against his hard chest and my nipples tingled at the contact. Liath pulled me even closer—his bronze eyes were burning with desire. Then I closed my own eyes as he bent towards me.

His lips met mine and I gave a soft moan. This was my first kiss—a kiss I had never expected to get. Calista had always told me I was too ugly for anyone to want to kiss me and somehow I had believed her. Now I knew she had been lying—she and Asfaloth both.

But I didn't want to think of them. I pushed the thought of my cruel cousins out of my head and felt myself melting against my new husband as he kissed me, showing me things I had never thought could be.

I felt the tip of his tongue probing gently at the seam of my lips and I parted for him instinctively. His tongue darted in, tasting me lightly, and then he was leading my own tongue back to his mouth.

Daring greatly, I slipped my tongue between his lips and he sucked it gently. His mouth tasted hot and sweet and slightly spicy and his big, warm hands were rubbing up and down my bare body, sliding over my back and hips and bottom. He gripped my ass hard and brought me against him, pressing against me until I felt the ridge of his shaft rubbing against my naked sex, parting the outer lips to rub against the forbidden button again.

I gasped in pleasure and writhed against him and then his hands traveled back up to cup and squeeze my breasts and tease my nipples until I moaned restlessly.

"So fucking beautiful," I heard his magical voice growling in my head again. How was he doing this? I had never heard of magic that allowed one to transfer thoughts.

"There's a lot you haven't heard of, little bird," Liath murmured. *"And I'm going to teach you all of it...but that's enough for tonight."*

And he broke the kiss, pulling back from me.

By this time I was panting, filling to overflowing with the unfamiliar sensations. I felt as though part of me had been asleep all my life and my new husband had somehow awakened it. I didn't have a name for it yet—this new part of me—but it was *hungry*. And it wanted *more*.

"More!" I whispered, half-ashamed of begging, but unable to help myself.

But Liath shook his head, a slight smile curving the corners of his sensuous mouth.

"These things can't be rushed, little bird. Besides, we need to save something for your lessons."

"My lessons?" I asked, frowning uncertainly. "What lessons?"

"Your magic lessons." Liath smiled mysteriously. "Don't worry—you'll see. We'll start tomorrow."

"But...I don't *have* magic," I protested.

"You do. And I'll prove it to you tomorrow," he promised. "Now put your gown back on—you're too damn temping all naked and hot like that."

I looked down at myself and realized all over again that I was completely nude and that I had been pressing myself against him wantonly as he kissed me. What was wrong with me? Why had I done that—acted like that? It must have been his magic working on me, I thought—making me do things I wouldn't normally do.

Liath rose from his seat on the end of the bed and headed towards the bathing chamber.

"Where are you going?" I asked. "I mean, why are you leaving?"

"Because as I said—you're too damn tempting," he growled. His bronze eyes flashed. "Got to take care of myself before I can trust myself to sleep beside you—especially if you're going to sleep naked, like that." He raised an eyebrow at me. "Which might be dangerous—better put back on the gown, like I said."

Blushing, I found my gown on the floor and scrambled to get back into it. By the time I finished, Liath was in the bathing chamber with the door closed.

I got into bed and slid under the covers, filled with confusion and unfulfilled tension and longing. But what was I longing for—for Liath to take me? Of course not! The very thought filled me with horror...didn't it?

Actually, it didn't anymore. If anything, I felt intrigued by the idea. The image of him on top of me, spreading my legs, filling me with himself, flashed across my mind's eye again. It had shocked and horrified me before...now I felt a warm flush of desire as I considered it.

Stop it—what's wrong with you? I scolded myself. *He killed Quill!*

But had he? He had said he wasn't my brother's killer and now that I thought of it, Asfaloth was the only one who claimed to have seen the killing. Who did I trust more—my cruel cousin or my new husband, whom I barely knew?

I couldn't honestly tell. I felt that I *wanted* to trust Liath—but I wasn't sure I could. He was Unseelie—the enemy of my people. All my life I had been warned against the unnatural monsters and creatures that inhabited the Winter Court.

And now I inhabited it too—what did that make me?

I didn't know anymore—I didn't know anything. Maybe I would find out tomorrow...

I settled down in the bed, with the warm, dark blue comforter pulled up to my chin. The pillow I pressed my face to had Liath's scent on it—warm and spicy. It smelled a little like leather and a bit like smoke. I also detected notes of fresh cut cedar and snow, which had been unfamiliar to me before, but was distinctive. And under all that was a masculine musk that was at once and entirely Liath.

I couldn't help breathing it in…and wondering what he was doing in the bathing chamber. He had said he was going to "take care of himself." Did that mean what I thought it meant? Surely not! But what if it did?

I was so innocent I wasn't even sure how a male would go about "taking care of himself"—or indeed, what a male looked like with his breeches off. But that didn't stop me from trying to imagine what might be happening behind the closed door.

These thoughts and imaginings made me restless and I tossed and turned, wishing I could stop the strange feelings that Liath had somehow caused in me when he touched me and kissed me.

I wished I could touch myself—I wanted to run my hands over my breasts and nipples and maybe even press the magic button between my legs that gave such intense pleasure—but I knew I must not. My early lessons, where my old nurse had bound my arms to my sides for days for the sin of reaching between my legs, were too strongly ingrained in me. I must *not* touch myself or take pleasure in my own body—it was *wrong*.

I closed my eyes and tried to think of calming things—the shadows of the forest and the cool breeze blowing through the trees… It wasn't easy, but slowly I began to feel calmer and even drowsy.

At last, just as I was finally drifting off, Liath emerged. He was freshly bathed and was wearing a long pair of soft sleep trousers. His eyes flicked to the night table, where his dagger was still where he had put it.

"Have you decided not to kill me after all, then, little bird?" he asked, as he slid into the bed beside me.

I frowned up at him.

"Not now, anyway. Not until I find out what really happened to my brother."

Liath's face went grim.

"You're not the only one who wants to know. But there's no finding out tonight."

He yawned hugely and settled into his side of the bed—which was also part of the middle, since he was so big. "Will you come here and cuddle with me on our first night of marriage?" he asked, raising his eyebrows at me and spreading out one arm in invitation.

"*Cuddle* with you?" I looked at him mistrustfully. "Is that all we'd do—just cuddle?"

He raised an eyebrow.

"Did you forget that just a little while ago you were naked in my arms begging for 'more,' little bird?"

I felt my cheeks get hot with embarrassment and I frowned at him.

"That was your magic making me act that way. I couldn't help it—you made it feel like soft fur was brushing over my body."

Liath gave me an interested look.

"Is *that* what my magic feels like to you?"

"You know it does," I protested, but he shook his head.

"No, of course I don't. I can't make it 'feel' any particular way—I just do it. But the very fact that you're so sensitive to the feeling of someone else's magic proves you have strong magic of your own."

"It proves no such thing," I said, frowning. "All my life I've tried to do magic—and all my life I've failed."

Liath arched an eyebrow at me.

"All your life you thought you weren't beautiful and yet now you know you are."

I felt my cheeks get hot and opened my mouth to protest, but he beat me to it.

"Don't say you're not again—you're fucking gorgeous. *Own* your beauty, Alira."

I didn't know what to say to that. I was still tempted to feel uncertain about my looks, but the way Liath was looking at me, his bronze eyes half-lidded with desire, gave me a shot of self confidence. He saw me as beautiful and that enabled me to see myself the same way.

So what if I didn't fit the Seelie Court's definition of beauty—neither did Liath, with his horns and his gray skin and his scar and his huge stature—but I found him extremely handsome and desirable—much more so than I should, I was sure. Why should only skinny, pale Fae maidens be beautiful? Why couldn't I, with my full curves and dark hair and eyes, be beautiful too?

"You *are* beautiful," Liath rumbled. "So fucking gorgeous it makes my shaft ache—though I shouldn't say that since I don't want to scare you."

I frowned at him.

"Are you reading my mind?"

He shook his head.

"No—I only catch thoughts here and there." He pointed to his horns. It's because I'm part Manticore. Also, you think very loudly, little bird. I knew you wanted to kill me long before you snuck out of the bathing chamber and took my dagger—I just wasn't sure why."

"You knew?" I demanded. "So…you were just pretending to be asleep earlier? Why?"

He shrugged.

"Thought we might as well get it over with. Also, I was curious to see how far you'd go."

"Not far enough, apparently," I muttered. I wasn't happy to know he could read my thoughts.

"Come on now—you don't really want to kill me anymore," Liath rumbled. "What you *want* to do is come here and get close to me—because this big bedroom gets cold at night and I'm always warm."

"You are?" I asked, nibbling my lower lip.

He motioned for me again.

"Why don't you find out? I'm tired of begging so I'll order you as your husband." He gave me a stern look. "Come press your soft, curvy, beautiful body against mine, Alira. *Now*."

His voice was a low, seductive rumble and I felt that something he had woken in me—the thing I'd tried so hard to put back to sleep—stir in response.

Still somewhat unwillingly, I scooted over towards him. I wasn't sure how this was going to work—I had never slept with anyone before. But Liath wrapped one long arm around me and drew me close to him.

I gave a little gasp as I felt my breasts press against his warm side. I would have resisted and drawn back but he had ordered me as my husband. And besides…I rather liked how it felt to be close to him. He was so big and warm and muscular and he smelled so good…

"Mmm…thank you, little bird. I think you smell fucking amazing too." He looked down at me, his bronze eyes half-lidded.

After half a mesmerizing moment I had to look away from his intense gaze. There he went again—picking thoughts out of my brain. An ability he said he had inherited from an ancestor.

"I didn't know that Manticores had horns," I remarked, looking up at him.

He shrugged.

"My ancestor did, apparently. The legend in my family is that my great-great grandmother risked bedding with a Manticore because she wanted a child with special powers."

"Did she get one?" I asked, curious despite myself.

"She got one son who could read minds and see into the hearts of others…and one that was a fucking monster. It took half the Court to kill him," Liath said grimly.

"By the Shining Throne," I murmured. "Really? They killed a royal Prince?"

"They had to or *he* would have killed them and laid waste to the whole fucking Court." Liath frowned at me. "You know all those scary stories you've been told all your life about the Unseelie Court?"

"Yes?" I whispered, looking up at him.

"They're all true," Liath said grimly. "The Winter Realm is a fucking dangerous place—so until you master your power, you're going to want to stick close by my side. All right?"

I didn't see that I had a choice.

"All right," I whispered.

"Hey—don't look so frightened. I'll protect you, little bird." Liath squeezed me gently. "Tell me, can you feel other's magic too?" he asked, returning to our earlier topic. "Or is it just mine?"

"I can feel anyone's magic," I admitted. I explained how Tansy's magic had felt like a rough scrubbing brush and Asfaloth and Calista's magic felt like stinging insects, biting me all over.

Liath frowned.

"That must have been fucking difficult—being so sensitive to all the magic around you and not being able to get to the magic inside you."

"I don't know why you're so sure I have magic," I told him. "I'm afraid you're going to be disappointed and want to send me back to the Summer Court."

"Never!" Liath growled deep in his throat and I felt the vibrations through my whole body. He drew me even closer to his big body, his arm tightening possessively around me. "You're *mine* now, Alira," he told me. "And I'm *never* letting you go."

Then he turned the lights from the chandeliers all the way out with a word, plunging the room completely into a gray, twilight gloom. I lay there, pressed against him and wondering what I had gotten myself into.

I had thought I was marrying my brother's killer—I had sworn to get revenge. Now, I wasn't sure of anything.

My mind was racing but little by little it started to calm down. I found myself soothed by the deep, steady rhythm of Liath's breathing and the beating of his heart, which I could hear since my ear—along with the rest of me—was pressed to his side.

Without knowing when it happened, I drifted off to sleep with thoughts of my new husband and my new home still buzzing like bees in the back of my brain.

10

I woke to the same gray twilight I had gone to sleep to, but the chandeliers had turned themselves up to shed a golden glow, rather like early morning sunshine over the bed chamber.

Liath was already up and getting dressed. He had on another pair of black breeches and his enormous black boots. Once more he was shirtless—I wondered if that was the regular mode of dress for the Winter Court. I would have asked if he ever got cold—but I was pretty sure I knew the answer to that. He had kept me toasty warm last night, despite the drop in temperature. His big, muscular body seemed to put out heat like a furnace.

"Come on—it's time you met your subjects, future Queen of Shadows," he said to me, when he saw I was awake.

"*What* did you call me?" I frowned as I slipped out of bed, shivering as the cold marble floor touched my bare feet.

"Queen of Shadows—she who sits the Shadow Throne is always referred to as the Queen of Shadows," he told me.

"But I can't! I would never even *try*," I exclaimed. "You even told me that if the wrong person sits on the Shadow Throne, it *kills* them!"

"But you're *not* the wrong person. You're the exact fucking right one. Come—we don't have much time. Get dressed," Liath rumbled.

"What am I dressing for?" I asked, deciding not to fight with him about his ridiculous statements. He would learn soon enough that I didn't have a magical bone in my body.

"To meet your subjects—and for breakfast in the Great Hall," he told me. "And afterwards, we're taking a walk. Don't worry," he added. "Just wear something comfortable."

I went to the closet in the bathing chamber and selected a simple dark green gown which went extremely well with my blue hair. It had a deep V-neck which showed a lot more cleavage than I would have been comfortable with if I had still been in the Summer Court. But here at the Winter Court, I found I wanted to make an impression.

I just wished that I had a necklace or any kind of jewelry to wear to go with the gown's deep décolletage. I paired the dress with soft black shoes that molded to my feet and felt as comfortable as though I'd been wearing them for years.

A look in the mirror standing in the corner of the bathing chamber made me smile at my newly-beautiful reflection. I was glad to see that Liath's magic—if that was what it was—hadn't worn off. I still felt lovely as I looked at myself in the mirror.

"That's because you *are* fucking lovely," Liath growled, coming up behind me. "And don't fucking forget it. Here."

He pulled out his dagger and pricked his finger. Then he re-sheathed it, made a gesture, and began pulling things out of the air.

First came a dazzling silver necklace set with moonstones, much like the ones on the dagger's hilt. Then came a pair of dangling moonstone earrings and a delicate filigreed tiara also set with the same pale, sparkling gems. Last was a ring with an oval moonstone as large as my eye.

"Only those of the Royal house may wear or use moonstones," Liath explained, as he fastened the necklace around my neck and arranged the tiara on my head. "This jewelry marks you as mine and under my protection. Always wear at least one of these pieces, anywhere you go in the Winter Realm. That way, no one will dare to fucking to touch you," he added, sliding the ring onto my finger.

"Thank you." I looked in the mirror again and was surprised at how regal the pale, gleaming stones made me look.

"Like a true Queen of Shadows," Liath rumbled approvingly. "Come on—let's go."

He led me out of his rooms—our rooms, I supposed—and through the Palace again. It was a bit of a maze but since it was a mirror image copy of the Summer Palace, I thought I would be able to find my way around.

Not that I would be spending much time exploring on my own—Liath had warned me to stay close to him and considering the frightening stories I had heard of the Winter Court, I was inclined to obey my new husband.

Are you really trusting him now—so quickly, so easily? a skeptical little voice whispered in my head. *How do you know he's telling the truth and he's not the one who killed Quill?*

I didn't know, of course. But until I could find out the identity of my big brother's killer, I felt I had little choice other than to trust Liath. Besides, I rather liked his company. He wasn't the huge, evil brute I'd been led to expect. He was…I wasn't sure *what* he was yet, but I wanted to find out.

The Great Hall was in the same place the Banquet Hall was in the Summer Palace and it was set up the same too, with a long table up on a raised dais for royalty and many smaller tables below for the nobility and other important people of the court.

Liath led me to the front of the room, to stand before the dais. When he stopped, everyone went silent. He didn't even have to call for quiet as my father often had his favorite courier do when he wished to make a speech—everyone simply hushed when they saw the massive Unseelie warrior standing there.

"My people," Liath said, raising his deep voice to be heard to the far corners of the hall. "May I introduce my bride—Princess Alira. Though she comes from the Seelie Court, she has Unseelie blood in her veins and thus she is one of us. More importantly, however, she is *mine.*" He paused for a moment, looking around at the assembled nobles and notables. "I will only warn you once—anyone who hurts or attempts any malicious magic against my bride, I will treat you as though you attacked me directly. And I will *show no mercy.* Do I make myself clear?"

His voice was a deep, menacing rumble and I couldn't help feeling a shiver run down my spine. Was his Court really so dangerous that he had to threaten them all to keep them from attacking me? What kind of snake pit had I married into? Also, what did he mean when he said I had "Unseelie blood in my veins?" I had no such lineage that I knew of. Was he lying about me in order to get his people to accept me?

There was a murmur of ascent from all those assembled which seemed to satisfy Liath. He nodded his head.

"Good. May I encourage you to come up and pay your respects to your new Princess—my new bride. Please be respectful and remember she is unused to our ways."

Then he led me up onto the dais. He sat in the middle of the long table and put me at his right hand—a place of honor reserved for the person who was closest to the ruler. I had never been given that seat beside my father—I was lucky if he even let me dine at the Royal table. Even then, I was usually squeezed in on the end as an afterthought. But Liath treated me like his queen.

"Hello, my dear," said a soft, cracked voice beside me.

I turned and saw a little old lady—almost bent double with age. I thought she must be ancient, since the Fae age much more slowly than mortals do. Her face was a mask of wrinkles and her hair was gray, but she gave me a kindly smile and a little wave. She was wearing fingerless gloves, I saw, and though her fingers were crooked, she went back to knitting something rapidly after she waved.

"Oh, hello," I said awkwardly. "I'm, uh, Alira."

"So I heard." She nodded graciously. "I am Liath's great, great Aunt Acosta."

"I was about to introduce you two, Aunt Acosta," Liath rumbled from my other side. "Alira, meet my great, great Aunt. She's been at the Winter Court almost since it came to be in the first place."

"That I have." The ancient lady nodded and smiled at me again. She had very white, obviously fake teeth the likes of which I had never seen before. She also had tiny, curling horns on the sides of her head—much smaller than Liath's and almost hidden in her salt and pepper hair.

"I got them from a doe," she said to me, still knitting.

"Pardon?" I frowned. "Got what?"

"My teeth, dear—I saw you admiring them." She tapped her white, even teeth with one of her knitting needles. "Brought it down myself—by magic of course. I can still hunt, you know."

"You...can?" I looked at her blankly. My father's Court rode out to hunt every now and then but I hadn't known the denizens of the Unseelie Court did as well. After all, all their lands were cold and barren—what was there to hunt?

Well, deer apparently.

"I certainly can." Great Aunt Acosta lifted her chin proudly. "I killed it and pulled the teeth and used a binding spell to fix them together. Used a whitening spell too." She grinned again, that white grin of hers. "And then do you know what I did?"

"Er...no. What did you do?" I asked politely.

"Why, the cooks made venison stew that night and I used that doe's own teeth to eat her up!" She cackled with laughter and repeated, "Ate her up—with her own teeth!"

"How...nice," I said, unsure what else to say.

"Don't mind Aunt Acosta," Liath leaned down to rumble in my ear. "She's a little mad. Harmless, though."

I simply nodded, not knowing what else to say.

"Liath has certainly got you all fixed up, doesn't he, dearie?" the old lady said. She nodded at all the moonstone jewelry I was wearing. "You've got on Queen Mab's entire regalia, you know. I wonder how she'd feel about a Seelie girl wearing her things?"

"Now, Aunt Acosta, Alira has Unseelie blood too," Liath protested.

"She does, does she?" The old lady frowned at me. "Where's her horns then? Or her wings? A tail?" She peered at me closely. "*Are* you hiding a tail under that pretty dress, my dear?"

"Oh, I...I'm afraid not. Sorry to disappoint you," I said politely, though it had never occurred to me I might have to apologize to anyone for *not* having a tail or any other animal-type abnormality. But maybe here in the Unseelie Court, it was normal.

"Ssspeaking of her pretty dresss, *I* am the one to thank for that."

The hissing voice came from the front of the dais. I looked up and had to school my face not to display shock.

There in front of the Royal table was a spider woman. That is to say, her bottom half was that of a large spider—and when I say "large" I mean a spider the size of a horse. Her torso began where the spider's head would have been and she had four long arms that had two elbows apiece. The top half of her was clothed in brilliant, poison green, which matched the green stripes on her black spider's body. Her face was mostly human, except for the cluster of extra eyes on her forehead.

"Ah—this is Shellya—our Royal seamstress. She made everything in your closet—except for the shoes, of course," Liath said, introducing us.

"Oh—thank you so much," I said politely. "I, er, love your work! The fabric is so soft."

"It should be—I ssspin it myself," she hissed proudly. "Jussst let me know if you need anything elssse."

"Actually, Alira and I are taking a walk outside after we have our breakfast and she's not used to the cold of the Winter Court," Liath told her. "Do you think you could make her a nice warm cloak to wear? With a hood to keep her ears warm," he added, looking at me.

"But of courssse, my Lord!" Shellya seemed extremely pleased to be asked. "I ssshall retire to the corner and begin work on it at once," she promised. With a final nod of her head, she scuttled off to one corner of the Great Hall and began spinning, dipping low to grasp a thin line of silk which came from her bulbous abdomen, which she then began knitting into a cloak with her four arms.

"She'll be finished in no time," Liath told me. "She's remarkably fast."

"She, uh, certainly is," I said, trying not to stare at the spider woman at work. She would have been considered a monstrosity at the Summer Court but here she was a normal person with a job. I liked that—liked that people weren't automatically excluded or hated just because they were different here in the Winter Court.

"Have some blueberry pancakes," Liath rumbled, putting some on my plate before I could protest. "Bacon?"

"Well..." I hesitated uncertainly. I loved this kind of substantial breakfast food but I knew it would do me no favors. "I'd better not," I said at last. "It will go straight to my hips."

"Let it," Liath said, forking a small mound of bacon onto my plate. "More of your gorgeous curves to hold onto." He gave me a wolfish grin and offered me a pot of syrup.

I was eating what was possibly the most delicious breakfast I had ever had, when a new person approached the Royal table—a centaur.

I stared at him in wide-eyed wonder. Everyone knows of the wisdom of centaurs but they left the Seelie Court long ago. They study the stars and know many things before they happen.

"Ah, Master Stableforth." Liath actually rose to acknowledge the visitor, reaching across the table to clasp his hand.

"Your Majesty." Stableforth the centaur bowed from his human waist. "And this must be your new bride—she who shall straddle the divide between night and light," he said, bowing to me as well.

"Um, excuse me?" I asked, raising my eyebrows. "I'm not sure what you mean by that."

"The ancient texts speak of a Fae maiden who is raised in the Summer Court but maries into the Winter Court," Stableforth explained. "It is said that she will have the power to rend the veil between the Courts so that the inhabitants may venture back and forth, as they did before the Great Divide was put up."

The Great Divide was the barrier between the Summer and Winter Courts—which technically occupy the same physical space, just at different times of the year. I had been shocked on our wedding day to see Liath breach it so easily—but the idea of actually tearing a permanent hole in it had never occurred to me. The amount of magic such a thing would cost to accomplish was almost unthinkable.

"I'm afraid you have the wrong maiden," I said politely. "I do not possess powers capable of such a feat, Sir. Or indeed, any powers at all," I added, shooting a sidelong glance at Liath.

"She won't believe she's got magic," he explained to the centaur, who was looking at me with some surprise in his mild brown eyes. (His hind quarters or "horse half" was a palomino, if you're interested.)

"But the ancient texts and the stars both agree," he said, frowning at me. "One or the other might very occasionally be wrong—but not *both*. It's simply impossible."

"Yet here I sit with no magic, Sir Centaur." I lifted my empty, powerless hands to show him what I meant.

"She just hasn't learned to access it yet—she still thinks Summer Court magic is the only kind there is," Liath said to Stableforth.

The centaur's bushy eyebrows drew down low.

"Summer Court magic is *stolen* magic," he proclaimed in a ringing voice which was almost approaching a neigh. "It is a fake—no true magic at all!"

I thought of telling him that I had seen Asfaloth actually turn a man inside out using this 'fake' magic but decided it would be an unforgivably rude thing to say—especially at the breakfast table. So I kept my mouth shut.

"*You* know that and *I* know that, but Alira is still an innocent," Liath told the centaur.

"Innocence must be lost if knowledge is to be gained," the Centaur said obliquely.

"Yes, Master Stableforth—of that I am aware," Liath said. "We'll be having our first magic lesson this afternoon. But first I must convince Alira that she has magic in the first place."

"Of course, of course." The Centaur nodded his head. "Well, please let me know if I may be any help."

"Thank you. I certainly will." Liath nodded politely back and Master Stableforth trotted sedately away.

"I've never seen a Centaur in the flesh before," I murmured to Liath.

"They are becoming increasingly rare, which is a great pity. Master Stableforth is one of my advisors," he told me. "In fact, he's the one who advised me to ask for your hand."

"Really?" I gave him a sidelong glance. "So you can blame *him* when you find out I have no magic, then," I remarked.

"We'll see." Liath didn't sound worried a bit. "Would you like more to eat?"

"No thank you," I said hastily. "They'll have to roll me away from the table if I take another bite."

It was a bigger breakfast than I'd had in...well, ever. As I said, I had been on what felt like a starvation diet in the Summer Court, though it was normal fare for the other High Fae. But a diet of candied flower petals and rose water tea just didn't fill me up—or make me slender, even though that was the goal.

"If you're ready, we'll go as soon as we've met a few more of your new subjects," Liath remarked. "Look, here comes Striath the Satyr now."

We wound up staying almost an hour more as a line of people, who would not have been considered people at all in the Seelie Court, came to make my acquaintance. I met the aforementioned Satyr, who had a muscular man's torso and a goat's shaggy legs, as well as a gaggle of giggling pixies no taller than my knee, some grumpy redcaps, a sweet young dryad who was to be my personal maid, and too many more to count.

They all came to nod and bow and wish Liath and me well on our marriage. We both nodded and accepted their well-wishes. I smiled graciously until the corners of my mouth ached—if I learned nothing else in the Seelie Court, I *did* learn faultless manners.

Finally everyone who was anyone had been met and Liath rose from the table. Taking my hand, he helped me rise too and also offered a hand to his Great Aunt Acosta.

"Thank you, my boy," she said, as he pulled her to her feet. She smiled at me. "And you, my dear—you're one of the family now. So you'd best hurry and give my great nephew a baby."

"Oh, um..." I could feel the color rising in my cheeks and I wasn't sure what to say.

"Now, Aunt Acosta, we only just got Joined yesterday," Liath said heartily. "It's a bit early to be thinking of babies."

"No, it's not! Not if you hope to ever hold the Shadow Throne," she said grimly. "Just you mind you put a baby in her belly as quick as ever you can!" she added as she shuffled away from the table. "We *must* keep the Throne in the Blackthorn family. It is *imperative*."

"I'll keep your advice in mind, Aunt," Liath said politely.

I thought the embarrassing incident was over, but the old lady grabbed me by the arm.

"Walk me down the dais, will you dearie?" she said to me, giving me a puckered smile from her mouthful of stolen teeth. "At my age, it's so easy to trip."

"Oh, well—of course." As off-putting as I was beginning to find Liath's Great Aunt, I could hardly refuse to help her.

Aunt Acosta gripped my arm more tightly as we navigated the few steps down from the Royal table. I expected her to let go of me as soon as we reached the bottom, but she only clutched me tighter.

"Listen to me, dearie," she whispered loudly. "If you're a shy one and have trouble parting your legs for a male, I can send along a passion potion to your room. Just slip some in your tea or wine and you won't have a bit of trouble letting your new husband breed you."

I felt shocked at her language—the more so because it was coming from what ought to have been a proper old lady.

"Thank you, but I do believe I shall manage," I said frostily, wondering how in the world I was ever going to extricate myself from her grip. Liath was no help—he was across the room, talking to the spider woman seamstress, so he couldn't rescue me from his Great Aunt.

"Just listen before you wave me off," she insisted. "I can be sure the baby he plants in your belly is a female! For only a woman can sit the Shadow Throne, as you well know. I would have tried it myself, but I'm too old! Too old by half!" She cackled, showing her bright white, stolen teeth again.

"Er, thank you for your offer," I said, not sure what else to say. "It's...very kind of you, I'm sure."

"I'm sure, too!" she laughed again and squeezed my arm in her claw-like grip. It was really beginning to hurt!

Just then, Liath finally extricated himself from his conversation with the spider seamstress and came to find me. He had a soft, twilight blue cloak over one arm.

"Oh, there you are, little bird," he rumbled. "Aunt Acosta, we must go now," he added. "I have something important to show my new bride."

"Well, I hope it's the shaft between your legs, my boy!" she exclaimed and cackled while I blushed helplessly. "Look at her—turning pink as a rose in bloom," she added, pointing at me. "You've got a proper virgin for your bride, Liath. Best break her in easy but don't wait too long—you've got to plant a babe in her belly as soon as you can!"

What was the old woman's obsession with Liath breeding me, I wondered indignantly? It was so embarrassing!

Liath must have seen my pink cheeks because he laughed as he sent his great aunt on her way.

"Don't be so shy, little bird. Aunt Acosta means well."

"*Does* she?" I muttered, watching her bent back retreating. She was shuffling away with surprising speed—apparently she could really move when she wanted to.

"Yes, she does," Liath said firmly. He held out a hand to me. "Come on now—forget about her. I have something important to show you and then we'll have your first magic lesson."

Doing my best to forget Aunt Acosta's odious words and offer, I took my new husband's hand. I was interested to see whatever it was he wanted to show me but as for giving me a magic lesson, well...I was still convinced he was going to be gravely disappointed.

There was no way he could teach what I didn't have.

11

"Those won't do at all," Liath remarked, surveying the little black shoes I had on which were clearly only for indoor or Summer wear. "The snow is fucking deep in places—I don't want you freezing your pretty little feet off."

He had already tied the new cloak and hood, made by the Spider seamstress in the time it had taken to eat breakfast, around my neck. But now he stared in consternation at my footwear.

"I'm sorry—I should have thought to wear something else," I apologized immediately.

Liath shook his head.

"No, don't say you're sorry for something that's not your fault. I should have told you to wear boots. Here."

He pulled out his dagger, pricked a finger, and a moment later I was wearing thick, comfortable leather boots with warm, woolly socks beneath them.

"Oh!" I gave a gasp at the sudden change. I was used to magic being done all around me, but as always, when Liath did it, I could *feel* it so clearly. In this case, the soft fur rubbing against my most delicate parts seemed extra intense.

"You all right, little bird?" He arched an eyebrow at me. When I nodded, he said, "Good. Then let's go—the Pool of Seeing is a fair piece from here and you can't reach it by magic. You must go there physically."

"The Pool of Seeing? What's that?" I asked, frowning as we stepped out the doors of the palace. The Winter weather was cold and crisp and I could see my breath puff out in a cloud in front of me—something I had never experienced in the eternal Summer of the Seelie Court.

"You'll see," Liath said mysteriously. "Come on."

And he led me into the woods surrounding the Winter Palace, despite the fact that there was a perfectly good road leading in the same direction we were going.

"Hey, why can't we use the road?" I huffed as we tramped through the snow.

"Because the Pool of Seeing cannot be found by following any road," Liath said over his shoulder. "You simply have to get lost in the forest around the Winter Palace and eventually you'll come to it."

I wondered how long "eventually" was. Traveling through the forest in Winter was much more difficult than it had been in Summer. There were roots and tangles of dead vines and underbrush, all of which were hidden by the snow. These kept tripping me and since I have never been graceful like a Fae maiden is supposed to be, I kept having to catch myself by grabbing tree trunks to keep from falling. This was hard on my hands, which were already numb with cold. Still, I tried to keep going—I didn't want Liath to think I was a burden or too weak to keep up with him.

But keeping up with his long strides really *was* beginning to be a problem. I was falling further and further behind and I was too proud to ask him to wait for me. Meanwhile he kept on tramping tirelessly

—his enormous boots simply crushed the vines and tangles that tripped me—so he was able to go more quickly.

"Oh!" I gasped at last, as a tangle of roots hidden by the snow caught my booted foot. And that was followed by an, "Ouch!" Because the trunk I caught myself on to keep from tripping happened to be covered in a thorny vine.

I pulled my hand away and examined my bleeding palm as I sank to my knees in the snow. It *really* hurt—there was a stinging sensation and the flesh was already swelling, as though the thorns that had pierced my flesh had some kind of toxin on them.

"Alira? Little bird?" Liath was suddenly at my side. "What are you doing way back here?" he demanded, kneeling beside me. "And why have you touched the touch-me-not vine?"

"I didn't do it on purpose!" I exclaimed, blinking back tears as he examined my palm. "I tripped and I was trying to catch myself."

"Well, this is bad. I need to heal it immediately—before the poison gets into your blood."

"I'm sorry," I said as he drew his dagger.

"Sorry for what?" he asked, as he drew the tip across his broad palm, not even flinching as it drew blood.

"Well…we've barely been married a day but it seems like you're always…always *hurting* yourself to help me or heal me in some way," I said.

"Don't be silly, little bird—you're my wife. It's my job to take care of you. Here—take my hand. No—like this. Entwine our fingers."

He gripped my hand in his much larger one, twining our fingers together so that his bleeding palm was pressed to my injured one. Then he closed his eyes for a moment, getting a look of concentration on his face.

Once more the feeling of soft fur brushing my private areas swept over me, but this time it didn't stop. It felt like the magical fur was rubbing me over and over, stimulating my body more and more until

I could barely *stand* it. I could feel my nipples getting tight and the forbidden place between my legs—what Liath had called my "pussy" felt incredibly wet and swollen.

It felt so good I wasn't sure how much more of the sensuous sensation I could stand. It was like my body was reaching for something—attempting to reach a peak or pinnacle of pleasure that I hadn't even known was possible—but I couldn't quite manage to get there. And still Liath kept our hands clasped tight as he murmured something under his breath—probably a healing.

"Oh!" I moaned as his magic continued to tease and caress me. "Oh, please!"

Liath's eyes opened and he gave me a quizzical look. We were still kneeling in the snow, facing each other but I barely felt the cold. I was nearly panting with the sensations his magic was causing in my body. I saw his bronze eyes go half lidded as he seemed to realize what was happening to me.

"Just a moment more, little bird," he murmured. "I've had to do both a healing and a purification. The touch-me-not vine is no joke—if the poison enters your blood, it can kill you. Is it bothering you?"

"It...it's your magic," I confessed, still panting. "It...it feels like it's *teasing* me—*touching* me."

"Touching you *where*, exactly?" Liath rumbled, though I was fairly sure he knew.

"Here," I admitted, gesturing with my free hand to my breasts. My tender peaks were tight under the silky gown I wore—they pressed against the thin material which molded to them, so that one could see the outline of both my nipples and large areolas.

"Hmm..." Liath cupped one of my breasts with his free hand. "Does it feel like this?" he murmured, and lightly brushed his thumb over my tight peak.

"Oh!" I half gasped—half moaned. "Yes...a little. But it's more like really soft fur touching me there."

"And where else is my magic 'touching' you?" Liath pressed as he rubbed his thumb lightly over my tight peak again. "Tell me and remember you vowed me your honesty."

"Well..." I bit my lip. By the Shining Throne, it felt so good when he touched me! "Also...also between my thighs," I admitted at last. I was trying to keep my legs pressed together but it was difficult because I felt so swollen and hot. I had on a thin pair of panties but I feared they might be soaked now. I felt extremely wet there for some reason.

"Mmm-hmm," Liath rumbled, a slight smile quirking the corner of his sensuous mouth as he continued to tease my nipple. "And does it feel good, little bird? When my magic *teases* you?"

"It feels...overwhelming," I admitted. I had the urge to press my breast further into his hand, almost as though I was offering myself to him, though I didn't know why. "I...it feels like my body is trying to... to reach something...some peak. But I can't quite get there," I tried to explain.

"Hmm, well I'm afraid the peak will have to be reached another time," Liath told me, withdrawing his hand from my breast at last. He also let go of the hand he was healing. His palm was already healed and when I turned my hand over, I saw that mine was as well.

"But...why does it *feel* that way?" I demanded, as he rose to his feet and put a hand under my elbow to help me up as well. "Your magic, I mean."

Liath shook his head.

"Don't know. Possibly because we're meant to be together. Though I've never heard of any other couple being able to affect each other in this way. Never heard of anyone who could feel magic on their skin like you do either though," he added. "Hold still. We're both wet from kneeling in the snow and I need to dry us."

"Oh, do you *have* to?" I exclaimed.

He frowned.

"You'd rather be wet and miserable?"

"No, it's not that..." I broke off, biting my lip. "I just feel like... it's...it feels so *good* when you...when you do magic on me and it seems like that can't be right."

"Can't be right?" He frowned. "What does that mean?"

"I mean, well...it's forbidden. For a maiden to...to have that kind of pleasure. To be touched in such a way," I nearly whispered. "At least, in the Seelie Court, it is."

"What fucking nonsense is that?" Liath exclaimed, frowning. "Why shouldn't you have pleasure?"

"Because it's *forbidden*," I emphasized again. "You *do* know what forbidden means, don't you?"

"What I know is that it sounds like someone filled your head with a lot of nonsense," he rumbled. "But I don't have time to deal with it now—we need to get to the Pool of Seeing. Just hold still—I promise the drying spell isn't nearly as intense as the healing and purification."

He pricked his finger and made a motion with one hand. Suddenly a warm, dry wind seemed to spring up around both of us. It swirled around my skirts—and even reached under them to tickle the spot between my thighs which was still wet and swollen from Liath's earlier intense magic.

"Oh!" I gasped, putting my hands to my skirt to try and keep it down as it tried to fly up and show my legs. "You did that on purpose!" I accused Liath, who was laughing at me.

"Maybe." He gave me an unrepentant grin. "But at least you're dry now."

It was true, I was. Well, my skirt was. The place between my legs was most definitely still wet from all the magic he'd been doing on me.

"Come on—we need to get going," Liath told me. I expected him to forge on ahead of me again. Instead, he bent down and lifted me off my feet, making me gasp.

"Oh! What are you doing?" I exclaimed.

"Carrying you so we don't have any more accidents," he said shortly. He held me as easily as though I weighed no more than a fluff of thistledown—which I assure you is *not* the case.

"You can put me down if I get too heavy," I said quickly as he continued tramping through the forest. "I really *can* manage—I'm just not used to walking through the woods in Winter with all the snow."

He frowned down at me.

"What makes you think you're heavy?"

"Well...I mean, compared with the other Seelie maidens..." I began.

Liath gave me a stern look.

"Listen to yourself, Alira—do I need to show you your beauty again?"

I thought of how he had stood behind me, cupping my breasts and teasing my nipples and bit my lip. Just thinking of it made my pussy feel even more wet and hot than before.

"No," I whispered. Though to be honest, I rather wished he would.

"Has it ever occurred to you that the reason the males of the Seelie Court like stick-thin females is because they're too damn skinny themselves?" Liath said.

"Er...well, no," I admitted. Certainly none of the tall, slender, blond males I had grown up around was as muscular as my Unseelie husband. I doubted any of them would be able to lift me and carry me through the snow as he was—not that any of them would want to.

"Forget all the bullshit they taught you at the Summer Court," Liath advised me. "Half of it was meant to control you and the other half is just plain lies."

"How do you know what I learned growing up in the Summer Court?" I demanded.

"I've had Seelie friends in the past," was his answer. Surprising, since our Courts have been at war for centuries. "Well, one friend, anyway. A good friend," he added.

"Who was it?" I asked. "Do I know them?"

But Liath shook his head, his face going dark.

"Never mind. I'll tell you later."

I wondered how much later but didn't dare to ask. The look on his face was foreboding, as though the memory of the friend was a bad or possibly a sad one. Also, I noticed he had spoken of this friend in the past tense. Perhaps he or she was dead? It was certainly something to consider...

"There it is."

Liath's voice made me glance up and I saw where he was looking. Right ahead of us was a clearing in the forest where the trees had not quite lost all their leaves. But the leaves they retained were blood-red. They waved like flags from the skeletal branches, blown by the icy breeze.

In the center of the clearing was a perfectly round pond, not much larger than the tub back in Liath's bathing chamber.

"There it is," Liath said again. "The Pool of Seeing." He set me down on my feet and took my hand, drawing me towards the pool. "Come—let us see what it might show us."

12

The Pool of Seeing was perfectly calm and still, without a single ripple and the water in it remained unfrozen though the rest of the forest was blanketed in snow and ice. The strange thing about it was that it didn't reflect the sky above or the branches of the trees growing around it. It showed nothing at all and its waters were dead black, so that it looked like a kind of dark hole in the forest floor.

I was reluctant to approach it but Liath drew me forward.

"It's all right," he told me. "The Pool won't hurt you. Don't touch the waters, though—they're deadly poison," he added, almost as an afterthought.

"Deadly poison?" I exclaimed, trying to step back. But he pulled me right up to the edge.

"Just don't touch. The Pool can show you much if you know what to ask," he said.

"But what should I ask?" Looking down into the black hole in the forest floor made a shiver go down my spine.

"You can't ask it anything until you reach your powers and learn to use them," Liath told me. "Also, it requires a sacrifice of blood. But that's nothing new."

He unsheathed his dagger again and prepared to cut his palm. I wondered if he had used blood magic so often he was immune to the pain.

"I brought you here to show you something, little bird," he said to me. "Something that should prove to you that you have magic inside you—more magic than anyone ever fucking dreamed of."

I didn't see how that could be true, but I simply nodded.

"All right—show me."

Liath drew the blade of his dagger over his palm. Then he held his clenched fist over the black waters of the Pool of Seeing and let the ruby blood drip into its dark depths. It looked like a hungry mouth to me, swallowing his sacrifice eagerly and strangely the drops made no ripples in the water. After a few moments, the glassy surface turned from midnight black to a pale blue.

"There—now it's ready," Liath murmured under his breath. Then he spoke loudly. "Show us the Punishment of Princess Talandra of the Seelie Court," he said.

The Pool rippled for the first time—a ripple that started in the center and went all the way to its perfectly circular edge. Then, suddenly, a Fae maiden appeared in the center of the water. Her image was so clear it was as though she was standing right in front of me.

I marveled at the image—I could see every detail from her pale pink dress to her long curls of dark gold hair. Her eyes, though, were gray—gray like mine, I thought.

"Oh...who is she?" I bent over the Pool, half reaching for the mysterious maiden but Liath pulled me back.

"Poison, remember?" he growled. "This is the Lady Talandra—your ancestress, if I am not mistaken."

"But I've never heard of her," I protested. "She is not listed in the family tree of the Royal Seelie house."

"That is because she was scrubbed from your history texts," Liath said grimly.

"She was? But why?" I protested.

"Watch and you'll see," he murmured, pointing at the Pool of Seeing.

I did as he said, watching as the maiden looked about her, as though she was trying to be certain she was quite private. She appeared to be in the forest, just as we were, but instead of the trees being full of green leaves or laden with snow, they were many different colors of red, orange, golden yellow, and bright vermillion.

"What is that forest she's in?" I asked.

"It's our forest—the Fae forest which shelters both the Summer and the Winter Courts," Liath told me. "But this was back before the Great Divide was put up to separate the Seelie from the Unseelie. Back then, all the people of the Fae lived in the same place and time and the forest had four seasons, not just two."

"Oh," I breathed, intrigued at the idea of two more seasons—not to mention the inhabitants of the Seelie and Unseelie Courts mingling together. "But what happened to Talandra?"

"She was a Princess—the daughter of the King who sat upon the Shining and the Shadow Throne—for back then, they were one," Liath continued, in a deep, mysterious voice. "Unfortunately, she fell in love."

"She fell in love? What's so unfortunate about that?" I asked, frowning.

"It was *who* she fell in love with that sealed her fate," Liath told me. "Watch."

As he spoke, a new person entered the forest glade where Talandra was concealed. It was a Satyr, I saw—a male with the muscular torso and head of a human man, but the shaggy hocks of a goat. Tall horns rose from his forehead and he had a goatee beard on his handsome, dark face. He and Talandra came together in a passionate kiss and I couldn't help remembering the way Liath had kissed me the night before.

"Their love was true…but the King, Talandra's father found out about it," Liath murmured, still narrating the tale the Pool was showing us.

Suddenly an angry figure with golden hair stepped into the picture. He was wearing the Sun Crown, just as my father always did and for a moment I thought he looked exactly like him.

"King Oberon—another ancestor of yours," Liath told me. "He was the one who created the Great Divide that keeps the Seelie and Unseelie Realms separate. All because he was angry that his daughter was willing to bed with an Unseelie—and a creature that was a half-breed at that."

"Oh no—what did he do to them?" I asked. In the Pool, the angry king had grabbed his daughter's hand and was pointing at the Satyr. Fae guards rushed up to flank him, tying his hands behind his back and dragging him out of the forest glade.

"For his daughter's lover, he decreed death," Liath said flatly and the Pool showed us a terrible image—a guard beheading the Satyr. An axe blade rose and fell and the sightless head rolled on the ground, the mouth still working soundlessly.

"Ugh!" I exclaimed involuntarily. "That's horrible! That poor Satyr!"

"Talandra's fate was fucking worse," Liath growled. "For her willingness to bed with an Unseelie, the king decided on a punishment that held a special level of shame. He strung her up naked at the crossroads in the middle of the forest and decreed that since she was so willing to bed with an Unseelie, that any who wanted her should have her."

To my horror, I saw the princess with eyes like mine stripped of her clothes. She had full breasts and curving hips too, I saw—also like mine. She was dragged by the Fae guards to the crossroads I knew well—it was at the border of the Unseelie territories and the Summer Court—the place where the Great Divide that kept the two Realms separate was thin.

Talandra's hands were tied together and raised above her head, where they were fastened to the post at the center of the crossroads. Then her legs were spread, showing her naked sex clearly, and tied in the open position as well.

"You might want to look away, little bird," Liath rumbled in my ear. "What comes next isn't very fucking nice."

I covered my eyes with my hands but I couldn't help peeking through my fingers—as you do when watching a scary or horrible sight. I didn't want to see it fully but I couldn't help looking just the same.

"How…how long did they leave her there?" I whispered, almost afraid to ask.

"Her punishment was to be bred by any male who wanted her for a whole day and night," Liath told me.

As he spoke, a new figure came into the picture. It was a goblin, I saw with horror. A huge one—they get quite large—with green, warty skin and stumpy, bow-legs. Its arms were too long, the hairy knuckles dragging on the dusty road. But it was the legs my gaze kept returning to. Between them hung a set of what I could only assume were male genitals—they were quite grotesquely large.

As I watched, they got even larger, the shaft in the middle swelling to the size of an enormous sausage while the two heavy balls below swayed with each bow-legged step.

The goblin came up to the bound Talandra, who was weeping silently and—

But I couldn't watch any more because Liath had covered my hands with his own, much larger one, blocking my vision completely.

"It occurs to me that you don't need to watch a rape when you've had so little experience, little bird. It'll scare you to fucking death," he growled in my ear. "Hey, can't you speed it up some?" he added, and I got the sense he was talking to the Pool itself. After a moment he said, "All right, that's better."

"Can...can I look now?" I asked as he pulled his hand away.

"You can." He took my hands from my eyes and I saw that the Pool was showing a picture of Talandra, though this time she was clothed. Her pale pink dress couldn't hide the unsightly swelling of her midsection, though—clearly she was pregnant.

"But...how many males...?" I began.

Liath shook his head.

"You don't need to know that. The point is, that punishment changed her life—and not for the better. Of course, everyone assumed that since she'd been bred by so many Unseelie 'monsters' that she would give birth to a monster herself. But she didn't."

"She didn't?" I asked, surprised.

"No—look."

The Pool showed us a picture of Talandra holding a beautiful, cherubic looking Fae infant. I couldn't tell what sex it was, but it had curly golden hair and bright, jewel-like blue eyes.

"Oh," I said in surprise. "It looks just like a regular Seelie Fae baby!"

"That he did—and since the king and queen had no other children besides Talandra, they chose to adopt their grandson as their heir," Liath said.

"They did? But what about the baby's real mother? What about Talandra?" I asked.

Liath looked grave.

"Dead—not a month after her child was born," he said shortly. "By her own hand. She couldn't bear the shame of what was done to her."

"Oh..." I breathed and my eyes filled with tears when I thought of what my ancestress had endured. The Pool of Seeing made it all so real—she wasn't some dusty figure from a history text. She had been a real, breathing female—a girl not unlike me and she had gone through a monstrous ordeal.

"Her death is sad and what was done to her is fucking unforgivable," Liath growled. "But her son passed on the Unseelie blood, which has remained dormant—even in you."

"So this is why you kept telling everyone I have Unseelie blood in my veins?" I asked, looking up at him. "But it must be so faint after all these years!"

"Faint or not, it's there and the power of mixing the blood of the Seelie and Unseelie Courts is undeniable," Liath said firmly. "You *do* have magic, Alira—you're the one foretold in the prophesies and in the stars—I'm fucking *sure* of it. You just have to reach down inside yourself and tap into it."

"But...how?" I asked as the pictures in the Pool faded and it went back to being dead black.

"I'm going to show you once we get back to the Palace," Liath promised. "Come—we need to go."

"Wait!" I stopped him when he started to lift me. "Wait—I know what I want to ask the Pool—ask it who killed my brother!"

Liath's face was grave.

"We can try but the Pool doesn't always answer—or show what you want it to. Sometimes it shows something completely unrelated."

"Can we just try, though?" I begged softly. "I need to know, Liath! Please!"

"Very well." My new husband nodded. Unsheathing his dagger, he drew it across his palm again. Then he squeezed his hand into a fist and held it over the dead black waters. "Show us who killed Quill," he said in a commanding voice.

Once again the Pool swallowed the drops of his blood eagerly and then the surface rippled and showed the hazy outline of a warrior. At least, I *thought* it was a warrior—he had on the sleek, golden armor of the Seelie army. But his face was obscured as though by a cloud—I couldn't get a gook look at him, no matter how I peered and squinted.

"Why is it doing that?" I asked, feeling a rush of pure aggravation. "Why is it hiding him? Hiding his face?"

"Whoever it is, they're using some pretty strong obscuring magic," Liath said grimly. "They're hiding what they've done from everyone —it won't be easy to find their true identity."

"But, then how am I *ever* going to find out?" I demanded. "I need to know who to go after to avenge my brother!"

Liath gave me a look that seemed to hold grudging admiration.

"You really mean to kill him, don't you? Whoever he is."

"Yes!" I said fiercely. "I don't know how, but I'm going to do it! He's going to die for what he did to Quill!"

"Well, to find him, you're going to have to have strong magic— stronger than his—strong enough to break the obscuring spell," Liath told me. "If you can break his magic, you can break *him*."

Suddenly the pool rippled again and the warrior with the cloudy face faded. In his place, I suddenly saw Asfaloth and Calista. Neither of my cousins had clothes on and they were kneeling on a bed—or rather, Asfaloth was kneeling behind his twin sister while she was on all fours in front of him.

"Oh Gods, brother—*deeper!*" she moaned, tossing her long golden hair over one shoulder. "Fuck me deeper!"

"As deep as you need me to go, sister," Asfaloth panted. He had his hands on her hips and he was ramming into her, I saw—ramming his shaft between her legs as her tiny breasts jiggled with every thrust. And though I couldn't quite see everything because of the angle the Pool was showing, I was fairly certain where his shaft was going.

Deep in her pussy, whispered a little voice in my head. *That's where it's going—he's ramming his shaft deep into his own sister's pussy.*

"By the Shining Throne!" I gasped, as it dawned on me exactly what my cousins were doing. It was no more than what I had accused them of, but I hadn't actually *believed* they were doing it! I hadn't really thought that Asfaloth would breed his own sister!

I could feel my face going hot as I watched the two of them rutting together, unable to look away. I wondered what Liath would think of them—of *me*. They were *my* kin, after all. And the thought of what they were doing together made my skin crawl.

I dared to look up at my new husband, and saw that he had one eyebrow raised.

"Well, how very *unsurprising*," he growled. "I thought the two of them seemed awfully fucking close."

"Why is the Pool showing us this?" I demanded, my cheeks still hot with embarrassment. "I can't believe it! I mean, it's so...so *humiliating!*"

"Not for you, little bird," he assured me. "You knew the two of them were scum long before you saw this. And as for why the Pool showed us..." He shrugged, his broad shoulders rolling. "Who knows? As I said, it won't always answer questions or show what you want. And sometimes it shows you things you definitely *don't* want to see. Hey—stop it," he added, talking to the Pool, which abruptly went dark.

I was relieved that the carnal scene between my cousins had ended, but I couldn't explain the strange feelings in my own body that seeing them do *that* together had caused. On one hand it was revolting—they were brother and sister! But on the other hand, the way they had been moving together, taking pleasure in each other...

I wondered how the act would be with Liath and how long he would wait before he took me. But he seemed to have already pushed the lurid scene out of his mind, for he only shook his head.

"Come on," he said, lifting me again and setting off into the forest. "Before you can find Quill's killer and vanquish him, you have to find your magic. And before you can do that, you first have to understand the different *types* of magic…and why the magic you've been seeing all your life is false."

13

"There's nothing false about Seelie magic," I argued, as Liath carried me through the forest. "I once saw my cousin, Asfaloth, turn a male inside out using it. All his organs were on the outside of his body." I shivered in revulsion at the awful memory. "You can't fake that kind of power."

"Yes, but you *can* steal it—and that's what Seelie Magic is—it's *stolen*," Liath told me. He wasn't even breathing hard though he'd been carrying me through the thick snow for quite some time.

"Stolen how? Stolen from who?" I asked, frowning.

"From nature mostly—from the bounty around them. And by extension, from the Unseelie Court," he explained. "Every time a Seelie Fae does a bit of magic, the power has to come from somewhere—the place it comes from is the forest around them. Which is also the forest around *us*."

"But I already knew that," I protested. "I mean, the part about the power being drawn from nature."

"No, you don't understand," Liath argued. "What do you think happens when a Seelie maiden does a working to fix the clasp on her favorite locket that got broken?"

"I don't know." I shrugged. "She reaches out and pulls the power from the natural world around her?"

"Yes, and somewhere a flower wilts or a tiny creature—a toad or a frog or an insect—dies," Liath told me. "There are *consequences* when you draw power—the life power—from a living creature or plant. The consequences are *death*. And the more power you draw, the bigger the death. In Asfaloth's case, turning a male inside out probably killed an entire tree somewhere in the forest."

"But…I've never seen any flowers wilt or anything die when someone did magic and I've been watching magic done around me all my life!" I protested.

"You haven't seen the Unseelie Court before, though—have you?" he countered. "The reason we live in eternal Winter is because we bear the brunt of the Seelie Court's constant drain of power. It withers our plants and keeps our Realm plunged into the season of death."

"I…didn't know." I shook my head. "But what about the plants inside the palace?"

"Protected by wardings," he said succinctly. "My mother, Mab, used to say that the greenery inside the Winter Palace was the only thing that kept her sane," he added.

"I'm so sorry," I murmured. "I had no idea that the Summer Court was, uh, sucking all the power out of the Winter Court."

"It's the reason we've been at war all these years," Liath growled. "The Great Divide which separates us allows the Summer Court to steal from the Winter Court without consequences. And the Seelie Fae don't care—they just want an easy source of power they don't have to pay for."

"The way you pay in blood," I whispered. A new thought came to me—a rather awful thought. "Are you going to teach me to, er, find my magic by cutting me?" I asked, my voice coming out tight and high.

"What?" Liath gave me a convincingly horrified look. "Of course not, little bird! Besides, blood and pain isn't the only way to pay for magic—you can pay for it with pleasure too. The greater the pleasure, the greater the magic you can generate and the more you can do with it."

"Is that why your magic feels so good to me?" I asked, feeling my cheeks get hot. "I mean, when you…you know, touch me with it?"

Liath shook his head.

"I still don't know why my magic affects you as it does, but my guess is because your own magic will be more pleasure based when you find it."

"But how will I find it?" I asked. We had reached the Palace by now—it had taken a much shorter time to get back than it had to find the Pool of Seeing in the first place.

"You'll see," Liath said mysteriously. "Let's go inside and get you nice and warm. Then we can start your first lesson."

14

"All right...there." Liath put a crystal vase with a single dead rose on the nightstand beside the bed. It was desiccated, its petals as thin and crispy as onion skin. They might have once been fresh and red but now they were the color of old, dried blood.

"All right, *what?* What do you expect me to do?" I asked blankly. We were sitting on the bed together having removed our boots and cloaks—Liath had said we needed to be comfortable. But I still had no idea what he wanted me to do. I was simply leaning against his side—which seemed natural after the way he had carried me home. I liked the feeling of his big, warm body against mine and the warm scent of his skin made me feel safe.

"I expect you to bring the rose back to life—to use your magic to breathe life into it and make it green and blooming again," he said, as though it was the easiest thing in the world.

"But...I can't," I protested. "I don't know how to even *begin*."

"Don't go looking for the power outside yourself to start with,"

Liath lectured. "I know that's probably what every tutor you ever had told you to do."

"Yes, that's true," I admitted. "They all told me to reach out and take power from the natural world around me. But if I can't do that, where will I get power?"

"From *inside* yourself, little bird…when you pleasure yourself," he murmured.

"Pleasure myself?" I looked at him with wide eyes. "But…I can't do that! I wouldn't even know where to start."

"You start by touching yourself—making yourself feel good," Liath said patiently. "Look, do you want me to show you?"

I bit my lip—what would I see if I said yes? But I wanted to know if he was right—wanted to see if I really did have any magic in me at all. And they say that you first learn by watching. So I nodded.

"Yes," I said. "Show me."

"All right." He had his left arm around me as we sat on the bed, so he reached down and unfastened his trousers with his right hand.

My eyes got wide as I saw him open them and reveal a perfectly enormous shaft.

"Wait—what are you doing?" I exclaimed, staring at him wide-eyed.

"Showing you how to use pleasure to gather power and magic," Liath said matter-of-factly. "I'm sorry if it shocks you to see my shaft, but you were going to have to see it eventually anyway, little bird. We *are* married, you know," he reminded me.

"I know," I said rather faintly. "I've just never seen…um, I mean…aside from what the Pool showed us today, I haven't seen any males, er, *unclothed*."

"I know you're innocent," he murmured. "Which is why we're going to take things slow. In fact, I'll make you a promise right now —I won't take you until you beg me to."

"You…you won't?" I looked up at him in surprise. "But we're

married. You could...could do whatever you wanted with me any time."

"But I won't," Liath said firmly. "Like I said, not until you want it so badly you beg me. Besides, we need to bring you along very slowly—first to find your magic and then to build it and help you master it. Now watch."

"Er...what am I watching?" I asked, but my eyes were already glued to his big hand curled loosely around his shaft. It wasn't like the goblin's shaft in the awful scene the Pool of Seeing had showed us. It wasn't warty or green or crooked. (Did I mention the goblin's shaft had a strange bend in it? Because it did.)

Instead, Liath's shaft was long and straight and capped with a broad, mushroom shaped head. It was also extremely large, however, and I wondered how he could ever fit it into a female's sex. Luckily, I didn't have to worry about that for the foreseeable future, since he had promised not to take me until I "begged" him and there was no way I was about to start begging to be split in two by the huge thing between his legs.

"Watch me and watch the rose," Liath told me, answering my question. "Now, my own power works best with blood—I'm a warrior and I generate a hell of a lot more pain than pleasure. But I *can* use pleasure as well when I need to," he added.

I watched, mesmerized, as his big hand moved along the thick shaft. Liath's head was resting against the headboard and his bronze eyes were half-lidded as he stroked himself. I wondered as I watched if he also had two heavy balls hanging below his shaft like the goblin had and if so, what would they feel like if I touched them.

"Don't just watch my shaft, watch... watch the rose," Liath growled, somewhat breathlessly.

I dragged my eyes from the erotic sight of the big warrior stroking himself and looked at the dried rose in the vase. Only it wasn't so dry anymore, I saw. The dark edges of the curling petals had gone from the color of dried blood to a vivid crimson and as I watched, the color began to spread. It licked down the curled petals and the leaves of the rose like fire, but instead of destroying, it healed. Soon the crisp petals were soft and velvety, curved into a tight bud, and the stem had gone from a dried stick to a lush green stalk with spreading green leaves.

"Gods!" I heard Liath groan and when I looked at him, I saw his thick shaft jerk and pulse in his hand. As it did, a large quantity of pearly white cream shot from its tip and painted his bare, muscular abdomen. And at the exact same time, the newly healed rosebud burst into bloom—fully alive again.

"Oh!" I exclaimed in surprise, looking back and forth from the blooming rose to the puddle of cream that had formed on Liath's flat belly. "That's *amazing*. And…what is this?"

I reached out to touch the white cream and Liath let me, though he kept a watchful eye on me.

"It's my cum, little bird—my seed," he rumbled. "It's what a male shoots inside a female's pussy to plant a baby in her belly."

"Oh…" I looked at my fingertip uncertainly. "Is *that* how it happens?"

Liath huffed a laugh.

"How did you think it happened?"

"Well, I knew that a male put his shaft, er, into a female," I said with as much dignity as I could muster. "But I *didn't* know about this creamy white cum stuff. No one ever told me—I've only been able to pick up bits and pieces here and there, listening to other girls gossip," I admitted.

Indeed, even Tansy had been reluctant to tell me about the way in which a male and a female came together to make a baby. She always said, "You'll learn when your husband teaches you." Well, Liath was teaching me, all right—and I was surprised at how interesting the lesson was.

"This 'creamy white cum stuff' is fucking sticky, so I'd better clean up—and get a new rose." Liath sat up, reaching for a bathing sheet he'd put on the side of the bed—though I'd had no idea why—before we started.

"That was truly amazing and, er, very instructive," I said, as he tucked his still rigid shaft back into his trousers. "But I still don't understand how you expect *me* to do it."

"The same way I did, little bird—by touching yourself. By giving yourself pleasure."

He removed the living rose and replaced it with another dead one. Then he settled on the bed beside me again and looped his arm around my shoulders.

"Go on, baby," he murmured in my ear. "Make yourself feel good —then just capture the energy you feel and send it towards the rose."

"Oh, but...but I *can't,*" I exclaimed, feeling horrified when I realized what he meant for me to do. "It's forbidden—I told you that earlier," I reminded him.

"Why should you be forbidden from touching your own body?" Liath asked, frowning.

"I... I don't know. I only know that I *am.*"

Briefly, I told him about how my old nurse had fixed my arms to my sides when I was little, after she caught me "touching my button" as she called it.

"I...I was so *ashamed,*" I whispered and as I spoke, I felt the old shame rising in me—the feeling of being bad and dirty and twisted for wanting to feel the sweet pleasure it gave me to touch the tingling little spot between my legs.

"Hey, hey..." Liath turned me to face him and cupped my cheek in one big hand. "What are these for?" he murmured, swiping one thumb over my cheek. It came away wet and I realized I was crying.

"I don't know." I sniffed. "My nurse...she called me a 'dirty, filthy girl' and said how disgusting I was. Her magic felt like a rough, prickling rope around my arms, tying them to my sides. It *really* hurt but she refused to lift it for days and days until she thought I'd learned my lesson."

"The only lesson she was teaching was how to be fucking cruel to an innocent child." Liath's face was as dark as a thunderstorm but I recognized that his anger wasn't directed at me. "It's all right, little bird," he murmured, drawing me closer and cuddling me against his side. "You're not a bad girl or a dirty girl, I promise you're not."

I was moved by his tenderness. He was so big and frightening looking, but he cradled me against him as though I was a hurt child—and at that moment, reliving the memory of what my nurse had done to me, that was what I felt like.

"Can you see why I don't want to touch myself, though?" I asked, daring to look up at him. "It's so scary—I mean, I still feel so *ashamed.*"

"I understand." He pressed a gentle kiss to my forehead. "It's something you're going to have to get over though—if you ever want to access your power on your own. But maybe we can try something else."

"Something else?" I felt my stomach do a flip. "Are...are you going to cut me after all? Or ask me to cut myself to try and bring up my power?" The way he was always slicing and pricking himself with his moonstone dagger was fine for him—he seemed inured to the pain and he could heal himself almost instantly. But I didn't like the idea of doing that to myself at all.

Liath shook his head.

"No, little bird," he rumbled. "I told you—your magic is almost certainly pleasure-based and pleasure is what we need to reach it and bring it out. So I'm going to help you with that—help you learn to touch yourself."

"But...how can you do that?" I whispered uncertainly.

"You'll see." Liath stroked my cheek. "Do you trust me?"

Strangely, I did. We hadn't been married that long—he ought to still be a stranger to me. But...he didn't feel like one. The way we talked so freely and the way I felt so calm when I was around him made it feel as though we had known each other forever. So far he hadn't hurt me as I had feared he would before we married—he had only healed and comforted me. He *looked* absolutely terrifying with his curling horns and burning bronze eyes...but he treated me as though I was his most precious treasure.

"I trust you, Liath," I told him, looking into his eyes. "And...I *like* you."

He rumbled with laughter.

"You sound surprised about that."

"I am," I said candidly. "Asfaloth and Calista...they told me you'd hurt me. They said you'd...you know, tear me apart on our wedding night."

His face darkened.

"Don't speak their names in our marriage bed, little bird. You know by now that the two of them are poison—they have nothing to do with what we have together."

"You're right." I nodded. "They were lying—I see that now. But I never expected you to be...well, so *gentle* with me."

His eyes softened.

"How else could I be with such an innocent maiden?" he murmured. "Such a sweet little bird?"

I felt myself blushing at the way he was looking at me—I saw a mixture of tenderness and lust in his bronze eyes and it made me feel hot and cold all over. It also made me want to kiss him.

Reaching up, I grasped one of his curling horns and tugged at him, wanting him to bring his face down so I could reach him. Liath obliged, his eyes holding mine the whole time.

"What do you want, Alira?" he rumbled softly.

"I want...I want to kiss you. The way you kissed me last night," I confessed.

One corner of his sensuous mouth went up.

"Do it, then. I'll not stop you."

I took him at his word—as I took his lips in a kiss. He tasted spicy and wild and I thought I could still taste a bit of the sweet syrup we'd had at breakfast.

Liath let me kiss him for a while and then he kissed me back, parting his lips for me to deepen the kiss.

Feeling bold, I slipped my tongue into his mouth, tasting him more fully. I liked how hot and sweet his mouth was—and liked it even better that he let me explore him as long as I liked. He growled softly and ran his big hands up and down my back and sides and I had the feeling he was holding himself back in some way, but I trusted him enough to know he wouldn't lose control and hurt me.

At last, I felt like I wanted more. My heart was pounding as I pulled away from him, looking into his eyes.

"I *want* to do this—I want to find my magic, if I have any," I told him. "But I still don't know how you're going to, uh, teach me to touch myself."

"I'll show you," Liath rumbled. "But first we need to rearrange things a bit…"

15

The rearranging involved moving things around. First Liath brought the tall standing mirror in its marble stand around to the end of the bed so we could see ourselves in it. Then he moved the nightstand with the dead rose right beside it, so I could see that as well.

Finally, he came back to the bed and arranged some pillows against the headboard. He leaned back against them and patted the space between his legs.

"All right, little bird—come here," he ordered.

I came to him at once and settled between his legs with his broad chest to my back. I felt surrounded by his big, muscular body—little and protected in a way I hadn't since...well, since *ever*. I liked how safe he made me feel.

"Good," Liath murmured in my ear. "Now just lean back against me and relax, sweetheart."

I did as he said, watching in the mirror as I did so. I had never thought of myself as "petite" but I looked so small, leaning back against him. I liked our size difference, though—it made me feel delicate and feminine in a way I had never felt when I was comparing myself to the sapling-slender maidens and tall, thin warriors of the Seelie Court.

"Are you...are you going to touch me with your magic?" I asked, meeting Liath's eyes in the mirror. I could feel a warm tremble in my belly as I asked him this—the desire to feel his magic stroking over my sensitive, vulnerable places again.

"Mmm...actually that's not a bad idea," he rumbled. "But first, open your gown for me. And pull up the skirt. I need to see those beautiful full breasts of yours and that sweet little pussy."

I felt a nervous thrill of pleasure at his words but I answered him with a saucy tilt of my chin.

"Are you ordering me to do this—to show myself to you—as my husband?"

"Hmm, you're a spicy little thing, aren't you?" Liath growled. "*Yes*, I'm ordering you as your husband. Show me your breasts—and your pussy, little bird."

My heart was pounding but I no longer felt shy to let him see my body—not after the way he'd shown me my beauty the day before. There were many tiny buttons down the front of my gown and now I unfastened them and pulled the soft fabric aside, baring my breasts for my husband.

"Gods!" Liath murmured, his deep voice hoarse. "So fucking beautiful, sweetheart!"

"Thank you," I whispered, feeling my cheeks get even hotter. "Er...what are you going to do to me?"

"Just this, to start with."

He murmured a word in my ear that I recognized as a warming spell. I felt a rush of warmth come over me and the familiar sensation of soft fur brushing my nipples and between my legs made me gasp and give a little moan. I noticed that for once, Liath hadn't had to prick or cut himself to make the magic work and wondered if that was because he was calling on pleasure for his power instead of pain or blood. It seemed reasonable to think so—but it was hard to think when his magic was touching me so intimately.

I moaned again and writhed against him, pressing my bare breasts out even as my hips undulated. I still hadn't pulled up my skirt as he had commanded and now I felt shy about it because I was certain I was getting wet all over again.

"Mmm, you like that, little bird?" Liath murmured in my ear as he worked the warming spell again. "It feels good on your tight peaks?"

As he spoke, he reached around and cupped my breasts, teasing my nipples with his thumbs as well as his magic.

The double sensation made me gasp and writhe again.

"Yes," I whispered. "By the Shining Throne…that feels so *good!*"

"It's going to feel even better," Liath promised me. "Pull up your skirt now, little bird. Let me see your pussy."

I bit my lip, unwilling for the first time to do what he asked. I was getting so *wet* down there—it seemed shameful.

"Do…do you really have to see it?" I asked in a small voice.

"Of course I do," Liath said reasonably. "How else can I teach you to pet your sweet little pussy unless we can both see it?" He met my eyes in the mirror and frowned. "What's this sudden shyness about, little bird? What's wrong?"

"I don't know if it's *wrong* exactly…" I said, looking down at my lap. "It's just…when your magic touches me—when *you* touch me—I seem to get all…all *wet* down there. And I don't know why."

Liath surprised me with rumbling laughter in my ear.

"Is that all? You're ashamed that your sweet little pussy is getting wet?"

"Isn't it shameful, though?" I asked, meeting his eyes in the mirror.

"No, of course not. Here—lift your skirt. Let's look together," he told me.

Biting my lip, I did as he said, pulling the skirt of my gown up until my white panties came into view. I couldn't help the rush of shame I felt when I saw that my fears were true—my pussy had made so much moisture the white fabric was nearly see though—and it was clinging to every little bump and curve.

"Oh, dear!" I started to lower my skirt and hide myself but Liath stopped me.

"No, don't hide it, sweetheart," he murmured in my ear. "Your little pussy is fucking beautiful."

"But…but I'm so *wet*," I protested. "I…I never had this problem before we were married," I added. "I *swear* I didn't."

"It's not a *problem*," Liath told me. "It's just your soft little pussy getting ready to have a shaft deep inside it."

"It is?" I met his eyes in the mirror and noted that my own eyes were wide with shock. This was another detail no one had ever told me—like the white cream that shot from the tip of his shaft.

"Of course," Liath murmured. "Here—take off your underthings and let's explore a little together."

Feeling naughty and hot all over, I lifted my hips and let him slide the damp panties down my legs. Then Liath had me part my thighs wide so that the two of us could watch in the mirror.

"How much do you know?" he asked softly, framing my wet, pink pussy with his big hands, but not quite touching me yet. "Almost nothing, I'm guessing, since you haven't even been allowed to touch this part of yourself."

"It's forbidden," I whispered, feeling my heart leap into my throat. I was all right with him touching me—even if it *was* embarrassing how wet and shiny my secret area had become. But still, the thought of putting my own hand to myself made me feel shame and anxiety.

"No, it's not—not anymore," Liath said firmly. "This is *your* body, Alira. From now on, you're allowed to touch yourself however you want." He rumbled a sigh. "But of course, I know that's easy for me to *say*. Let's talk about it..."

He cupped my mound in one big hand and then ruffled the small patch of midnight blue curls at the top of it. The sensation sent a shiver through me and I quivered in his arms.

"Oh! *Liath*..." I protested a little breathlessly.

"Don't 'oh, Liath' me, little bird—we're just getting started," he growled softly in my ear. "Your curls are a sweet part of you, but I like what's below even better. Like these—your outer lips." Gently, he traced the parts in question with one long finger, making me moan and shiver against him again. "Feels good?" he asked.

"Y-yes," I stammered. But I had a feeling it could feel even better. Liath proved me right with his next action.

"Your outer pussy is beautiful, but so is your inner pussy," he lectured softly. "Your inner folds..." He traced them lightly with a gentle finger. "And then, of course, there's your sweet little clit."

As he spoke, he found my special place—the little button I had been forbidden to touch all my life. He began to circle it lightly—very lightly—with just the tip of his finger.

Sparks of pleasure ran through my entire body at his gentle touch and I arched my back and moaned in surprised delight. It felt so good —even better than I remembered when I had explored this place before—back before my old nurse had punished me for it.

"Oh...oh, Liath!" I gasped, writhing in his arms. "You're barely touching me but it feels so *good*."

"Of course it feels good when I pet your soft little pussy," he rumbled in my ear. "It's made to feel good—just like your sweet, curvy body is made to experience pleasure."

I moaned again and trembled as I watched him stroking me in the mirror. I could see my inner thighs were getting wet and shiny as more moisture came from inside.

"You...I...I think you're making me wetter," I panted, nodding at the image in the mirror.

"Gods, so I am, little bird," he growled softly and his eyes in the mirror were lazy with lust. "But that's all right—like I told you, it's just your body helping you get ready to take a shaft deep inside. The wetter you are, the more easily it can slip into your tight pussy."

"But...but surely not a shaft as big as *yours*," I protested breathlessly. "I don't see how I could...could fit something that size inside me!"

Liath's long fingers slid lower and I felt him probing gently at the entrance of my pussy. He slid them a little way inside me and I winced as I felt them encounter resistance.

"You still have your maiden barrier, then? Of course you do," Liath answered his own question, sliding his fingers out again. "Well, I won't lie to you, little bird—the first time can be a bit painful, due to the barrier and the fact that your little pussy is so tight and my shaft is on the larger size. But I promise I'll get you ready to take me when the time comes. And it gets easier with practice."

What he was telling me was a little scary but I was glad he was being honest. It made me trust him more.

"All right," I whispered. "But...I'm not ready quite yet."

"No, I know you're not," Liath told me. "And we're not here for that anyway—we're going to try and help you learn to touch yourself and find your power."

I nibbled my lower lip.

"I still don't know about...about touching myself, Liath."

"That's all right," he murmured. "Because I'm going to do it with you. Look here..."

He took my right hand in his much larger one and placed it between my legs. The moment I was cupping my pussy, I felt my heart starting to hammer in my chest.

"What...what do you want me to do?" I felt frozen...uncertain of my next move.

"Just cup yourself for a moment," Liath said softly—his breath was warm against the side of my neck and his deep voice was calm and soothing. "Feel how sweet and soft she is, your little pussy. The springy mound of curls...the soft outer lips and your sweet, slick inner cunt..." He kept his own big hand cupped over mine as he talked. "She's so *beautiful*," he told me, pressing lightly so that my fingers made more contact with my inner folds. "And so worthy of pleasure—just like you are yourself, Alira."

I tried to feel myself as he felt me—to explore the different areas he had mentioned. I liked running my fingertips through my soft curls, I found. The feeling was ticklish and teasing at the same time. And it didn't seem too wrong to trace my outer pussy lips with my finger. But it was when I tried to touch my inner pussy that I felt another wave of shame overcome me.

Dirty girl! whispered my old nurse's voice in my head. *Filthy girl!*

"I...I can't," I whispered, feeling my chest tighten with anxiety as I met Liath's gaze in the mirror. My reflection echoed the shame I felt. "I can't touch myself. Not *there*."

"You mean your clit, sweetheart? The little button between your legs?" Liath murmured.

"Yes," I whispered, nodding my head. "*There*. That's the part I was touching when...when my nurse caught me. It feels so good but...but it makes me feel dirty, too."

"You're *not* dirty and she has no power over you anymore," Liath assured me. "You can touch yourself—it's *your* body, sweetheart. Here...let me help you."

Gently, he took my hand in his much larger one. With his two first fingers over mine, he guided my fingertips to the aching center of my sex. Slowly, he helped me stroke myself, sending shivers of pleasure and shame through my whole body.

"Good girl, Alira," he growled softly in my ear as he helped me touch myself. "You're being such a *good girl* right now…touching yourself for me, giving yourself pleasure. Such a good girl to pet your sweet, soft little pussy for your husband."

His words of praise made me feel even hotter than I already was and the shame seemed to fall away.

"Oh…*ohhhh!*" I moaned, arching my back as he helped me stroke myself. "Oh, Liath—it feels so *good!*"

"I know, baby—it's supposed to," he murmured. "Gods, you're gorgeous when you give yourself pleasure! Now take that pleasure and push it outward—towards the rose," he instructed.

I moaned as I continued to stroke lightly around my button—with Liath's help—and tried to do as he said. I concentrated on the sparks of pleasure shooting through me—visualizing them almost like sparks coming off a fire. Then I imagined aiming them at the dead, dried rose sitting in the vase beside the mirror.

As I did, I couldn't help watching myself in the mirror at the same time. It was an extremely erotic sight—the girl with long, midnight blue hair cradled against her husband's broad powerful chest while he helped her stroke her soft little pussy. Her large breasts were fully on display, her tight pink nipples and large areolas showing as she explored herself for the first time in what felt like forever.

And all the time, Liath was murmuring praise into my ear.

"Good girl, Alira. You're my good girl," he growled softly as he slowly drew his hand away, leaving me to touch myself. "Don't stop—pet your pussy for me—stroke your hot little clit. Give yourself pleasure—it's all right."

His stream of encouragement and praise helped me keep going, even after he withdrew his hand. I watched in fascination as the girl in the mirror stroked herself, her fingertips sliding nimbly around and around the little pink button at the center of her sex.

"Gods, look at how wet your little pussy is getting," Liath groaned softly. "So fucking hot, baby—keep going. Keep petting your sweet little pussy."

I did as he said, mesmerized by what I was seeing—what I was doing. And at the same time, I tried to capture the sparks of pleasure and send them towards the rose. But as I did, I kept feeling the same way I had earlier when Liath was healing my hand—like my body was struggling to reach a kind of peak that I had never felt before.

"Liath," I gasped, as I continued to stroke myself. "I feel...feel like I'm trying to find something...like all this power is building up inside me and it has to go somewhere but...but I don't know where it's going!"

"You're probably going to come soon, little bird," he murmured soothingly. "That just means your body is going to release all the built-up sexual energy."

"Is that what happened to you when...when you made all that creamy stuff?" I gasped, my fingers still working between my legs.

He rumbled soft laughter in my ear.

"Exactly, little bird."

"And if...if you were taking me...you would... would spurt it between my legs instead?" I panted.

"That's right, sweetheart." His eyes were burning as I met his gaze in the mirror. "Deep in your sweet little pussy. I'd fill you up with my cum until you overflowed."

"Oh!" I gasped. Somehow the mental image of him doing that—of his thick shaft stretching my pussy open and spurting deep inside me—appeared in my mind's eye and excited me even more. It was frightening to think of something so big and thick going inside me...but incredibly arousing too.

"Mmm, you're getting close now, little bird," Liath told me. "Soon you'll feel the pleasure peak inside you. When you do, push it all outward—right at the rose."

The rose—*right*. It was difficult to keep the rose I was trying to bring back to life in mind when the pleasure inside me seemed to be taking all my attention. I was close…so *close*. But I needed something more.

"Liath, please," I begged as I stroked myself. "Please, I need…need something else."

"Does this help?" He cupped my breasts in his hands and began to tug gently on my tight nipples.

"Oh!" I moaned, arching my back. "Yes, that helps! But I need…I want…"

"Tell me what you want, little bird—if it's in my power, I'll give it to you," he growled.

"Call me your 'good girl' again," I begged, the words leaving my mouth in a gasp. "Please, I like it when you do that. And…and it makes me feel like…like it's all right to…to let go."

"It *is* all right to let go. Because you *are* my good girl, Alira," he rumbled in my ear, still tugging and twisting my tight peaks. "Such a *good girl* to pet your sweet, hot pussy for me."

It was exactly what I needed—my new husband's words of praise seemed to send me over some kind of edge. Suddenly I felt the pleasure peaking inside me—wave after wave of sensation rolling through me. My nipples got almost unbearably tight, my toes curled, and a cry of pure emotion broke from my lips.

"Liath!" I gasped, arching my back as the pleasure flooded and overwhelmed me. "Oh, it feels so…so…*oh!*"

"That's right, little bird—let it go," he growled in my ear. "Let it all go and let yourself come. Gods, you're gorgeous when you're coming!"

The girl in the mirror was indeed beautiful in the midst of her pleasure. Her cheeks were flushed and her eyes were bright as she writhed against her husband, who was caressing her full breasts and murmuring in her ear.

"Look at you coming so fucking *hard*," Liath rumbled, tugging my nipples some more. "Let yourself go, little bird—but don't forget the rose."

The rose! I really had almost forgotten—but I think I can be forgiven since I was caught up in my first ever sexual release. I tried to gather the sparks of pure sensation shooting through me—I could almost see them in the air around me—and throw them at the rose.

Live! I thought fiercely at it as my body pulsed with pleasure. *Grow, thrive! Be alive!*

And then I closed my eyes as another wave of sensation overcame me—for a moment I glimpsed what seemed to be a whole sky full of stars... and then, finally, everything went still.

16

"Alira? Little bird—are you all right?" Liath's deep voice brought me back from the warm place I'd been—a place of peace where the overwhelming pleasure ebbed slowly away, leaving a sense of sleepy contentment in its place.

"Hmmm?" I opened my eyes to see him peering anxiously down at me.

"Are you all right?" he repeated. "You had a really intense release and then you seemed to faint for a moment—fucking scared me."

"Sorry..." I sighed deeply and stretched luxuriously in his arms. "Oh..." I looked at my hand—the one I had touched myself with. "I, er, think I need to clean myself up," I told Liath.

"I can help you with that." Taking my hand in his, he sucked my fingers into his mouth, cleaning them with his tongue until the last traces of my wetness were gone.

"Oh..." I watched him with wide eyes. "You, er, like that?"

"The taste of your pussy honey? Fuck yes, sweetheart." He gave me a half-lidded look as our eyes met in the mirror and I realized there was something hot and hard pressing against my back.

"Oh!" I exclaimed, turning to look down between us. "You're, uh, shaft is hard again."

"Because it's fucking arousing to watch you pleasure yourself, sweetheart," he growled.

I bit my lip.

"Do you...do you want me to help you with it? With your shaft, I mean? The same way you helped me touch myself?"

"Mmmm, now *there's* an idea," he murmured. "But first let's check on your progress."

He got out from behind me and went to the end of the bed to examine the rose. I bit my lip, waiting for the result. The rose looked healed from where I was sitting but maybe—

"Fuck! I knew it!" Liath's excitement was palpable.

"What? What is it?" I asked anxiously.

He came back onto the bed with me, holding the rose.

"Look—I told you that you have magic!" He showed me the rose which was as fresh and blooming as the one he had healed himself with pleasure. "And look at this..." He twisted the stem and I saw that there was another blossom growing from the side, right beside the first one—it was as red and fresh as the other and it most definitely had *not* been there before.

"Oh..." I touched the silky petals with one finger. "Are you *sure* you didn't help me do this?" I asked, looking up at Liath doubtfully.

He shook his head firmly.

"No, baby—this was all you. You healed it perfectly—but I've never seen anyone cause a dead rose to bud and form a new bloom like that. Told you that your magic was going to be something special."

"But how can making a rose bloom help me find Quill's murderer?" I asked, feeling troubled. "It's a nice trick, but I don't see how I can use it to defeat a killer."

"You're trying to run before you can walk," Liath said practically.

"You just found your magic—now you have to train it. And that might take a little while."

I looked up at him, my heart pounding.

"Does that mean we'll do more of this? More touching. More...coming?"

He gave me a lazy smile.

"Count on it, little bird."

"In that case...would you like me to help you with your shaft?" I asked again. I was extremely interested in his male equipment—I wanted to touch him intimately, as he had touched me.

"Mmm, you're a curious little virgin, aren't you?" Liath rumbled. "Yes, I think you can help me. Would you like to learn how to touch it?"

"Yes!" My heart started beating even harder. "Yes, I want that, very much," I confessed rather breathlessly.

His eyes went half-lidded.

"And would you like to be my good girl and learn how to suck it? Suck my cock to get the cream out?"

A moment before I had been feeling completely sexually content but now I felt the tingling and heat start between my thighs again. I pressed my legs together, trying to ease the ache.

"Yes, please!" I murmured demurely, looking up at my new husband. "Please teach me how to suck your shaft, Liath. I want to be your good girl every way I can."

"There are lots of ways to be my good girl, sweetheart and I'm going to show you every single one," he promised. "But let's start with this..."

He taught me how to handle his long, thick shaft—how to curl my hand around it and stroke it, though my fingers wouldn't fit all the way around his thickness. I learned to suck the head too, exploring the little slit at the top with the tip of my tongue for a taste of what he called his "precum"—a clear liquid that flowed out before the actual creamy cum was released when he came.

I loved his dark, spicy, masculine scent and the way his shaft was so hot and hard in my fingers…and yet the skin was silky smooth when I rubbed my cheek against it. I couldn't get much of it into my mouth—it was too thick and long. But Liath didn't seem to care. He stroked my hair and praised me as I pressed hot, open-mouthed kisses up and down his length. He even let me handle the large, heavy balls which hung beneath.

"Be very careful with those, little bird," he growled hoarsely as I weighed them in my hand, fascinated by his male equipment. "They're extremely delicate."

It made me smile to think of any part of my big, muscular husband as "delicate" but Liath assured me it was so. In fact, I got the distinct impression that he was trusting me by letting me touch and handle him there.

As I touched him, I could see the little sparks of pleasure coming from him—just as I had seen my own sparks when Liath had been teaching me to touch myself. I wondered if I could use those sparks to work magic too, or if only my own sparks would work. When I asked Liath, he rumbled,

"Why don't we find out?"

We paused for a moment and he got another dead rose—he had gathered a whole bundle of them for practice purposes—and set it in the vase. Then I went back to handling him to make the sparks fly—literally.

"All right now, little bird," he murmured, putting his hands behind his head and nodding down at his fully erect shaft. "It's up to you—see if you can make me come and heal the rose at the same time."

I licked my lips and gave him a naughty smile.

"I'll be happy to."

Then I went to work on him with my mouth and hands. Liath watched me, his eyes burning, as I stroked him up and down and sucked the broad, mushroom-shaped head of his shaft into my mouth. His precum was flowing freely now and I lapped it up eagerly. I liked his flavor—it was spicy and salty and sweet all at once and I was eager to taste his cream.

Liath groaned softly as I stroked and sucked him and tickled his balls lightly, as he had taught me. Then I had a new idea. Leaning over him, I pushed his thick shaft between my bare breasts. At the same time, I leaned down to lick the head some more.

"Gods, little bird!" Liath groaned, his eyes blazing with lust. "Where did you learn *that* little trick?"

"Nowhere," I said primly. "It just seemed to me that since you like my breasts so much, you might like them around your shaft. Was I right?"

"*So* fucking right, sweetheart!" he groaned. "Gods, don't stop—I'm going to come!"

"Not yet!" I exclaimed. "I want to taste your cream when it comes out."

He arched an eyebrow at me and his voice dropped to a low growl.

"Are you saying you want me to come in your mouth, Alira?"

I bit my lip.

"Is that bad?"

"No, of course not, sweetheart." He stroked my hair with one big hand. "It's just—I tend to come a lot. And not every female likes the flavor."

"I like the flavor of your precum," I said. "I *think* I'd like your cum—your cream—as well."

"All right, but you don't have to swallow if you don't want to," Liath told me. "And you can pull off at any time—don't feel like you have to take it if you don't want to." He frowned. "You know, this might be too much, considering how innocent you are."

"I want to feel you spurting in my mouth," I said stubbornly. "I want to taste your cream on my tongue when you come."

Liath groaned softly.

"Gods, little bird! All right, but don't say I didn't warn you. Go on—make me come. And don't forget the rose," he added.

"I won't," I promised.

I stroked his long, hard shaft with my soft breasts and bent to suck the crown once more, savoring the unique flavor of the precum that flowed from the tip. I could see Liath watching me so I made a show of it, sliding my tongue around and around the broad head before sucking it deep into my mouth again.

"Gods, sweetheart!" he groaned and then I felt his shaft growing even harder and hotter between my breasts. He was coming—or he was about to, anyway. I could feel it—could feel the pleasure building up in him, almost the same way I felt his magic when he used it on me.

I saw the sparks again too. When the first salty spurt of his cream hit my tongue, I saw them flying all around him, like a swarm of fireflies.

Reaching out with my mind, I captured the sparks and aimed them at the third dried rose. At the same time, I was swallowing as fast as I could—Liath hadn't been lying when he said he came a lot, but I found that I enjoyed every drop. It was creamy and hot and it warmed my throat and my belly going down.

"Gods, Alira!" Liath gasped hoarsely as he stroked my hair. "Such a soft, sweet little mouth! Such a good girl to suck my cock so nice and deep—such a good girl to swallow all my cream!"

I felt a warm glow at his praise and I used that too—sending the positive emotion towards the dead rose along with the sparks. I loved the feeling of pleasuring my lover—my husband. I loved the sound of his groans...the feeling of his big hand stroking my hair...the taste of his cream and the feeling of his thick shaft pulsing between my lips.

In fact, I loved *everything* about this experience though I hadn't expected to like my "wifely duties" at all. It was surprising in the best possible way.

"Mmm!" I moaned around his thick shaft, still sucking. "*Mmm...*"

At last Liath's shaft stopped spurting and I felt him begin to get a little softer between my lips. Which meant I was finally able to get all of him in my mouth. Moving my breasts away, I leaned over, taking as much as I could, only to hear Liath rumble with low, exhausted laughter.

"Gods, sweetheart—what are you trying to do, kill me with pleasure?"

I looked up, letting his shaft slide from between my lips.

"No, of course not! It's just that you're so big there's no other time I can get you all into my mouth," I explained.

"Well, you can stop for a minute, little bird. Let's have a look at the rose," he told me.

I sighed and pulled away—though I would have been happy to keep sucking him—while he got the third rose. When he saw it, he let out a low whistle and twisted it in his hands.

"Did it work?" I asked eagerly. "I was trying to use a mixture of your pleasure and my own."

"Oh? Did it feel that good to suck me, then?" He raised his eyebrows at me.

"Well, of course it felt good to suck you, but I was actually talking about...about when you called me your 'good girl,'" I admitted, blushing. "*That* was the pleasure I used."

One corner of his mouth quirked up.

"You *really* like that, don't you?"

"Well...I've never been called a 'good girl' before," I told him. "I've never been 'good' enough for *anyone*—not at the Seelie Court, anyway. You know how my nurse treated me and my father has always blamed me for killing my mother when I was born. And of course my cousins are horrible. None of my tutors ever praised me either, because I could never do magic."

"Well, you can now. Just *look* at this."

Liath showed me the rose—or should I say *roses*. For this one had budded too—but it had done so multiple times. It almost looked like he was holding a bouquet in his hand, except that many of the new roses were still just buds.

"I bet with a little more practice you could make them bloom," Liath rumbled speculatively.

"Do you want me to suck you again?" I asked, giving him a naughty smile.

"Gods, you're an eager little virgin." He stroked my hair. "No, I want to see you touch yourself again. Pet your sweet pussy for me, little bird. And let's see if we can't make those roses bloom…"

17

That was the beginning of my magic lessons but certainly not the end. We practiced for hours nightly and sometimes during the day too. I found that my appetite for my new husband only grew and since Liath always seemed to want me as well, both of us were always eager to work on my magic skills.

I was getting better and better at controlling and manipulating my power. I still saw it as sparks, like swarms of fireflies, and I was learning to see it even when the situation wasn't sexual. I spent an entire morning watching the little dryad who was my maid standing out in the courtyard on a rare, sunny day, soaking in the sun's rays and enjoying herself.

The sparks of pleasure and joy that came from her branchy arms and mossy hair were beautiful to behold. I knew that she must love the warmth of the sun so much because she was tied to one of the trees in the forest—she was in fact, its spirit. Because of this she couldn't get too far from her tree, though luckily the Winter Palace was within her range.

I thought about the other trees in the forest on the Unseelie Lands and how long it had been since they had been allowed to bud and bloom and grow leaves. The Great Divide which separated the Seelie from the Unseelie Court and kept it always Summer on the Seelie side and always Winter on the Unseelie side had been in effect for centuries.

It seemed so unfair that the people in my new home almost never got to see the sun or feel its warmth on their faces. Something ought to be done about it, but it was impossible. My own ancestor, King Oberon, had raised the magical division after his daughter had been brave enough—and foolish enough—to love one of the Unseelie Fae. The magical wall had been born of hatred and malice and prejudice—what was strong enough to tear down that barrier and reunite the Realms once more?

Stableforth the Centaur seemed to think that *I* was the answer to the problem, but though I continued to progress with my magic, I couldn't say that I believed that to be true. I was getting very good at bringing dead roses back to life and I had also been able to channel my magic to heal as well, but there's a big difference between healing and tearing down a magical barrier that's been in place for hundreds of years.

I practiced the healing with Liath often. He would cut himself with his dagger and then let me send my "sparks" as I called them, to his wound. I envisioned his flesh knitting together, becoming whole again and it worked.

The only thing he wouldn't let me try to heal was the scar on his face.

"No, little bird," he said, when I suggested it, his expression growing grim. "This scar is a remembrance of something I deeply regret. I do not deserve to be rid of it."

I wanted to ask him what this secret pain was—the old memory that went with the scar, but I didn't quite dare. We hadn't known each other long enough, I told myself. When our marriage was a little older and I was more sure of my Unseelie husband, I would ask. Until then, I simply continued practicing healing other, fresher wounds with my sparks.

Liath nodded, when I explained how I captured the sparks with my mind and showed them what to do and where to go. However, he told me this *wasn't* how he healed himself when he did Blood magic. He didn't see any sparks—his method was more direct.

"I just command the wound to heal and it heals," he told me. "But you do what works for you, little bird. Magic is different for everyone."

I did as he said and continued to work with my "sparks." Now that I had learned to see them, I could find them everywhere there were happy and positive emotions. But my best source of magic turned out to be *me*—the number of sparks I could generate when Liath and I were "practicing" my magic together seemed to grow every time. I just wished I had a way to store them somehow and use them later instead of having to make or find new ones every time.

Of course, Liath had to cut or prick himself every time he did a spell or a working—if he wasn't using pleasure magic with me—so I supposed that was simply how magic was. If you were using your own magic, you had to generate it or find it every time. It was a price I was willing to pay—I was just so happy to find out I wasn't some kind of Royal dud, as I had believed all my life.

But though I was glad to have it, so far my magic seemed only good for positive things like healing and reviving. I didn't see how I could use it for any kind of death or destruction—I would need it to be, though, if I was ever to find Quill's murderer.

Even in the middle of my joy, I hadn't forgotten my big brother—I was going to avenge him if it was last thing I did. I had even been considering another trip to the Pool of Seeing. I had thought of some questions that might lead me to the killer in a more round about way, since the Pool seemed unable or unwilling to show me the murderer outright. But for the time being, I was content to work on my magic.

Despite the fact that I still missed my big brother, my time in the Unseelie Court was one of the happiest periods of my life. Liath and I were growing closer and closer—which wasn't difficult to do when we spent hours in each other's company, exploring each other's bodies. The big Unseelie warrior was the ideal husband—he was always kind and never cruel to me. He was patient and protective and a wonderful lover...though he still insisted on taking things slowly.

"We have to work up to certain acts, little bird," he explained when I pouted because I wanted to do more. "We need to hold something back to help your magic grow."

Having magic for the first time in my life—as well as the unconditional love and approval of a male I was beginning to fall for—made me incredibly happy. I also loved my growing power. It felt like I had looked inside myself and found a live coal glowing at the center of my heart—and now that I had found it, I could use its heat to keep me warm or do a hundred other things. I walked everywhere surrounded by clouds of the sparks of my own pleasure and joy—which only I could see, of course.

And then Liath decided to take me to the Mortal Realm.

"Are you sure it's safe?" I asked for the hundredth time as he took out his moonstone dagger and prepared to cut a passageway from the Unseelie territory to the Mortal Realm.

"Of course I'm sure, little bird. I used to go there all the time with... I used to go there all the time," he finished, leaving me with a confused frown. Who had he gone to the Moral Realm with and why didn't he want me to know?

Before I could ask those questions, Liath muttered a word of transportation and pierced the empty air with his dagger. He drew it down sharply, creating a black rift, just as he had on our wedding day. Then he took my hand and we walked through it, out of our own world—and into another place entirely.

18

"What *is* this place?" I murmured, looking around me with wide-eyed wonder. The Mortal Realm was so busy—and so *loud*! There seemed to be music blaring everywhere and people were shouting and dancing and laughing and drinking. There were glowing signs on the walls that must be magic. One said "Bud Light" and another said, "The King of Beers." I wondered where this king was and how he proposed to rule over all the malt beverages of the world.

"This is amazing!" I looked around me.

"No, this is just a tavern—a human tavern," Liath told me, raising his voice a little to make himself heard. "It's called 'Harry's Bar' in fact—I know the owner. Do you want a drink?"

"Can we look around some first?" I asked.

I was fascinated by the humans. They were almost all dressed in tight blue trousers—even the females. And the few I saw that were *not* dressed like males were instead wearing incredibly short, tight skirts which seemed barely long enough to cover their crotches. Both modes of dress would have been considered unseemly for a maiden in either the Seelie or the Unseelie Realm, but here they appeared to be normal.

The humans were all dancing and drinking and laughing and none of them seemed to have noticed that Liath and I had appeared out of thin air. Though in their defense, we *had* come from the darkest corner of the bar.

"Look all you want," Liath told me. "Don't worry—humans are mostly harmless. But be careful—you won't be able to do any magic here because of all the iron they use in their buildings."

Iron, of course, saps Fae power—be it Seelie or Unseelie. I could feel its presence faintly in the frame of the building around us, but I couldn't say that it bothered me much. And I could still see the sparks —they came freely from the humans, though they didn't have any magic. So the sparks must be just positive emotions then, I thought to myself. I wondered if I could use the sparks coming from the patrons of the tavern to do magic the same way I could use Liath's sparks or the sparks of the other Fae?

"Go on—explore," Liath urged me. "I'll keep an eye on you."

"But...won't the humans think we're strange?" I asked uncertainly. After all, we weren't dressed like them at all and in Liath's case, he couldn't be mistaken for human in the least. His huge height, gray skin, bronze eyes, and white hair stood out in the room filled with mortal beings.

But he only laughed.

"Maybe in the past, but the Mortal Realm has changed. You'll see —you won't ever have to make an excuse for your appearance—the humans themselves will make excuses *for* you."

As he finished speaking, a mortal girl who looked to be around my age walked past us, heading for the back of the bar. She had on tight blue trousers and a short-sleeved shirt made of some soft-looking material. Her clothing emphasized her figure and I saw she was a curvy girl like me. Her long brown hair swished as she walked.

There was something different about this human, I thought, as she approached us. She had more sparks coming from her than almost anyone else in the noisy tavern combined. And they had a golden hue—the way my own sparks did. I wondered if she might have a bit of Fae blood in her somehow—was that possible?

Sometimes the fairies of the Seelie Court stole a human child and replaced it with one of their own—just for the sake of doing mischief. Such children were called "Changelings" and they often had no idea of their true heritage and origin.

To my surprise, the girl stopped right in front of us. She looked us up and down and grinned.

"Hey, is there a *Lord of the Rings* con in town?"

"A what?" I asked, frowning.

"Maybe *World of Warcraft?*" she continued, not answering my question. She pointed at me, "You're an Elf maiden, right?"

"Oh, well…yes," I said, uncertain if it was right to reveal myself to a mortal.

"I knew it! I *love* your ears—they look so real!"

Reflexively, I reached up to touch my pointed ears which stuck out through my hair.

"How did you ever get your hair that shade of blue?" the human girl continued. "It's *gorgeous.*"

"Yes, my wife *is* quite beautiful," Liath agreed amiably, which made me blush with pleasure.

"She really is," the girl said sincerely. She studied Liath with a look of concentration on her face. "And you must be…hmm, you're not *quite* an orc…"

"I am an Unseelie warrior," Liath said helpfully.

"Oh, right—of course!" The girl frowned. "Uh—what franchise is that from? Never mind," she said, before Liath could answer. "Anyway, great cosplay! You're both killing it!"

I had no idea what the mortal girl thought we were killing, but she had already past us, heading for a sign that said, "Restrooms in the Rear."

"Wow, you were right," I said, looking up at Liath. "They don't seem to mind that we look different at all!"

"They think we are dressing up as characters from some of their favorite books," he explained. "Stories of the Fae Realms that have bled into the Mortal Realm which human authors write about."

"I had no idea there was that much crossover between our Realms," I remarked.

"There is—though a human has to have at least *some* Fae blood in their veins to visit either the Seelie or the Unseelie Court," Liath told me as he led me to the counter at the front of the crowded tavern.

"What about Changelings?" I asked, thinking of the girl we had just met and how her sparks were different from everyone else's.

"You mean the babies the fairies leave in the place of human babies they snatch?" Liath asked.

I nodded.

"Can they get back to the Fae Realm?" I had never heard of such a thing happening in the Seelie Court, but maybe I had just been sheltered.

"Oh yes." Liath nodded. "But it doesn't happen very often," he added. "They mostly go through their lives thinking they're human. And of course, the older they get, the less magic lives in their blood. Eating human food and drinking human drink makes them more and more human every day. The same way eating fairy food and drink changes the human children which are stolen away."

I did know a few fairies who had been human by birth—but they were male. And male fairies, while still good looking, weren't nearly as lithe and ethereal as the female fairies.

We walked up to the counter and I saw the girl who had spoken to us return as well. I watched her as Liath ordered us both some of the human beverages which he wanted me to try. She ordered a drink too, and started speaking to a human male who had just come up to her. They seemed to be meeting for the first time but I didn't think the girl liked him very much. She simply nodded at most of what he said and then turned her attention to another male on her other side.

It was then that I saw the first male—a grungy looking human with a scruffy half-beard and shifty eyes—reach into his pocket and slip something into the girl's drink.

Alarms went off inside my head. Why had he done that? What was he planning to do? What substance had he put into the friendly human girl's drink—was it some kind of poison?

I wanted to ask Liath about it, but he was busy talking to the bartender behind the counter. So I continued watching the scene playing out in front of me.

The human girl with the special sparks kept talking to the male on her other side and as she did, she absently reached for her drink and raised it to her lips.

I felt a surge of fear—I couldn't let her drink poison! I opened my mouth to shout for her to stop, but she had already taken a gulp of the liquid in the cup. Oh no! I bit my lip, watching to see if she would die. Poor girl!

She didn't die, to my relief, but after a moment more, she put a hand to her head and took a staggering step to one side.

"Hey—whoa!" I heard the man beside her say. He took her arm solicitously and I thought with relief that he was going to help her.

That was when I saw the first man—the one with the shifty eyes who had dropped the strange substance into her drink in the first place—nod at the man who was holding the girl's arm. Understanding raced through me—the two of them were in on this scheme together! To my horror, they each took one of the girl's arms and started dragging her away from the wooden counter.

"Wait...wai..." she said, her words beginning to slur. "I don'...don' know where 'm goin...Wha's happenin'?"

"Don't you worry, baby," one of the men said, smirking at the other as they dragged her away. "We're going to have a *lot* of fun together—you'll see."

It was clear to me that whatever poison or potion they had slipped into her drink, it was meant to incapacitate her and distort her sense of reason. And it was equally clear that the two men were intending on taking her virtue though she had not offered it to them.

I couldn't stand by just watching any longer. Leaving the counter abruptly, I ran over to them.

"Stop!" I shouted, grabbing the girl's arm to try and pull her away. "Leave her alone!"

The men gave me irritated looks.

"Hey, what's your problem?" the shifty-eyed one demanded. "We're just taking our friend here, home."

"Yeah, she's had a few too many drinks," the other man said, shrugging.

"No she hasn't—she only had one drink. But you put something in it—some sleeping potion!" I exclaimed.

People in the tavern were beginning to look at us and I saw the two men exchange uneasy glances.

"Uh, I don't know what you mean, lady," the first one said.

"Yes, you do!" I insisted. "I saw what you did—you drugged her drink!"

"Fuck off, lady!" the second man growled. Taking a firmer grip on the human girl's arm, he started dragging her more forcefully towards the door.

"Yeah—this is none of your business." The other man gave me a one-armed shoved that sent me sprawling—or it would have, anyway, if someone hadn't caught me.

"You *dare* to touch my wife?" The deep, growling voice behind me belonged to Liath, who had left the counter and was now right behind me. He set me carefully back on my feet and grabbed the male who had shoved me by the throat. "I ought to break your fucking neck!" he snarled, lifting the male high into the air.

"Holy shit!" I heard the first man mutter. He dropped the girl—who he had mostly been supporting—and rushed for the door.

I grabbed the human girl before she could fall, noting that her sparks were much diminished—probably because she had been drugged.

"Quickly, Liath—don't let the other one get away!" I told my husband. "They were both in on it together!"

Liath dropped the first human male on the floor and went for the second, who was nearly at the door. He clearly hadn't counted on an Unseelie warrior following him. Liath's long arm reached him before he could make his destination and his big hand caught in the back of the man's collar. He dragged him back, choking and gagging, and dumped him by the first male.

"Hey, what's this—what's going on?" One of the human bartenders—a male one—had come out from behind the counter. "What's happening here, Liath?" he asked, frowning. Apparently, he knew my husband.

"These two were trying to drug the little female," Liath growled, nodding at the human girl I was mostly supporting. She had one arm slung around my shoulders and her head was lolling onto my shoulder. Clearly whatever potion they had given her, it was an extremely strong one.

The human bartender looked angrily from the two males cowering on the floor to the human girl.

"That's not true—we were just helping her home!" the first one babbled.

"Yeah—she's had too much to drink. She's my sister!" the second one exclaimed.

"Your sister, huh?" the bartender looked at him with a frown. The human male *did* have the same shade of brown hair as the girl, though I didn't think they looked alike at all, other than that.

"He's lying!" I exclaimed indignantly. "He slipped something into her drink—I *saw* him."

"No, I didn't—I'm telling you, she's my *sister*, man!" the human male insisted. "I don't know what you think you saw, but I wouldn't drug my own *sister*." He apparently thought he had found a lie that worked and intended to stick with it.

I wished the girl wasn't so drugged. She needed to speak up for herself in this matter and let the bartender know the human male was lying.

Without thinking about it, I gathered some of the many swirling sparks in the room and knotted them together with a bit of mental dexterity. Then I pushed the ball of sparks at her, whispering a word of cleansing under my breath. I needed to clean her of the toxin that had been given to her so that she could speak in her own defense.

The girl took a deep breath, gasped, and then lifted her head. She looked at me in a confused kind of way.

"Elf...maiden?" she whispered. "What...who are you and what happened to me?"

"I am Alira of the Unseelie Court," I told her truthfully. "And what happened is that these men drugged you and were trying to drag you away from the tavern."

"The...tavern?" she looked confused.

"The bar," Liath growled. He shook the human he was still holding by the collar. "Is either one of these males your brother?"

"My brother?" the girl frowned and straightened up. "No, of course not. I don't even *have* a brother."

"You see, Harry?" Liath growled at the bartender. He glared at both of the human males who shrank back from him in fear and confusion.

"I see all right," the bartender who must also be the owner of the establishment said grimly. "You watch them, Liath—I'm calling the cops."

"Hey, no!" one of the men begged.

"You can't arrest us—we didn't do nothing!" the second one exclaimed.

"You drugged this girl and you were dragging her away to take her virtue!" I snapped at them.

"Her what?" the first one demanded. But the second man apparently thought that now was the time to run for it. He scrambled to his feet and headed for the door, barely evading Liath's big hand as my husband reached for him.

Without thinking of it, I gathered more sparks and threw a binding at his legs. I felt the magic wrap around his ankles and he fell on his face, full length on the floor.

As he went down, he knocked into a woman holding an enormous glass filled with sloshing liquid. She gasped in surprise and the contents of the glass spilled directly onto the man's head in a pink waterfall that smelled sharply of alcohol.

"Oh! My eyes!" he screamed, rubbing at the streams of pink drink that were pouring down his face. "Fuck, that *hurts!*"

"You want to try and run too, bub?" Harry the bartender asked the other male as Liath went and dragged the first one back, away from the door.

"No, but I still say we didn't do nothing," the human male muttered sullenly.

"You'd probably better put a binding on that one too," Liath murmured in my ear, when he got back to me with the soaking male, who was still pawing at his eyes. "Though I'm not sure how the fuck you're doing it with all the iron in this place."

I looked up at him, surprised.

"You…felt that?" I asked. "The same way I can feel your magic?"

A smile quirked one corner of his sensuous mouth.

"Well, it didn't feel like anyone stroking me off or anything—like my magic apparently feels to you," he murmured. "But yeah, I felt it. Felt like a stream of hot, sizzling power shooting right past my head. You're packing a real punch, sweetheart. How the hell are you doing it?"

I shrugged.

"The same way I always am, I guess. I just reach for the sparks and—"

"Hey, I need to thank you." It was the human girl. I still had my arm around her waist but she was supporting her own weight now and her eyes, which had been clouded by the drug, were clear now.

"No thanks are necessary," I told her quickly. "I just saw what those two human males were doing and I didn't want you to lose your virtue against your will."

She gave a little laugh.

"I guess you're staying in character, huh? I admire that kind of commitment."

I remembered what Liath had said about humans thinking we were dressing up as characters in their favorite books and nodded.

"Yes—exactly," I told her. "Are you well now?"

"I'm feeling a lot better than I was. Thank goodness whatever they gave me seems to have worn off really quickly. I'm Lily, by the way," she added. "Is there anything I can do to thank you two for saving me?"

"Just be more careful about your drink in an establishment like this," Liath told her. "There are too many males who would be happy to take advantage of a female alone."

"Um, yeah. I will be." She nodded seriously and ran a hand through her long, brown hair. I noticed that her sparks had started again and they were as bright as ever. There was something special about this human girl—I wondered what it was.

But I wasn't given a chance to find out. Just then, the peace keepers showed up—what Harry had called the "police"—and started asking what had happened. After some explaining, they hauled the two human males away—hopefully to some kind of prison where the two of them couldn't hurt any other females, I thought.

Lily thanked us again and left and I was about to say to Liath that maybe we ought to leave too—it would be time for the evening banquet at the Unseelie Palace soon—when Harry the bartender came back.

"Well, *that* was a little adventure," he said, speaking to Liath. "I don't see you for months and then you show up with a beautiful lady and keep one of my customers from being date raped." He nodded at me. "Thanks for that, by the way."

"Happy to help," Liath said, nodding. He seemed to want to go but Harry the bartender kept talking.

"Where have you been all this time, anyway?" he asked, frowning. "And where's Quill?"

"What?" I exclaimed before I could stop myself.

Harry looked at me.

"Liath's best friend Quill—haven't you met him? I figured if you're here with Liath, you must have. Those two used to come in every Wednesday night to drink and play darts—always dressed up like their Elvin characters. Then suddenly, they just stopped coming." He frowned up at Liath. "Is he okay?"

"No," I blurted. "Quill is...is *dead*."

I could feel the grief and disbelief washing over me as I realized something awful. Liath had known my brother as more than an adversary—the two of them had been friends. Maybe even best friends as the bartender had suggested.

My husband and my big brother had been friends and for some reason Liath had kept that fact from me.

I felt incredibly betrayed.

19

"Look, little bird—" Liath started as we stepped through the rift between the Realms and it closed behind us.

"Don't call me that!" I exclaimed, rounding on him. "You knew about my nickname because Quill told you, didn't you? Go on—admit it!"

Liath blew out a breath and ran a hand through his hair.

"Yes, I did. I fucking admit it," he said. "But you have to give me a chance to explain."

"Explain why you never told me you were best friends with my big brother?" I demanded. "How could you not tell me that, Liath?"

"Because I didn't think you'd believe me!" he exclaimed. "Who would believe that the two princes of the warring realms could find friendship in the midst of war?"

"*I* would have believed," I said, though I wasn't sure I would have—not at first, anyway.

"You would have thought I was tricking you—trying to get close to you by telling lies," Liath growled. "And I wouldn't have blamed you—it's pretty fucking unbelievable."

"Tell me, then." I walked over to a fallen log. Brushing the snow from it, I had a seat. I was much more used to the Winter weather now and being out in the cold didn't bother me as it had when I had first come to the Unseelie Court. I patted the log beside me, but Liath didn't come and sit. Instead, he began to pace in front of me, like a male who is too anxious to settle.

"It started at Harry's—the place I just took you," he said, talking as he paced. "I went there because I was curious about the Mortal Realm. And I happened to see your brother—to see Quill, there."

"How long ago?" I asked tightly.

He sighed and ran a hand through his hair again.

"Five years," he admitted. "At first I was ready to fight him—he was a Seelie warrior and I wanted to take him down."

"What happened? Why didn't you?" I asked, curious despite myself.

"Well...your brother happened. He waved me over as though I was an old friend—and then he bought me a drink!" Liath laughed. "Can you fucking believe it? Bought me a fucking drink." He shook his head.

"Actually, that sounds like something Quill would do," I said slowly. "He was always slow to anger." Well, except when he knew that Asfaloth and Calista had been tormenting me.

"I was so surprised I sat with him and had a drink," Liath said. "And we talked...just talked. About Court life...what it's like to have the burden of being next in line to the throne on your fucking head. Things like that." He shrugged. "You know."

"Did he talk about me?" I asked tightly, wondering what my big brother might have said.

"Oh yes, little bird—he talked about you a *lot*," Liath said softly. "He loved you dearly, you know." His voice dropped. "He told me how your cousins tormented you—how fucking cruel they were."

My skin felt hot all over. How much had Quill told Liath? Had he revealed all the horrible, embarrassing things that Asfaloth and Calista had done to me? There were so many humiliating incidents I just wanted to forget—and I certainly didn't want my husband knowing about them!

"I see," I said stiffly. "Is that why you decided to ask my father for my hand? Because Quill was killed?"

"Partially," he admitted. "I...started going to the Pool of Seeing—just to watch over you, you know," he added. "I knew Quill would have wanted me to."

"You think my brother would have wanted you to *spy* on me?" I demanded, glaring up at him.

"It wasn't *spying*, exactly," Liath said defensively. "I was just keeping an eye on you. I wanted to be sure they didn't hurt you."

"What did you see?" I asked him, my voice shaking. "Did you see the time Asfaloth did a transformation and gave me a sow's head for a whole day and forced me to attend a Court banquet that way? Or what about the time Calista used a filth spell to smear all my dresses with pig shit as soon as I stepped out of the doors to my room? They kept me locked up a whole month that way because every time I tried to leave, I was magically covered in filth—it was really *hilarious*," I said fiercely.

"Alira...little bird—" he began.

"I told you, don't call me that!" I snapped. "How about the time my cousins caught me swimming naked and then made me look at my reflection in the pond while they told me how ugly I was? Did you see that—*did* you? Is that why you were so eager to show me I was 'beautiful' on our first night together?"

"You *are* fucking beautiful!" he growled. "None of what they did to you can make that otherwise, Alira!"

"Just admit it!" I jumped up from the frozen log. "You asked for my hand and married me because you felt *sorry* for me! Because Quill was your best friend and you thought you had to look after his little sister after he was killed!"

"That's not it—or not *all* of it," Liath objected.

"Well, it's all I need to hear." I turned and started making my way back to the Winter Palace.

I couldn't help feeling hurt and betrayed. Liath had probably seen all the incidents I had mentioned—and others too awful to recount. I felt humiliated that he had seen how Asfaloth and Calista had tormented me—and betrayed that he had asked for my hand just because he felt sorry for me and thought he owed it to Quill to take care of his helpless little sister.

He had acted like I had value to him—like he knew I had incredible magical ability and that he thought I would be able to help him take the Shadow Throne of the Unseelie Realm. He had made me feel important—beautiful—*special*.

I felt none of those things now. I just felt hurt and angry and betrayed. So I ignored his calls and walked back to the Palace alone.

I had nothing left to say to my husband, I told myself. And I didn't care if he had anything to say to me—I wasn't listening.

20

Dinner in the Banquet Hall that night was a silent affair. I sat at Liath's right hand as always with his Great Aunt Acosta on my other side. The food was delicious and plentiful as always, but I found I had no appetite.

After trying several more times to speak to me, Liath seemed to have given up. He was brooding in silence, his face like a thundercloud, and I was keeping quiet as well.

I couldn't get over what I had learned. I kept picturing Liath looking into the Pool of Seeing, watching me be tormented by my cousins and feeling sorry for me. And then telling himself it was his duty to marry me and watch out for me, since I was his best friend's little sister. Poor little thing with no magic and no beauty and no way to protect herself—how sad. How pitiful.

How *pathetic.*

"Well, you're certainly not eating much tonight, dearie," Liath's Great Aunt Acosta remarked, breaking into my dark thoughts.

"Oh, er—I'm not very hungry," I mumbled. Making small talk

with Liath's mad Great Aunt was the last thing I wanted to be doing, but of course I couldn't be rude to her either.

"Well, more for me!" she exclaimed, taking a large helping of venison from the steaming platter in front of us and grinning at me with her white, stolen teeth.

"I wish you the joy of it," I said coolly. "I have no appetite myself."

"Mayhap you're pregnant, then!" she said brightly. "Having a baby in your belly can often make you sick to your stomach, you know my dear."

"No," I said shortly. "I'm certain it's not that."

"No?" She looked disappointed. "What a shame! And you so ripe for childbearing, with those nice wide hips of yours!"

I bit my lip. I would never tell her, of course, that there was no way I could be pregnant since Liath and I hadn't actually consummated our marriage yet. When I asked about it—timidly, since he was so very large—Liath always said there was no hurry. He told me he wanted to take his time, learning my body, helping me grow my magic, bringing me along slowly because "some things just can't be rushed, little bird."

Now I wondered if he was making excuses not to take me. What had seemed like a kindness before seemed suspicious to me now. Was he planning to get rid of me? Until our Joining was consummated, it wasn't fully legal. He could simply say I was still a virgin—which I was—and throw me over the moment he got bored of me.

Such awful thoughts were filling my mind and distracting me that I hardly noticed when Great Aunt Acosta asked me if I would like to try some of the "special wine" she had brought. I simply nodded my head, and when she poured it into my glass and urged me to try it, I lifted the goblet to my lips and drained it, scarcely tasting the bitter flavor that lingered on the back of my tongue.

"Good, good—you drank it all!" Great Aunt Acosta clapped her withered hands in apparent delight. "That will take care of any problems you have conceiving, I'm sure of it, dearie!"

I had no idea what she was talking about—I thought her words were simply the ravings of the mad. So I only smiled as well as I was able and thanked her for the wine.

It wasn't until later, when I was getting ready for bed, that I felt the effects…

21

"I'll sleep on one of the couches—you can have the bed," Liath growled at me, the moment we entered our bed chamber.

My stomach knotted unhappily. I didn't actually *want* to sleep away from him. From the very first night I had slept in his arms, curled up against his muscular side and breathing in his warm, spicy scent. I didn't like the idea of spending the night alone in the big, empty bed.

It was on the tip of my tongue to apologize and say I didn't want to sleep apart...but he had already turned his back to me and was heading to the living area.

Head drooping, I made my way to the bathing chamber. I would take a long soak in the tub, I told myself—just as I had on my first night here. I would pamper myself and use the bath salts and the special hair ointment which was meant to make my long, midnight blue tresses shine like glass.

Then I remembered that it was Liath who had given me the ointment as a present and frowned. Perhaps I *wouldn't* use it after all. Maybe I would use something else—or else not bother with washing my hair. It didn't really need to be washed since Liath had done that for me, just the other night when we had taken a bath together.

I tried not to think of how nice it had been splashing playfully in the tub with him, laughing and tickling each other. And then later when he had washed me everywhere, his big hands, soapy with bubbles, cupping my breasts and rolling my nipples to make me moan and writhe against him.

He had held me against him with my back to his front so that I could feel his long, hard shaft pressing against my bottom while he washed me. And then he had growled in my ear,

"Are you ready for me to wash you lower, little bird?"

I had moaned and writhed in his arms, loving the feeling of his big, hard, naked body against my own.

"Yes, I...I think I am," I had whispered.

And then Liath had reached between my legs...

I came back to myself, realizing that I had been just standing there, remembering how good it felt to have my husband touch me. In fact, I could almost feel his big, warm hands on me, rubbing everywhere...teasing my most sensitive areas.

"Stop it!" I muttered to myself. "You're being ridiculous. Just forget the past and draw yourself a bath!"

I followed my own orders, going to get the water running in the tub. There was some magical means of controlling the temperature and I made sure that the water rushing from the golden faucet was good and hot.

I went to my side of the closet and took off my gown. But as I was sliding it over my head, I couldn't help remembering how Liath had helped me take off my gown the night before. He had slipped it over my head but my arms had still been caught in the long sleeves. Liath had pulled them gently but firmly behind my back and then started talking in his deep, growling voice, right in my ear.

"Well, little bird, it looks like you're trapped," he had murmured. "What are you going to do to get free?"

"What...what would you have me do?" I had whispered breathlessly, my heart pounding.

"You're going to be my good girl and suck my cock," he'd informed me.

"What? Right here?" I had exclaimed breathlessly.

"Yes, right here, little bird. Now on your knees and take me nice and slow and as deep as you can."

I had sunk to my knees before him, eager to be his "good girl." I just couldn't get enough of his praise—I loved it when he stroked my hair with his big, warm hands and rumbled about how good and perfect and sweet and beautiful I was as I took his cock deep in my mouth and swallowed his cream...

"You're doing it again," I muttered to myself. "Stop it, Alira! What is *wrong* with you?"

I tried to push Liath out of my mind as I pinned up my hair and went back to the tub, which was almost full of steaming water. I sprinkled a generous helping of the glittering pink bath salts into the tub, swirled them around twice to melt them, and then climbed in myself.

My teeth caught in a hiss as I lowered myself into the deep water which was almost hotter than I liked. Perhaps I had overfilled the tub? I was up to my neck in steaming, scented water and feeling rather overheated already.

But I told myself I was fine. I stretched out, allowing myself to float so that my large breasts bobbed at the surface. Everything was all right, I told myself. Everything would be—

Something in my line of vision caught my attention and cut off my positive affirmation. My large nipples were in plain sight since my breasts were floating but they were no longer pink—instead, they had turned a deep maroon color which was most disturbing.

I reached out to touch one experimentally and winced.

"Ow!" I exclaimed involuntarily as I yanked my hand away. My nipple was incredibly sensitive—to the point of pain. In fact, now that I thought of it, even the warm water lapping against my tight peaks felt like too much. What was going on with me?

As I realized this, I opened my legs to try and sit up from my floating position. This allowed a quantity of heated water to rush into my inner pussy, making me give a muted yelp. Ouch—that *hurt!* I couldn't remember when my clit had ever been so sensitive, but I clapped my legs closed, not wanting any more water to get inside. What was wrong with me?

It was at that moment, that I started noticing that my breathing was coming too fast and shallow. My heart was pounding and my throat seemed to be closing up.

Oh no! I clutched at my throat, gasping for breath, the air whistling thinly in the pinhole my airway had become. Why couldn't I breathe?

I tried to get up—to get out of the overfull tub—but I slipped and fell back with a splash that sent water over the side and all over the floor. There were huge black flowers blooming in my field of vision now—dimly I realized I was passing out.

I needed to get help but when I tried to call, I found that my throat had closed completely. Panic took me and I forgot I was angry with my husband—he might be the only one who could save me! And though I couldn't call him with my voice, I hoped he could still hear me when I "thought loudly" as he put it.

"Help! Liath, help me!" I thought-shouted. *"Help, I can't breathe!"*

Blackness was eating my vision by that time and I was just beginning to sink beneath the water when the door to the bathing room burst open and Liath appeared. His bronze eyes were wide with worry and he was wearing nothing but his sleeping trousers.

"Little bird?" He scooped me out of the bath, getting water everywhere and looked down at me frantically. "What is it? What's wrong?"

I shook my head and gestured weakly to my throat.

"Can't...breathe!"

"Hang on," Liath told me. "I've got you, baby. I'm going to help you—I swear it."

He rushed with me to the bed chamber and laid me, soaking and naked as I was, full length on the bed. Then he grabbed his moonstone dagger—which was never far from him—and slit his palm with its silver blade.

He placed his big hand over my throat and I felt the warm blood sliding down my neck as he whispered words of opening, clearing, cleansing, healing...

Slowly my throat began to open. At last I was able to take a huge, whooping gasp of air, filling my lungs until I thought they might burst.

"Alira? Sweetheart?" Liath knelt beside me on the damp bed, his bronze eyes worried. "Are you all right?"

"I...I couldn't *breathe!*" My voice came out in a hoarse, choked sob and then I was crying—tears pouring down my cheeks because I had come *that* close to dying and I knew it. If Liath hadn't been able to hear me, or if he had ignored my call for help because we were mad at each other—

"I would never ignore you, little bird. *Never!*" he growled fiercely. Gathering me into his lap, he cradled me close and stroked my trembling shoulders. "It's all right," he murmured. "All right now—I've got you, and I won't let anything happen to you."

I cried and buried my face in his broad chest as the fear slowly left me. Safe—I was safe in his arms, I told myself. Everything was going to be all right now that my husband was holding me and protecting me.

"I've only ever wanted to hold and protect you, little bird," he murmured. "And…I'm sorry I didn't tell you that Quill and I were friends. I should have—I admit it."

I looked up at him.

"Did you only marry me because you felt sorry for me? Or out of a sense of duty to your best friend?"

"No, of course not!" Liath said fiercely. He stroked the damp hair away from my face and looked down at me intently. "I asked to marry you because I fell in love with you, little bird," he murmured. "When I saw how brave you were—how you never let anyone break you, no matter how fucking cruel your cousins were. I admired your courage. And when I told Stableforth what I was considering, he was the one who researched your background and found the prophesies about one with the blood of both Courts uniting them again."

I bit my lip.

"But…you didn't just want me because you thought I was the one those prophesies were talking about? Because I don't think I am, Liath."

"I don't know," he remarked thoughtfully. "You were doing magic in the Mortal Realm today—I've never seen a Fae able to pull that off. At least, not in a building with that much iron in it."

"I only did what I always did—I just reached for the sparks and used them," I protested.

"Maybe you have some Mortal blood somewhere in the mix too," he remarked. "Under special circumstances—like what happened to your ancestress, Talandra—a Fae child may have more than one father, you know."

"No, I didn't know that," I admitted. "But…is that why you wanted me? For my magic?"

"I told you, I wanted you—*want* you—because I fell in love with your beauty and your courage," Liath said firmly. "I don't fucking want anyone else but you, baby. And no, I'm not thinking of getting rid of you just because we haven't consummated our Joining yet."

I bit my lip, realizing that he must have heard the thoughts I'd been thinking during the banquet, when I had drunk all that "special wine" his Great Aunt Acosta had given me...

"Special wine?" Liath asked, frowning. His face grew dark. "Gods, the mad old bat!"

"What? What is it?" I exclaimed, looking up at him.

"I think I know what happened to you just now."

Liath helped me sit up and reached for his dagger again, which he had left on the nightstand. He pricked his finger and did a warming spell first, since I was still damp and shivering. Then, once I was all dry and the bed was as well, he did a summoning.

In a moment, he had the elaborate golden goblet I'd been drinking from at the banquet that evening. It must not have been washed yet because it still held the sticky dregs of the wine Great Aunt Acosta had poured for me.

Liath dabbed his little finger in the wine and placed a single drop carefully on his tongue. After a moment, he turned his head and spat.

"By the Shadow Throne—that's the most concentrated lust potion I've ever tasted! And you say you drank a whole glass of it?"

"Yes—she was really excited that I drank it all," I admitted.

Liath shook his head.

"No wonder you had some kind of reaction to it! What can she have been thinking, giving you something like that?"

"I think she was trying to help me get...get pregnant," I admitted in a low voice. "She seems obsessed with the idea of me producing a female heir for you—one who can sit the Shadow Throne."

"I believe that in time *you* will be able to sit the Shadow Throne—and the Shining Throne too, if you wish it," Liath told me. "And don't say you won't, Alira," he added, when I started shaking my head. "There's something special and unique about your magic, which is why I've been bringing you along so fucking slowly."

"Is that why you haven't...haven't taken me yet?" I asked. I was very aware that I was completely naked with him and that my nipples and pussy were throbbing as I spoke.

"That's exactly why, little bird," he murmured, stroking my cheek. "Don't you think I *want* to take you? Want to thrust my shaft deep in your soft, sweet pussy and flood your womb with my cream? But the moment I take your maidenhood has to be special—it has to be *right*. It's going to be a moment of blood and power and pleasure like no one in this Realm or any other has ever seen. It has to be done at the right time. Besides, didn't I tell you I wouldn't take you until you begged me to?"

"What if I begged you now?" I asked, shifting restlessly on the bed. "Or at least begged you to do *something* for me? I don't know why, but I'm so sensitive and achy in my private places, Liath!"

I nodded down at my nipples and areolas, which were still dark maroon. The inside of my pussy felt hot and swollen too—my clit throbbing like a second heartbeat.

Liath frowned.

"Hmm...I'd bet the last drop of my magic that's a side effect of the fucking lust potion. I have to have a word with Great Aunt Acosta."

"You don't think she...she wouldn't do anything on purpose to...to hurt me, would she?" I asked hesitantly.

Liath shook his head.

"I don't think so. She's just mad—though in her day, she was a force to be reckoned with."

"Well, I'm never eating or drinking anything she offers me again," I said, shivering. "I drank the wine because I didn't want to be rude but I'd rather be rude than dead!"

"You're not going to die—not while I'm here to protect you." Liath stroked my hair away from my eyes. "And to pleasure and heal you. Do you want me to try and heal your nipples, little bird?"

I bit my lip.

"How exactly will you heal them? I mean, with your blood?"

The blood from his cut palm had already been wiped from my neck and I was grateful for it in the extreme—he had saved my life. But the idea of him rubbing blood over my nipples didn't really appeal.

Liath shook his head.

"I think this kind of healing is more suited to pleasure magic," he rumbled, his eyes going half-lidded.

"But...are you going to touch my nipples? I mean because I don't think I can stand it if you, you know, pinch or twist them like you do sometimes when you're uh, touching me or I'm touching myself," I confessed. "They're *really* sensitive, Liath."

"In that case, I'll have to heal you with my tongue—that's much more gentle," he murmured.

"Oh—all right." I didn't mind this a bit. Liath was very fond of sucking my nipples—he loved my big breasts and told me so every chance he got.

He frowned.

"I'm not just going to lick and suck your nipples, you know, little bird. I'm going to need to lick your sweet little pussy too."

"You...you are?" I squeaked uncertainly. This was something we hadn't done yet—though Liath had spoken of wanting to do it often. "I thought you were saving *that* for a special magic lesson," I said, feeling anxious and worried. After all, what if he didn't like it? Didn't like the taste of me there?

"I already know I'm going to love how your sweet pussy tastes," Liath told me firmly—clearly he was still attuned to my thoughts. "I lick your fingers every time you touch yourself, remember?" he murmured, his eyes going half-lidded. "You don't know how hard it's been to hold off from tasting your sweet pussy, little bird. Been wanting to lick between your legs from the very first."

"You...you have?" I asked.

"Fuck, yes!" Liath assured me. He sat back against the headboard and pulled me into his lap so that I was straddling him. "But first, let me take care of your beautiful big breasts," he told me. As he spoke, he cupped my right breast in his hand and brought my aching nipple to his mouth.

I bit my lip as I waited for the pain of contact—my tight peaks were so sensitive now that everything seemed to hurt them.

But Liath seemed to know how delicate this area was now. Putting out his tongue, he lapped very, *very* gently, bathing my aching peak with long, slow strokes of his tongue and then swirling it around and around the puffy areola as well.

I moaned softly and carded my fingers though his long, thick hair. By the Shining Throne, that felt so good! I thrust my chest forward, begging mutely for more.

Taking my invitation, Liath took my whole nipple into his hot mouth, sucking gently at first and then—when he knew I could take it—much harder.

"Oh, Liath..." I moaned softly as he switched to the other nipple and gave it the same treatment. I could see the sparks of my own pleasure floating around me like bright golden motes. Most of them flowed from where his mouth met my breast and then continued on down to my throbbing pussy. Looking down, I could see them pressing against my swollen clit and then melting into my flesh, which seemed to send shivers and tingles through my entire body.

"Mmm, baby—your tight nipples taste so good," Liath growled, releasing my second peak at last. "Love to lick and suck you."

"Does...does that mean you're going to...to lick between my legs now?" I asked shyly. I didn't know if I wanted him to do this or not. It seemed so intimate...so forbidden.

"Why should it be forbidden?" Liath asked reasonably. "You suck my shaft all the time, little bird. "It's about time I repaid the favor."

"I don't do it as a favor when I suck you—I do it because I *like* it," I protested.

"Well, I happen to fucking *love* the taste of your pussy honey and now I want to taste it straight from the source," Liath told me. His eyes grew lazy with lust. "Can you be a good girl and spread your legs so I can lick your sweet little pussy, baby? Can you be my good girl and spread wide for my tongue?"

I felt my heart start pounding in my chest. I couldn't get enough of his praise—probably because when I was growing up, nobody praised me for anything. I was never good enough. Now Liath told me how good I was all the time—and I *loved* it.

"Yes," I whispered, nodding. "Yes, I...I think I can do that."

"Good girl. Then let's get you all set up."

Liath had me come to the end of the bed where he propped a pillow under my head and another under my bottom.

"So you can see what I'm doing," he added, putting another one under my head. "It's hotter if you watch me lap your soft little cunt."

Then he took another pillow for himself and put it on the floor at the end of the bed.

"For my knees," he explained. His bronze eyes burned. "I'm expecting to be here awhile," he added.

I bit my lip.

"You really think it's going to, er, take that long to heal my pussy with your tongue?"

"I think it's going to take that long for me to get my fill of your sweet honey," Liath growled. "Like I said, been wanting to taste you from the very first."

He sank to his knees before me, kneeling at the end of the bed as I lay before him, open and waiting. I nibbled my lower lip and gripped the coverlet on either side of me. I couldn't help feeling nervous—my pussy was aching by this time. Great Aunt Acosta's lust potion had certainly had an effect! Also, I still felt anxious about Liath putting his mouth on me in such an intimate place. I expected that he would just dive right in, though I didn't feel nearly ready.

But Liath surprised me again. Instead of sticking his tongue in me directly, he leaned forward and placed a soft kiss on my mound of springy curls. Then he rubbed his cheek against it and inhaled deeply, as though he couldn't get enough of my scent.

"Gods, you smell so good, little bird..." His voice was almost a groan. "Love the sweet scent of your pussy."

"You...you do?" I asked, looking down at him.

"Mmm-hmm." He kissed my curls again and then looked up at me. "Are you ready to let me kiss you now?"

"Just...just a kiss?" I asked. I had thought that he would spread me open and lick me to heal my inner folds the same way he had lapped and sucked my nipples and areolas.

"Just a kiss to start with," Liath told me. "We'll get to everything else in time, but I'm going to take it slow with you since you've never done this before—or had it done to you."

"Thank you, Liath."

My heart was warmed by the sweet, patient way he was treating me. Once again it occurred to me that anyone who saw my husband would think he was a stone-cold killer—with his scarred face and huge, muscular body, it would be difficult to believe that he was anything but an Unseelie thug. No one seeing him on the battlefield would believe that he would kneel before me and coax my legs apart to give me sweet, gentle kisses on my vulnerable pussy.

I heard a rumble of laughter and realized that Liath must have caught my thoughts again.

"You're right, little bird—I behave differently in the bedroom than I do in the battlefield. But of course, I have a good reason—*you*." He rubbed his scratchy cheek against my inner thigh, making me gasp and squirm with the intense sensation. "So are you ready to let me kiss your sweet little pussy?"

"Yes, I...I guess so," I murmured, nodding.

"Good, then just relax for me," he murmured. "I want you to feel comfortable with my mouth on you before I spread you open and lick you, baby."

I took a deep breath and nodded.

"All right. I'm ready."

"Good girl," Liath told me. "Such a good girl to open your pussy for me and let me kiss you, Alira."

I felt the familiar surge of pleasure at his praise and then he was kissing me—kissing my pussy as gently and sweetly as if he was kissing my mouth.

I moaned and shifted my hips as I felt his lips part and his tongue began a slow, gentle caress up and down the slit of my pussy. He wasn't really probing inside me—not yet—but the feeling of his warm wetness caressing me was delicious. I could feel just the tip of his tongue sliding over my aching clit and the sensation made me shiver all over as the sparks of my pleasure rose to hover in the air around me.

I knew my husband must truly be enjoying himself, because sparks of pleasure were rising from him as well, mixing with mine to make a dancing pattern above our heads.

"Mmmm..." Liath sat back for a moment, his lips shiny with my juices. "Gods, you taste even better than I thought you would, little bird! Are you ready to let me spread you open and give you deeper kisses now?"

"Deeper kisses?" I whispered, my heart pounding in my chest.

Liath gave me a level look.

"You know what I mean, Alira. I need to open your sweet pussy and bathe every bit of your inner folds to ease your ache and heal you of the lust potion's effects. And you have to be a good girl and let me. Can you do that?"

"I think so," I whispered.

"Good girl," he growled softly. "Here we go, then."

Bending to the spot between my legs again, he put his thumbs on my outer pussy lips and gently spread them wide. I bit my lip when I saw how dark my inner folds were. My clit was extremely prominent—throbbing in the center like a dark pink pearl begging for attention.

"Gods, so beautiful," I heard Liath mutter, and then he leaned closer and took a long, loving taste of my pussy, dragging his hot tongue over as much of it as he could.

I moaned as his tongue touched the sensitive area. I was in such a heightened state of arousal from the lust potion that the intense pleasure he was giving me was almost *unbearable*. Yet I knew I must bear it, if Liath was ever going to heal me.

He looked up at me again.

"Good girl, Alira," he growled softly. "I know it's intense but you can do this—you can let me lick your sweet pussy and heal you."

"I...I'm trying to be good and hold still," I whispered. "But it's hard—I feel like...like I need something to hold on to."

Liath nodded.

"I can tell. If it feels too good and you can't quite manage to hold still, just hold on to me." He tapped one of his horns with a finger. "I have some built-in handles for you right here, sweetheart."

Thinking of his horns as "handles" made me giggle and feel a little less tense. But I was still hesitant.

"Um...are you sure I won't hurt you? I mean, yanking on your horns?" I asked.

He rumbled a laugh.

"Forgive me, little bird—you've immense magic inside you but your physical strength can't match it. No, I'm not worried about you hurting me. Although to be honest, sometimes I like a bit of pain with my pleasure."

I looked at him, wide-eyed.

"You do? But...how can that be good?"

"Just a tiny bit of pain can enhance your pleasure—the way a bit of salt brings out the flavor in a sweet dish," he explained. "It's not for everyone, but some find it very desirable. I happen to be one of them. So hold on to me and 'yank' as hard as you want to—I won't mind."

Leaning down, he nuzzled me gently, rubbing his rough cheek against my mound of curls again. I took his invitation and reached down to grip his horns. The way they curved, it almost seemed as though they were meant for my hands and I could feel their rough ridges against my palms.

Liath was kissing me again, but this time he was kissing my inner thigh. His hot, wet mouth felt delicious against my flesh, but I knew where it would feel better. Experimentally, I tugged at the horns, bringing his mouth where I needed it most—to my pussy.

He looked up, his bronze eyes burning with heat and desire.

"That's right, little bird—put me where you need me. You're in control now."

"I...I am?" I liked this idea—it made my heart pound to consider the idea of taking control and guiding my huge Unseelie warrior husband to exactly where I wanted and needed him.

Liath must have caught my thought because he gave me a lazy grin.

"That's right—sometimes it's fun to be the one in charge, isn't it, little bird? Give it a try, why don't you?"

Then he bent his head again, as though waiting for me to take control.

I did so, tugging on his curling horns as I guided him once more to my open pussy.

"There!" I gasped as he began to lap me, dragging his hot tongue over my inner folds. "Right *there,* Liath! By the Shining Throne—don't stop!"

It was clear he had no intention of stopping. He slid his big hands under my ass and scooped me up, lifting me to him as though he was a man dying of thirst and my pelvis was bowl of cool water. And then...he devoured me.

I gasped and moaned as his tongue lashed my sensitive clit, teasing and whip quick. Then, the next moment he was slipping his tongue inside me to lap up my honey and then back to my clit, which he sucked into his mouth and circled with just the tip of his tongue.

"Oh...oh, Liath!" I moaned his name like a prayer and both our clouds of sparks rose higher and higher. They were filling the room now—filling the bedchamber all around us. I had time to think that it was too bad we hadn't had time to set up a bunch of the dried roses that Liath kept for me to practice on. I bet I could have revived a whole bouquet with the pleasure he was giving me!

And then Liath's hands moved, though he kept his mouth on my pussy. They slid up to cup and knead my breasts. My pleasure rose even higher and I felt my release coming—rushing towards me like a rising tide. In a moment it would sweep over me and drown me...or else raise me to the highest peak imaginable.

For all the other releases I'd had—either by Liath's hand or my own—were nothing compared to the feeling of his hot, wet tongue exploring me. It felt so good, so right! I squeezed his horns and tugged hard, bucking my hips up to meet him. Close I was getting so *close!*

"*Liath!*" I panted. "Oh Gods, yes...*yes!*"

And then suddenly, I was *there*—I saw my pleasure sparks explode outward as my body reached the peak. I gripped Liath's horns so hard I was certain I would have ridges on my palms and fingers when this was over, but I didn't care. I was coming...coming harder than I ever had before...

And just at that moment, his fingers found my sensitive nipples and squeezed.

Just as he had told me, the little bit of pain increased my pleasure —brought spice to the sweet encounter. I felt my body jump another level and the sparks exploded outward again, filling the whole bedchamber like a symphony of stars.

THE THRONE OF SHADOWS

"Oh...*Oh!*" I gasped, my back arching helplessly as my toes curled. *"LIATH!"*

I think I must have lost consciousness then—all I could see were stars—stars everywhere and my heart was pounding so hard it felt like it might explode. I heard Liath calling my name and then he joined me on the bed and gathered me into his arms.

"Little bird? Alira?" he rumbled and I thought he sounded worried. "Come back to me, sweetheart," I heard him saying as he patted my cheek gently. "Please—come back!"

At last the field of stars faded and I was looking up into the worried face of my husband.

"Liath?" I mumbled, feeling disorientated and slightly dizzy. "What...how?"

"You came, little bird—came harder than I've ever seen anyone fucking come," he rumbled. "And you nearly passed out in the process."

"You were right," I whispered. "Just a little bit of pain—the way you squeezed my nipples just as my pleasure was peaking..." I shivered, remembering the intense sensations. My whole body still throbbed from the aftermath of my release.

"I'm glad you enjoyed it—though you scared the fucking hell out of me, collapsing like you did afterwards," he growled.

"Sorry..." I shook my head. "I was just so...it felt so *good*. I didn't know anything could feel so good—so intense."

Liath looked thoughtful.

"I'm not sure it does to most people."

I frowned.

"What do you mean?"

"You seem to have an increased capacity for pleasure," he told me. "Probably because it's tied to your magic."

"Oh, my magic." I shook my head. "I was just thinking—as much as I *could* think—that I wished we had set up some of the dried roses you use to help train me. I'm sure I could have revived a whole dozen or more with that release you gave me."

"You did better than a dozen," Liath said dryly.

"What do you mean?" I asked, frowning up at him.

"Just look around the bedchamber—look at the plants," he told me.

"What? Help me sit up," I said.

He did as I asked, lifting me easily into a sitting position so I could survey the bedchamber. I looked around and could scarcely believe what I saw.

All of the plants that were already growing in the room had burst into bloom—even those that weren't supposed to produce flowers! And the rest of the walls were covered in climbing rose vines. The air was filled with their heavy scent as the velvety blossoms nodded their heads at us.

"You've made our bedchamber a fucking jungle," Liath growled, but there was unmistakable pride in his voice. "Gods, little bird—when your power reaches full strength, no one will be able to stand against you!"

"Not even my brother's killer," I whispered, looking around.

Liath frowned.

"No, not even him—whoever he might be," he said in a low voice.

And I thought for some reason, he seemed troubled.

22

The next day in the Banquet Hall, Liath made certain to put me to his right hand and his Great Aunt Acosta to his left. He wanted to talk to her, he said—to try and explain why the lust potion she had given me was so dangerous.

I bore her no ill will for what she had done—well, not *much*, anyway. The aftermath of the lust potion seemed to have unlocked a new area of my power—magic came even more easily to me now. It was as Liath had said—the greater and more intense my pleasure, the greater and more powerful my magic.

Our bedchamber did indeed resemble a jungle bower now, which I rather liked. What I liked even more was my husband's reaction. I kept catching Liath watching me from the corner of his eye with a proud little smile playing around his lips. I loved that he supported me so fully.

But, though the aftermath had been exciting and gratifying, the lust potion *had* nearly killed me. So it was a good thing that Liath was going to say something to her.

I tried to look like I was concentrating on my meal, but actually I was listening as hard as I could to the conversation going on beside me.

"Aunt Acosta, you cannot offer Alira any more of your potions," I heard Liath saying in a low voice. "The lust potion you gave her last night was *much* too strong."

"What? My boy, I'll have you know I've been making potions since before you were a gleam in your mother's eye! The potion I gave her was just exactly right—perfect to help her conceive."

"And we appreciate you wanting to help, but you must not do it anymore." I could hear the impatient growl in Liath's voice, but he was clearly struggling to keep his tone civil. I was certain he was aware that all the Court was watching us—the nobles and the notables and of course, the servants, were keeping their eyes on us as we sat at the Royal table on the raised dais.

"*Someone* must help for it appears you're doing a poor job of it yourself!" Great Aunt Acosta said rudely. "Why is she not pregnant yet?"

"That is no business of yours." The growl in Liath's voice was more pronounced now. "I am asking you—politely—to keep your nose out of our business. Alira and I haven't been Joined for that long—she will conceive when we are ready and not before."

"How *dare* you!" Aunt Acosta exclaimed. "How dare you ask me not to take an interest in who sits the Shadow Throne?"

"I *dare* because your lust potion nearly fucking killed the woman I love!" Liath's voice rose to a roar and when I looked up from my plate, I saw that his bronze eyes were blazing.

"And who says that wasn't my intent in the first place?" Great Aunt Acosta pushed suddenly back from the table. She was moving much more fluidly than I had ever seen her move before, I noted. Her eyes were flashing with anger as she glared at Liath.

"What?" He frowned at her. "What are you saying? Be very careful, Aunt Acosta—it sounds like you just admitted to making an attempt on the life of the Princess of the Unseelie Court."

"I did!" the old woman snarled. "And why should I not? You're trying to supplant *me* with *her!* You want your bride—that mealy-mouthed little Seelie bitch—to take the Shadow Throne from me! *I* am the rightful heir to the throne—I should have had it long before your mother took my place!"

The rage had gone from Liath's face—now he simply looked shocked.

"Aunt Acosta, what are you saying?" he asked blankly.

"I am saying what we all know to be true—that *I* am the rightful ruler of the Winter Court!" she announced. "And I shall claim my place on the Shadow Throne *now!*"

She marched away from the Royal table, moving like a woman half her age. For a moment Liath and I both just sat there—I think we were both stunned. Then Liath rose quickly from his chair.

"I have to stop her," he muttered. "She doesn't know what she's doing!"

I thought it seemed like she knew perfectly well what she was doing. And I still couldn't believe she'd tried to kill me on purpose! I jumped up and ran after Liath, who was already leaving the dais. And of course, the rest of the Court left their tables in the Banquet Hall and came too.

We all followed Great Aunt Acosta en mass as she left the Banquet Hall and made her way towards the Throne Room, where the Shadow Throne sat silent and foreboding.

I caught up to Liath and reached for his hand. He took mine and gave it a distracted squeeze.

"I have to stop her," he muttered again, as though speaking to himself. "But surely she wouldn't be mad enough to actually try the throne?"

I thought she seemed mad enough to do anything. Her wrinkled face was set in tense lines of determination and her eyes still sparkled as she marched towards the dais where the Shadow Throne sat, wreathed in silence and darkness.

Liath reached out with his free hand to catch her by the elbow before she could ascend the dais where the Shadow Throne was waiting for her, its blood-filled carvings writhing on its black surface.

But there seemed to be some kind of barrier between Acosta and her great, great nephew. Even as Liath reached for her, his fingers slipped off, as though her arm was coated in butter or oil.

"Oh no—she's put a touch-not spell on herself!" I heard him mutter as she ascended the steps that led up to the throne. "Aunt Acosta—don't! The Throne won't fucking accept you!"

"How do you know it won't?" I asked, as he reached for her again and once more his hand slid right off. It was like he couldn't get hold of her, no matter how he tried.

"Because she's fucking *mad*," he growled and I saw real worry in his eyes. "The Shadow Throne won't accept a ruler who isn't sound of both mind and body! It won't—"

And at that moment, Great Aunt Acosta sat herself down on the blood-red cushion and put her hands on the arms of the throne.

For a moment, nothing happened. The Court was all gathered in the Throne room—Satyrs and nymphs and redcaps and ogres and goblins—Shellya the Spider Seamstress and Stableforth the Centaur and everyone else. All of us were watching—holding our breath as we wondered what would happen.

Then a low rumbling voice that seemed to come from the base of the throne itself spoke a single word:

"DENIED."

Then the ruby set in the back of the throne—which was as big as my fist—suddenly began to glow.

"Get out! Aunt Acosta—get off the throne! Go—*go!*" Liath roared.

But it was too late. Even as the realization of what she was doing seemed to dawn in Great Aunt Acosta's wrinkled face, a beam of blood-red light shot from the glowing ruby and hit the back of her gray head.

There was a sizzling sound and the elderly Fae appeared to be transfixed—she held perfectly still, like a butterfly pinned to a board. And then one of her eyeballs blew outward, splattering like a burst grape on the floor at her feet. At the same time, the red beam of light coming from the ruby to pierce the back of her head, shot out the empty eye socket. Clearly it had burned a hole right through her head and brain.

"Ware!" Liath roared, pushing me out of the way and gesturing at the members of the Court who had come too close. "The Shadow Throne is roused to anger. Go—all of you—*run!*"

The nobles and servants scattered and Liath took me in his arms and ran to the far edge of the room. There he stopped, though he pushed me behind him. But I peeked around his broad shoulder and saw what was happening.

For a moment the glowing beam continued. It still held Great Aunt Acosta in place, though she was clearly dead. Her other eye was open but unseeing and had the glassy look of an animal which has been stuffed as a trophy. The beam of light coming from her ruined eye seemed to be searching for other targets, it slid here and there on the floor and everywhere it touched, it etched deep grooves in the black marble flagstones.

"What's going on? What's happening?" I asked Liath.

"Shhh," he shushed me, though I hadn't been speaking that loud. "When the Shadow Throne is roused to anger, it takes some time for it to become inert again. Great Aunt Acosta was a poor fit for it and it takes exception to being offered such a bad candidate."

"I didn't know it was alive," I whispered.

"It is and it isn't...the whole thing is fucking complicated," Liath muttered. "Oh look—it's stopped. Thank all the gods that ever were."

He was right—the fist-sized ruby set in the upright back of the Shadow Throne had stopped glowing and the writhing lines of blood that filled its carvings were moving much more slowly.

As soon as the deadly red beam stopped shooting through her eye, Great Aunt Acosta slumped. Slowly, her body slid out of the throne and down the steps of the dais, coming to a rest on the ground in front of it. The Shadow Throne had rejected and killed her in the space of less than a minute.

I had never seen anything like it.

Liath started towards her inert body but I put a hand on his arm to stop him.

"Is it safe?"

"It is now," he told me. "Gods, I've only seen it do that once before—when my sister tried to sit the throne and take it from my mother."

"Wait...what?" I exclaimed. "You had a *sister*? And she tried to usurp the throne from your mother?"

Liath sighed.

"Yes, though I'd rather not fucking talk about it. It's one reason my mother abdicated. She loved my sister, you see—even after Gelenta tried to take the Shadow Throne from her. It broke her heart to lose a child and so...she left." He looked down at me and barked an unhappy laugh. "Do you see now why I didn't judge you when the Pool of Seeing showed us your cousins fucking? I've got no room to judge—my family has its own sordid past."

As he spoke, we finally reached the foot of the dais where Great Aunt Acosta lay. Her right eye was open but unseeing. Her left was nothing but a charred black hole in her head.

"Gods..."

Liath shook his head and ran a hand through his hair.

"I can't fucking believe she tried that! She's *never* been a candidate to sit the throne! Back before she went completely mad, she knew that."

"I'm sorry, Liath," I said awkwardly as he gathered the old Fae's body into his arms. Even if she had tried to kill me, she had been his last living relative and I felt his pain.

I could *see* his pain too, I suddenly realized—there were black motes clustering around his head like a swarm of gnats. I wished I could wave them away, but I knew his sorrow wouldn't be so easily dismissed.

I walked with him as he left the Throne Room and carried his Great Aunt down to the family crypt in the basement of the Winter Palace. It was cold down there—freezing in fact. I could see my breath coming out in white puffs but I said nothing as Liath laid his Aunt to rest on an unmarked gray marble slab.

"The mortuary attendants will come to tend her later," he said in a low voice. "I have done all I can for her." He squeezed his eyes shut. "If only I could have stopped her from trying for the fucking throne!"

"That wasn't your fault," I told him. "She was mad, as you said. And clearly her madness had been building for some time."

"Yes, well, *that's* clear enough." He sighed and looked at me. "I'm sorry, little bird—she tried to kill you. I should have protected you better—I should have known."

"How could you?" I asked reasonably. "She wasn't in her right mind, Liath. None of this was your fault."

He shook his head.

"I should have seen it—should have known the madness had eaten her mind enough to make her dangerous."

"The only thing that's really dangerous here is the Shadow Throne," I said seriously. "I know you think I should be able to sit it and take the crown of the Winter Court—"

"Not now—not for many, *many* years, little bird," he said quickly. "Your magic is coming along nicely, but you're not ready yet—not nearly." He took me by the shoulders and crouched down, to get to eye-level with me. "Swear to me now you won't try to take the throne until we both agree you're ready. I know all the prophesies say you should be able to, but I don't want to take a chance on losing you. I couldn't fucking bear it!" And he crushed me to him for a long moment.

I put my arms around him and hugged back, inhaling his warm, masculine spice and feeling safe and protected. I felt something soft on the top of my head and realized he had kissed me there.

"I have no problem giving you that promise," I said, tilting my head up to look at him. "I have absolutely no wish at all to wield the power the Shadow Throne commands."

"Good." Liath nodded. He gave me another kiss—this one on my forehead—and pulled me to his side. "Come—the attendants can't deal with her until we leave." He sighed. "Do you want any more supper?"

I shook my head.

"Somehow I've lost my appetite," I said dryly. "Why don't we go back to our bedchamber and cuddle?"

"You want to cuddle, hmm?" A smile touched the corner of his mouth, though his bronze eyes were still sad.

"*I* want to cuddle *you*," I said, to clarify.

His smile widened just a bit.

"But you're so small, little bird—how will you manage it?"

"You'll see," I told him. "Come on—back to the bedchamber."

We climbed the steps leaving the crypt and Great Aunt Acosta's body, already cooling on the slab where Liath had left her. But I couldn't forget the horrible way she had died...and couldn't help thinking of the day when I myself must try for a seat upon the Shadow Throne.

Would it accept me...or reject and kill me? I was glad I had years and years before I had to find out.

Or so I thought...

23

I had a feeling that my big, brave Unseelie warrior husband needed comforting—though of course he would never ask for such a thing. As mad as Great Aunt Acosta had been, he had loved her and she had been part of his childhood and his life. He had no one left now of his immediate family—no one but me.

So the moment we got back to our bedchamber, I suggested a bath.

"You want to take a bath together?" He raised an eyebrow at me. "That sounds nice."

"No, *I* want to bathe *you*," I said, a bit bossily. "The way you take care of me sometimes."

He rumbled laughter, but I thought it didn't reach his eyes.

"But it's easy enough for me to bathe and care for you—you're so small, little bird. How are you going to manage a big brute like me?"

"You'll see," I told him. "Now get undressed while I run the bath."

Liath did as I said and soon he was nude—and mouthwatering to look at. His broad muscular chest led down to narrow hips and long, muscular legs. But I couldn't help noticing that his shaft was undeniably soft. He was still thinking of what had happened in the Throne Room, no doubt.

I had him get into the steaming water and started with his long, moonlight colored hair. I washed it using his favorite shampoo and put in a moisture cream to make it sleek and manageable. I massaged his broad shoulders, working the knots of tensions loose until he groaned softly and relaxed under my hands—I even polished his horns with the special stone and gloss he kept for the purpose.

Liath had done this several times for me since our Joining—taking over my nighttime routine completely to wash my hair and body, scrubbing and massaging with his big hands until I went limp with pleasure. Now I did my best to return the favor and found that I liked it—liked it a *lot*.

I reached into the tub to scrub him with the extra-large sponge, paying special attention to his broad back, which made him groan appreciatively again. However, I didn't do anything overtly sexual. Now wasn't the time, I told myself. The time might come later on tonight, but it wasn't here yet.

At last I determined that he was finished. I had him climb out of the tub—I obviously couldn't lift him out, as he often lifted me—and then I worked a drying spell that acted like a kind of warm, miniature wind twister. It circled around and around him, howling softly to itself until he was completely dry upon which it promptly dissipated, leaving my husband standing huge and naked in the middle of the bathing chamber.

"Well?" He raised his eyebrows. "What now, little bird? Should I get dressed for bed?"

"If you like," I said lightly. "I suppose I should as well."

So we changed into our night clothes but I made sure to wear a dress with a loose top—I had a feeling I might need it.

I climbed up on the bed—positioning myself in the center, leaning against the headboard which was Liath's usual position. Then I patted my legs.

"Come here—lay your head down in my lap," I ordered.

He gave me an amused look but did as I said. Lying on his back, he settled his head in my lap.

"And now?" he asked, looking up at me.

"Now, I want to comfort you...and cuddle you."

I put my arms around him and leaned down to place some gentle kisses—first on his forehead, then one on each eyelid, which he closed obligingly for me, then the tip of his nose and finally, on his mouth. I stroked his hair, which lay like a moonlit waterfall over my lap and kissed him again.

When I finally lifted my head, Liath looked up at me and I saw that his bronze eyes were suspiciously bright.

There is a myth, you know, about how males ought to always be strong and brave and never shed a tear, no matter how badly they might be wounded within. I don't believe in that. When we are wounded, we should seek solace—for not all wounds are external and even the biggest and bravest of us can be cut to the quick.

"Little bird..." Liath's voice was thick with emotion as he turned his head and nuzzled against my breasts, which were loose under my gown.

I caught my breath—the lust potion was still in my system, at least in part—but I tried not to show it.

My husband seemed to know anyway.

"Let me suck your breasts," he murmured, nuzzling me again. "Give me your sweet, ripe nipples to suck."

Looking down at the tent rising in his loose black sleep trousers, I saw that he was no longer soft—quite the opposite, in fact.

I was more than willing to do as he asked. Loosening the string at the top of my gown, I let it fall open to reveal my breasts—the nipples still darker than was normal for me. Then I noticed something strange.

"Wait...what is this?" I frowned down as I examined my right nipple. Perched on its tip was a bead of amber liquid. Also, did my breasts seem fuller than usual?

"What is it?" Liath put out his tongue and tasted the droplet, though I hadn't asked him to. He frowned and licked his lips. "I think it's nectar—the lust potion must have had some kind of fertility components in it."

"Nectar?" I looked down at my breasts and saw that the other nipple had a bead of the same amber liquid. "By the Shining Throne—what is nectar?"

"It's something a female Fae's breasts can produce instead of milk if need be," Liath explained. "The fertility herbs that bring it on are often given to a female whose milk has dried up. Supposed to be full of life force and vitality—it's healing and nourishing for the babe."

"But...I don't have any babe to feed!" I protested. "And my breasts are full of this stuff! Just look!" I nodded down at myself. For whatever reason now that my breasts had decided to make the nectar, they had apparently decided to make a *lot* of it. The amber liquid was beading on my nipples and then running down the bottom curves of my breasts, making a sticky mess.

"You have *me*," Liath pointed out. His bronze eyes grew heavy. "Let me suckle you, Alira. "Let me empty your breasts—you must be aching with how full they are."

I bit my lip.

"You really want to? It doesn't seem...disgusting to you?"

"How could it? Your breasts are beautiful. And the nectar is sweet. Let me suckle you," he murmured again. "Give me your breast—comfort me that way."

I felt my heart begin to beat faster for some reason. His head was still lying in my lap and I leaned over him, offering my right breast again.

"If you think it will help you feel better, my love," I murmured, stroking his rough cheek as I fed my tight peak into his mouth. "Then suckle me—drink my nectar and be comforted."

Liath's answer was a low growl of pure lust as he took my nipple deep into his hot mouth and began to suck and swallow, suck and swallow, over and over again.

I moaned in pleasure and relief—my breast really had been *extremely* full—and carded my fingers through his hair. I had never dreamed of comforting my husband this way, but I found that I liked it—and wanted to give him more of myself in any way I could.

Soon Liath had emptied my right breast and so I gave him the left. At the same time, I reached down to pet the hard ridge of his shaft, which was still extremely prominent under the thin black silk of his sleep trousers.

He groaned around my nipple and arched up into my hand, as though asking for more.

"Do you like that, my love?" I murmured as he continued to suck my breast. "Does it feel good when I comfort you like this?"

Liath groaned wordlessly and thrust into my hand again. I rubbed the soft silk against his shaft, sliding my hand up and down, giving him as much pleasure as I could.

At the same time, I tried something new—I gathered the sparks of pleasure that both of us were generating and sent them down lower, to caress his heavy balls.

Liath's eyes went wide for a moment and he glanced down at my hand before releasing my nipple for a moment.

"Alira, are you—"

"Using magic to tease your balls?" I arched an eyebrow at him. "Yes, actually—I am. Do you like it?"

"Feels fucking *amazing*," he growled. "Do it some more."

"Keep sucking me then," I murmured, rubbing my nipple against his lips again. "That breast is still too full."

"As you wish, little bird," he growled softly and began sucking again.

I moaned softly and continued stroking him...and teasing him with my sparks. By the Shining Throne, I had never imagined how good it could feel to be married to the right male! I was so glad that Liath had asked for my hand—and I was glad I could be there for him, during this difficult time as well.

I was thinking I might be able to finish Liath off by the time he emptied my breasts of the nectar, but it was not to be. He was still hard and a long way from shooting his cream by the time the nectar finally ran dry. He lifted his face from my breast and gave me a half-lidded look.

"Mmm, little bird—that was delicious. But now that your nectar is gone, I want to taste something else."

"What?" I asked, rather breathlessly. I was still running my hand over his shaft and he was thrusting slowly into my loosely cupped fingers.

"You know what else." He reached up and pushed the bottom of my gown up, exposing my pussy. "Hmm...I see you didn't wear your panties tonight."

I bit my lip.

"I...forgot them."

"Good. Come here." Liath put his head between my thighs and suddenly I felt his hot, wet tongue parting my outer pussy lips.

"Oh!" I gasped, jerking my hips. "Oh, Liath—you don't have to do that! *I'm* the one who's supposed to be comforting *you* and you're making it awfully hard for me to reach you." I nodded at the way my arm was stretched out to the limit, trying to keep stroking him as he licked me.

"Don't touch me with your hand then—only use your magic,"

Liath challenged me. "And I'll only use my tongue—we'll see which of us can bring the other off first."

"Liath! Are you sure?" I asked uncertainly. "You really want to...to lick me again after all the time you spent doing it last night?"

His bronze eyes went lazy with lust.

"Sweetheart, I *always* want to lick you—always want to taste your sweet honey. Let me lap your soft little pussy—I'm sure I would find that *extremely* comforting," he added.

I felt myself melting under his gaze. My nipples were still tight from all his sucking and my pussy was throbbing with need and the remains of the lust potion.

"Well...all right," I whispered at last. Scooting down a bit, I spread my thighs wider for him and lifted my gown completely. "Come on, then," I told him, tugging on one of his horns. "Come lick me and taste my honey—tell me if it's as sweet as the nectar."

He made hungry growling sound in his throat.

"I can already tell you it's ten times sweeter. Gods, little bird—love to taste you."

And then he buried his face between my thighs and began lapping in earnest.

I moaned and bucked my hips up to meet his tongue and all the while, I kept using my magic sparks to stroke and tickle him. I imagined them as a hand much larger than mine—one big enough to easily encircle his thick cock. Liath groaned and bucked his hips as well...and so our contest was on.

I'm sorry to say, I can't remember who won. The feeling of his warm, wet tongue sliding over my throbbing clit made it very hard to think—and hard to concentrate on doing magic too. But every time I started to fail, Liath would look up at me for a moment and encourage me to go on.

"Come on, little bird," he would growl softly, his mouth shiny with my juices. "Come on—you have to learn to do magic when you're distracted, too. Be a good girl and stroke me with your sparks—make me shoot my cream."

I loved it when he talked to me like that—dirty talk, he called it—and I moaned softly and renewed my efforts.

So though I'm not sure exactly who won our little contest, I do know that we both came often and hard as we comforted each other all night long.

24

If you think my life at the Unseelie Court sounds more or less idyllic—well, except for Great Aunt Acosta trying to kill me and then subsequently bringing about her own death by attempting to sit the Shadow Throne—you would be right. It *was* idyllic—I had a husband who treated me like his most precious treasure, a life where no one teased or tormented me, and magic for the first time in my life.

I was perfectly happy and I would have gone on being perfectly happy if I hadn't had the idea to go and visit the Pool of Seeing on my own one day.

This was an idea that I had been mulling over in my head for quite some time. Liath had often warned me not to leave the Winter Palace grounds by myself, but the trip to the Pool of Seeing wasn't far, I reasoned to myself. In fact, it couldn't even be said to be outside the Palace grounds, since it was in the woods immediately around the Palace. Besides, I had my own magic now and I was perfectly capable of defending myself.

That was because I was learning to use other emotions to work my spells. True, pleasure sparks still worked the best, but I could use negative emotions like fear and anger too—if a bit less effectively. At any rate, I had no fear and I was certain I could make the Pool of Seeing bend to my will.

So I waited until Liath was off inspecting his troops—the Unseelie Army was stationed to one side of the Palace, since they often went to fight. Though at the moment, we were in a cease fire, because of the Joining between Liath and myself.

As soon as he was gone, I put on my warmest cloak and boots and headed into the woods. First, though, I put a spell of lightness on my feet, which allowed me to glide over the surface of the snow without sinking down into the underbrush and the tangled vines. Before I knew it, I was standing beside the Pool of Seeing.

As before, it looked like a black void in the forest floor—perfectly round and utterly black. I shivered as I looked into it, but I knew what I had come to do and I was determined to do it. The Pool, however, would not take my sparks. It was thirsty for blood and nothing else.

I took the small ceremonial dagger, which Liath had given me as a present, from the sheath at my waist. It was only as long as my middle finger and had moonstones on the hilt, just as his much larger one did. The blade, though tiny, was extremely sharp. I winced as I drew it across my palm and held my fist over the surface of the Pool.

I let several drops of blood fall into the black waters and waited until they began reflecting the sky and branches above before I voiced my question.

"Show me who killed my brother," I said. I had decided to at least try this query first—maybe the Pool would show me what I wanted, even though it had refused to show Liath.

But again, I only got an image of a figure wearing armor with his face obscured. I was disappointed, but it was no more than I had expected. However, I had another question that I thought might work.

"All right," I said, feeding the Pool of Seeing a few more drops of my blood. "Show me someone who knows who killed Quillian. Someone I can talk to," I added, hoping to narrow things down a bit.

I don't know who I expected to see but the image that surfaced after the Pool had cleared wasn't what I anticipated at all.

It was Liath who stared back at me—my own husband, with his familiar bronze eyes and scarred face.

My hand shook and I drew it back from the Pool as though I had been burned.

"No..." I whispered. "No, that can't be right."

The Pool's surface rippled and showed him again—this time on the battlefield. I saw his eyes blazing, his sword upraised as he rushed forward towards someone. His mouth was open in an angry shout but who he was shouting at, I couldn't see.

Because whoever it was, they were standing right behind Quillian. And the point of their sword was shoved through his back and protruding from his chest.

I watched in horror as my big brother cried in soundless agony and slumped forward, impaled from behind. But still I couldn't see the face of his assassin—it was obscured.

Liath knew who it was, though—and he had known it all along, I realized. He had been there that day on the battlefield when Quill was killed. He knew and he had been pretending all this time that he had no idea.

My husband had lied to me and I was determined to find out why.

25

I marched home—well, more like flitted home since the lightness spell was still on my feet, allowing me to skim swiftly over the snow. I was so angry I was ready to spit—just as I had that very first night when Liath had caught me trying to cut his throat. How could he lie to me like this? If he knew who my brother's killer was, why was he keeping it from me?

I went straight to our bed chamber and found him there—dressed in his armor—a fact, which I did not, at first, register.

"Little bird." He turned to face me, his face set in grim lines.

"I know!" I snapped, glaring up at him.

He frowned.

"You know what?"

"I know that *you* know!" I shouted at him. "You know who killed Quill and you've been keeping it from me all this time!"

His reaction was not what I expected. Instead of returning my anger with anger of his own, he ran a hand through his hair and sank down on one of the sofas.

"Gods," he growled hoarsely. "Not now, little bird."

"Yes, *now!*" I insisted. "I want to know who it is. I have magic of my own now—I can kill him! I want to avenge Quill!"

"Alira, listen to me..." Liath beckoned for me to come to him. I stepped up to stand between his spread legs and looked him challengingly in the eye.

"Who is it and why did you keep it from me?" I demanded.

Liath shook his head.

"You're not ready to know—your magic isn't strong enough yet."

"Yes, I am!" I insisted. "And I want to know!"

"You can't face him," he countered. "Not yet."

"Yes, I can—whoever he is, I can face him and I *will* face him!" I insisted. "Tell me now, Liath, or I will never forgive you for keeping it from me—I swear by the Shining Throne!"

"It was your cousin—it was Asfaloth, that little shit—all right?" Liath burst out at last.

I took a step backwards, feeling sick. I had always hated my cousin—well, both my cousins, since Asfaloth and Calista came as a pair. And I knew that they disliked me and Quill as well—mainly because he didn't let them torment me. But I hadn't known that Asfaloth would *kill* someone in his own family—that he would stoop so low.

"He stabbed Quill in the back," Liath said heavily. "It was cunningly done—he waited until both of them were in a shaded area of the battlefield and then threw up a see-me-not around the two of them." He tugged on one of his horns. "I saw what was happening—I have a spelled visor on my helmet that cuts through obscuring magic —but I couldn't get to Quill in time."

I felt my stomach twist.

"What...what happened?"

"I ran across to him—crossed the enemy's line. I got right up to Quill just as your bastard of a cousin stabbed him in the back. I tried to pull him away but all I got was his blade in my face." He touched the white scar that ran down his cheek. "That's why I wouldn't let you heal this, little bird. It's a reminder of my failure to save my best friend...I don't deserve to forget."

"So *that's* why Asfaloth was able to blame you," I whispered. "Because everyone saw you on the Seelie side of the battle, right near Quill."

Liath laughed harshly.

"Exactly. I wanted to cut the fucker down right there, but I was surrounded by about half the Seelie army and Asfaloth was surrounded by the other half—using his own warriors as shields. I couldn't get to him." He shook his head. "I still have dreams where I stay and just keep cutting them down until I finally slice his fucking throat."

I shook my head.

"I don't understand—why did you keep all this from me? I would have believed you—Asfaloth is horrible and he and Calista never liked Quill. Though I didn't think he would actually...actually..." I put a hand to my throat, unable to continue.

"I didn't tell you because I didn't want you going after your cousin before you're ready to face him," Liath rumbled, frowning.

"But I *am* ready!" I protested.

He shook his head.

"No, you're not. Not nearly. Because..."

"Because what? Why?" I looked at him anxiously because there was a grim look on his face.

"Little bird, I didn't want to tell you this way, but we're out of time," he said heavily. "Your father...he's dead. Asfaloth has taken his place, which means he has the power of the Shining Throne behind him. You're not strong enough to take him on—not with that kind of magic backing him."

I sucked in a breath. I had never been close to my father—I could not recall a single time that he told me he loved me or hugged me or even smiled at me. But he was still my father and the news of his death hit me like a blow.

"I'm so sorry..." Liath gathered me into his arms and took me on his lap. "I know it's hard to hear."

"I...I'll be all right," I said, lifting my chin and trying to keep the tears out of my voice.

"I wish I could stay here and comfort you the way you comforted me," Liath murmured. "But I'm afraid I must go."

"Go? Go where?" I demanded. Finally it registered with me that he was wearing his armor—mainly because the breastplate felt hard and cold against my side. "Not...not to battle, surely?" I exclaimed.

Liath nodded.

"I'm afraid so. Asfaloth has ended the peace between us by crossing the Great Divide and slaughtering some of my people. Such an act cannot go unanswered."

"What? No!" I exclaimed as fear gripped me. "No, Liath—please don't go!"

"I'm sorry, little bird—I *have* to." He put me gently from his lap and rose to tower over me. He looked immense in his suit of black armor but all I could think was Quill had been wearing armor too, the last time I saw him and how my cousin's blade had pierced it with ease.

"Liath, wait—why can't you make some kind of truce or peace?" I begged.

He shook his head.

"That might have been possible if Quill had lived. We used to speak of making peace between the two Courts—he was willing to give up stolen magic and to make the rest of the Seelie Court pay for their power as well. Your father would never agree to it, though," he added. "And I'm sure Asfaloth won't either."

I knew he was right, but I kept flashing on my last memory of my older brother—asking me for a kiss on the cheek for luck—

before he went to battle. And then he never came home...at least, not alive.

"*Please*, don't go," I begged again.

"I *have* to. But I will be back as soon as I can." Liath leaned down to kiss me gently. When he pulled back, his bronze eyes were unreadable. "Don't worry, little bird—I've gone to battle many times and always returned," he told me. "Besides, maybe this is finally my chance to avenge my friend and your brother."

Then, before I could say anything else, he swept out of the room, his black cloak swishing behind him.

26

"Your Majesty, there is news of the battle—none of it good, I'm afraid." The clip-clop of Master Stableforth's hooves was muted on the carpet of my chamber.

"Yes?" I looked up at him and as I did, I saw my own haggard reflection in one of the mirrors. I had been pacing in the living area of the rooms I shared with Liath, worrying about him obsessively. My husband had been gone for a week now—a week in which I'd had no news of him and not a single message.

Now I looked up at the centaur and felt my stomach drop at the look on his face. It was grim news then—very grim.

"Tell me quickly," I said to Stableforth. "Is he…is he *dead*?"

I could scarcely get the words out. Only now that I had lost him was clear to me how very much Liath meant to me. He wasn't just my lord and husband—he was my best friend, the one I turned to now, when I was upset or worried or blue. Slowly and quietly, I had been falling in love with him and I hadn't even realized it until now. Now that he was gone.

"He is *not* dead," Stableforth said.

I sank down to a couch, trembling as relief washed through me. But it was relief tempered with caution.

"If he's not dead, then where *is* he?" I demanded.

"Captured," Stableforth told me. "A prisoner of war—a prisoner of your cousin, King Asfaloth. Though to say the truth, I have heard that he rules jointly with his sister, the Lady Calista," he added.

"She's no lady," I said rudely. "Anymore than Asfaloth is really a king. He might wear the Sun Crown and sit the Shining Throne, but he's nothing but an imposter!"

"Be that as it may, he holds Prince Liath prisoner," Stableforth said grimly. "And it does not appear that he intends to set him free."

"He might not intend it, but he *will* set Liath free!" I felt my hands squeeze into fists. "I'll make sure of that!"

The centaur looked alarmed.

"My Princess, pitting yourself against the ruler who sits the Shining Throne is *not* wise. The only way you could defeat him is if you also had the power of the throne behind you."

"The Shadow Throne," I whispered.

"Exactly." Stableforth nodded. "But you are not ready to sit the Shadow Throne yet and so you cannot stand against your cousin."

"Who says I'm not ready?" I demanded, lifting my chin. "If trying for the Shadow Throne is the only way to get my husband back, then I'll do it."

"My Lady, please—pause…reflect!" Stableforth said earnestly. "You have seen what the Shadow Throne does to one who is not ready or able to claim it. Your magic is not yet ripe —you are not powerful enough."

"And when will I be powerful enough, then?" I demanded. "Am I to wait, year after year, pacing these halls alone without my husband, until I finally feel ready?"

"If that is what it takes." The centaur nodded.

"No!" I rose from the couch on shaky legs, but I refused to sit back down. "No—for I would rather be dead in an instant trying to get the power to save my Liath than live all the long, lonely years without him!"

"Please, my Princess!" Stableforth exclaimed. "Prince Liath would kill me if he knew I allowed you to try such a rash and foolish action just to save him."

"It's not your decision to make, Stableforth," I told him. "It's mine—and I'm making it now."

I strode out of my rooms, so empty now without Liath. I knew what I was doing was risky—maybe even rash—but I refused to back down. I couldn't stay here in the Winter Palace year after year while Liath rotted in an iron cell in the dungeons of the Summer Court.

I would sit the Shadow Throne or die trying, I told myself—that was all there was to it.

Stableforth followed me with a clatter of hooves, begging me to reconsider. But I refused to listen to him. I had magic now—strong magic—only I needed more. And only the Shadow Throne could give me the power it would take to stand up against my brother-murdering, husband-kidnapping, son-of-a-bastard cousin!

The sound of Stableforth's hooves on the marble floors seemed to draw the attention of everyone else in the Palace. Soon there was a whole crowd of Palace folk—both nobles and servants—following us to the Throne Room.

It reminded me uncomfortably of Great Aunt Acosta's fate. She, too, had marched to the Throne Room followed by the whole Court, determined to sit the Shadow Throne and she had been killed for her troubles. Who was to say I would be any different?

I say it, I told myself firmly. *And all the prophesies in the stars and books say it too. I have magic now—I can do this! I **will** do this.*

That was what I told myself all the way to the Throne Room. And yet, when I actually came to the dais the throne was mounted on, I felt my heart shrink within me.

The Shadow Throne was wreathed in darkness and the ruby whose lethal ray had killed Liath's Aunt Acosta was likewise dark and silent. But I knew how quickly it could come to life and send a deadly beam of light directly through my skull. I knew how fast my life could come to an end.

And yet, I had to try.

On shaking legs, I climbed the steps of the dais until I stood before the throne. The lines of blood flowing through its carvings like veins seemed to beckon me and the Shadow Throne itself almost seemed to call to me.

Come...try your luck, I thought I heard it whisper. *I may grant you unimaginable power...or I may kill you. You can't know until you try.*

"My Princess, please!" Stableforth had come to a stop directly before the throne with the rest of the Court gathered around him. "Please, I beg you not to do this!"

"I must," I said.

I sat upon the same blood-red cushion where Great Aunt Acosta had so lately been killed and settled myself upon the Shadow Throne.

27

At first there was nothing but a low humming buzz that I felt more than heard. It was pure power, I realized—magic so deep and vast it was like an ocean just waiting to be tapped. If I could reach into that reservoir my own magic would be enhanced to limitless proportions. I would have enough to battle Asfaloth and Calista both—enough to rescue Liath and bring him home.

But the power had not been granted to me—not yet. I could feel the Shadow Throne weighing me—considering if I was worthy of this immense and limitless gift. If I was judged unworthy, I would be killed—summarily executed just as Great Aunt Acosta had been.

Suddenly the ruby behind me lit up. Don't ask me how I knew—I was sitting with my back to it, after all. But I could see the glow of it in every courier and noble's eyes—all of them staring at me and getting ready to scatter the moment the deadly beam pierced through my skull and shot out looking for new targets. The floor in front of the dais was still etched with deep grooves from Aunt Acosta's attempt.

I tensed, my shoulders going tight and my stomach clenching like a slick fist. I would have liked to leap from the seat of the throne, but I felt as though invisible bands had closed around my arms and legs and I was being held in place.

I was about to die—I was sure of it.

I closed my eyes, not wanting to see the horror in my subjects' faces when the Shadow Throne killed me...

But for some reason, the deadly beam of killing light didn't come from the ruby embedded in the back of the throne. And the longer it didn't come, the more I wondered what was going on. The throne had taken less than a minute to decide that Great Aunt Acosta wasn't right for it—why was it taking so long deciding my fate?

At last there was a deep rumbling and I heard the same voice I had heard before Acosta met her fate. I was sure it would say either "Denied" or possibly, if I as very lucky, "Accepted." But to my surprise, it said neither of these. Instead the deep voice of the Shadow Throne intoned,

"NOT YET."

"Not yet? What does that mean?" I exclaimed, filled with a mixture of relief and disappointment. On one hand, the Shadow Throne had refused to lend me its power. Oh the other hand, I wasn't dead with a smoking hole burned through my brain, which was most certainly a blessing.

To my surprise, the Shadow Throne answered my question—not in the deep, booming voice but in a quiet whisper in my ear, which only I could hear.

"You are not ready yet, child—but you will be," it told me. ***"You must prove yourself worthy—you know what to do."***

And then, suddenly the invisible bands that had been holding me in place on the throne released me. Something that felt like a lot of invisible hands pulled me upright, out of the throne, and pushed me gently away. I found myself descending the steps of the dais while all the Court looked on with wide eyes.

"M-my P-princess," Stableforth stammered, his eyes wide. "I never dreamed...I have not seen such a reaction from the Shadow Throne and none such has ever been recorded in the annuls of the Winter Court!"

"Come with me," I told him. Keeping my head high, I swept through the Throne Room, aware that all eyes in the Court were upon me.

Stableforth trotted after me, his hooves *clip-clopping* on the flagstones. We made the trip all the way back to my chamber where we could at last be alone.

"My Lady, what happened?" the centaur asked anxiously, when the door was safely shut and the rest of the Court was left to gossip and speculate about the strange performance I had put on.

"Well, the Shadow Throne didn't reject me," I said. "I am alive, as you see..." I opened my arms and gave a little bow. "However, it didn't accept me either," I added.

"It was merciful to you and spared you for another attempt later—perhaps years from now," Stableforth said reverently. "It is as I said—your magic is not ripe enough yet to wield the power of the Shadow Throne."

"It spoke to me—in my ear," I told him.

His eyes widened.

"What? My Princess—what did it say?"

"It told me that I must prove myself worthy," I said. "And it said I would know what to do." I gave the royal advisor a level look. "And I do, Stableforth—I know *exactly* what to do."

"And what is that, my Lady?" he asked respectfully.

I lifted my chin.

"I might not have the power of the Shadow Throne behind me, but I'm going after Liath just the same," I told him. "I will not let him rot in my cousin's dungeons—I will go to him and find a way to bring him back."

"What way?" Stableforth exclaimed, looking more upset than ever. "My Princess, without the power of the Shadow Throne behind you, how can you possibly hope to stand against the one who wields the power of the Shining Throne?"

I frowned.

"Did not the Shining Throne and the Shadow Throne used to be one and the same?"

"Well, yes—before your ancestor King Oberon grew angry with his daughter for bedding with a half-breed Unseelie and created the Great Divide which broke the Fae Kingdom into two separate Realms," Stableforth acknowledged. "The difference is that the Shining Throne of the Summer Court does not judge those who sit upon it as worthy or unworthy."

"Which is how my bastard of a cousin was able to take it from my father, no doubt," I snapped. "You can mark my words, Stableforth—my father, the late King of the Summer Court, did *not* die of natural causes. Asfaloth murdered him—just as he murdered my brother, Quillian."

Stableforth sucked in a breath.

"Then your cousin has much to answer for. But I'm sorry, Princess Alira—I just don't see how you can make him pay without the power of the Shadow Throne behind you."

I took a deep breath, trying to calm the rage which had risen in my chest.

"The point isn't to punish him and make him pay—not right now, anyway," I said. "The point is to get Liath away from him and bring him home."

I was proud at how measured and calm my voice sounded. Could I have cheerfully wrung my evil cousin's neck with my bare hands? *Yes.* But would I attempt to do so? *No.* Right now my main priority was getting the one I loved most in the world back to the Winter Court—and back in my arms—where he belonged.

"How will you bring the Prince home, though?" Stableforth asked doubtfully. "Your cousin has said that he will refuse any offers of ransom. I believe he still holds a grudge for the way Prince Liath choked him at your Joining ceremony," he added.

"I'm going to beg," I said calmly.

"Beg?" Stableforth's eyebrows rose nearly to his hair line. "A Princess of the Winter Court begging at the Summer Court? I'm afraid that won't look very seemly."

"I don't care how it looks," I snapped. "I only care about getting Liath back! And Asfaloth..." I swallowed hard. "My *cousin* loves it when I beg—when I humble myself before him."

How often had I had to swallow my pride and beg him and Calista to remove some harmful or malicious spell they had cast on me? I had thought I was done with all that, but now I saw I must beg once more.

Just the thought of lowering myself to my cousins yet again sickened me—but I had a plan. And if Asfaloth would not release Liath to me, well—I only needed a few moments alone with my husband to carry it out.

Stableforth still looked doubtful but I was ready to go into action.

"Get me Shellya, the Royal Seamstress," I told him. "I must be dressed for Court for this to work."

"Well...as your Majesty says," he murmured and went to call the spider woman seamstress for me. "I hope you know what you're doing, Princess," he added, as he headed for the door.

"I do," I said, hoping it was true. "Don't worry, Stableforth—I have everything in hand."

Which was a complete lie but what else could I do? I would risk anything to get back the male I loved—anything at all.

28

"You look lovely, Your Majesssty," Shellya hissed, her eight legs skittering to move her bulbous body backwards so that she could see me in her latest creation. "Ressssplendant."

"Thank you, Shellya—truly you have outdone yourself." I swished the thin panels of blood red silk back and forth—the color complimented my midnight blue hair and made my gray eyes shine like stars. It was cut quite low in the front, showing the full swells of my breasts, though I had always tried to hide them before, when I lived in the Summer Court.

Likewise, it had a high slit right up the center with only a thin panel of white lace to cover my pussy. The panel could easily be pushed aside, and I wasn't wearing any panties beneath.

Why, you may ask, was I dressing in this provocative way in order to go beg at the Summer Court? It had to do with my plan. I had the tiny moonstone dagger Liath had given me hidden in a pocket in the folds of my dress, and though my magic might not be as strong as Asfaloth's—since he had the power of the Shining Throne behind him—I could still make a portal between the Realms. All I needed was a moment alone with Liath—a moment to cut a portal in the Great Divide—and then I could take him home.

But I had to see him first, and that would require some serious groveling. I hated the very thought of it, but it wasn't like I was unused to it. I had spent my childhood begging my cousins to reverse their cruel spells—I could lower myself once more if it meant I could save the male I loved.

"Lovely," Shellya said again, smiling with all her eyes.

"Thank you." I nodded my head.

We were standing out in the courtyard—the one which corresponded exactly to the courtyard in the Summer Court where Liath and I had been Joined. The sky overhead was overcast and gray and the chilly wind would have made me shiver if I wasn't too nervous to be cold.

"Truly, you are beautiful, Your Majesty," Stableforth said, stamping a hoof. "But are you certain it's safe for you to go to the Summer Court?"

"No," I said. "But I'm going anyway. I'm not sitting around here one more minute while Liath is stuck over there. I'm going to get him!"

"Well, you have courage—no one can doubt that," he murmured. "In that case, I wish you good luck in bringing the Prince home."

"You will be in charge while I am gone," I told him. "Since there are no other Unseelie Royals left and I trust your judgment."

Stableforth made a low bow with his human half.

"Truly, you honor me, my Princess."

"Don't get too excited," I told him. "I won't be gone long."

I hoped.

Then I drew the tiny moonstone dagger which Liath had gifted me from my hidden pocket, took a deep breath, and gathered the sparks flying around the air with my mind. They were mostly my sparks—motes made of my desperation and my determination to get my husband back. But I made them work as I stabbed a hole in the Great Divide and pulled the knife down, cutting a rift between the Realms.

I was going to get Liath back or die trying.

29

"You there! Who are you and how dare you enter the Summer Court without permission?" a deep voice barked at me.

I blinked and blinked again, trying to see who it was. One of the Palace guards, I thought. I simply wasn't used to the bright sunshine anymore—it made my eyes run with tears which I swiped away hastily as the guard finally reached me.

"Do you not know me?" I demanded, trying to sound imperious.

"Princess Alira?" The guard looked surprised. "But...what are you doing here?"

"I have come to see my Royal Cousin, Asfaloth," I told him briskly. "Kindly bring me to him at once."

"Oh, er..." To my surprise, the guard's cheeks and the tips of his pointed ears went rather red. "King Asfaloth and Queen Calista are, er, having a private consultation at the moment. I'm afraid the Throne Room is closed to visitors."

"I do not care about that!" I exclaimed. "And I am no visitor—I am a member of the Royal Family. Take me to the Throne Room at once!"

The guard bowed.

"As you wish," he said uneasily. "Though I must warn you, Princess, that you may see something that is not to your liking."

"I am confident I will—seeing my cousin upon the throne where my father used to sit is very *much* not to my liking," I snapped, as he escorted me briskly through the Summer Palace halls. My soft slippers made almost no sound on the white marble flagstones.

The guard made no answer and soon we were at the carved golden double doors which led to the Throne Room of the Summer Palace. The guard knocked loudly at the doors, as though he was trying to warn those within.

"Princess Alira, once of the Summer Court, now of the Winter Court, come to visit King Asfaloth and Queen Calista!" he bellowed in a voice that nearly sent me deaf. Only then did he push open one of the doors and escort me inside.

If my cousins heard the guard's warning bellow, they hadn't heeded it. Asfaloth was lounging on one side of the Shining Throne with Calista on his right. She was bent over with her head in his lap and after a moment, I saw that she was openly sucking his cock, which stuck out through the fly of his golden breeches.

I felt a moment of shock—they had never been so open with their incestuous relationship before. But then, there was no one to stop them now—no one to say no. So of course, they had grown bold.

"Ah, Cousin Alira," Asfaloth greeted me, while his sister continued to work on him. "To what do we owe the honor?"

"To the fact that you have my husband." I marched down to the front of the Throne Room and stood with my hands on my hips, glaring up at the two of them. "I am here to collect him—give him back at once!" I demanded.

I had calculated that it was best to appear proud at first and then look shaken and sad, as though they had beaten me when they refused my request to hand over Liath—as I was sure they would.

Sure enough, Asfaloth laughed at me.

"Do you hear this, dear sister? Our little cousin *demands* that we release that brute she calls her husband!" he chortled.

"Mmm-hmm," was Calista's only reply—but then, she *did* have her mouth full of cock.

"Now that you are King of the Seelie Realm, you can release prisoners of war," I insisted.

"Yes, now that I am *King*." Asfaloth smirked at me and I longed to wipe the smug expression off his face.

"How did my father die, anyway?" I asked.

"He passed in his sleep. So very *sad*." Asfaloth made a face of mock sorrow. "Alas, the Royal physician could find no cause of death."

I wondered if the physician had thought to check for traces of poison. I'd had a pet cat once—little more than a kitten—when I was a girl. Calista had given the poor little thing something that caused her to contort her fury body and yowl in terrible pain before she finally foamed at the mouth and died. After that, I had never dared to have another pet, for fear that a similar fate would befall it.

"So a Fae of healthy middle age simply dies in his sleep?" I demanded.

Asfaloth spread his hands.

"As you see. *Ah!* Have a care with your teeth, sister dear!" he added, in an undertone to Calista. He looked back at me. "And do you think now that *you* should sit the Shining Throne? The sad little Princess with no magic?"

I was glad that reports of my magic had not crossed the Great Divide. It was better if they thought me completely helpless.

I shook my head.

"No—you are welcome to the Shining Throne. All I ask is that you give me back my husband, so that we can return to The Winter Court together."

Asfaloth glared at me.

"After the way he humiliated me at your farce of a Joining? I think not! He's rotting in a prison made of iron bars down in the dungeon and that is where he's going to *stay*." He made a shooing motion at me with one beringed hand. "So you'd best just scoot on back to the Unseelie Court with all the half-breeds and monsters where you belong. For Liath Blackthorn is never leaving."

At this, Calista stopped sucking her brother and shot a venomous glare at me.

"Did you hear that, you little brat?" she hissed, swiping at her mouth which was shiny with spittle and her brother's precum. "You're *never* getting your beast of a husband back! So you might as well tuck your tail between your legs and scuttle back to the Winter Court where you belong!"

A hate for the both of them so great that it almost choked me rose in my throat, but I swallowed it down with some difficulty. This was, after all, no more than I had expected.

It was time to beg.

"Please..." I let the tears come into my eyes. "I apologize for what Liath did on our Joining day," I told Asfaloth. "But if you won't let him go, will you at least let me see him? He has become...very dear to me in the short time we have been married."

Calista gave an ugly laugh.

"What? Have you actually fallen in *love* with that big brute?"

"He's probably railing her every night," Asfaloth speculated, sneering at me. "Is he a good fuck, Cousin?" he asked. "Is that it? You just can't get enough of that half-breed Unseelie cock?"

"He is my *husband*." I gave a little sob. "I just want to see him —*please!*"

"Fine." Asfaloth tucked his shaft back into his breeches and leered at me. "But you have to beg us—get on your knees!"

I did as he asked, kneeling on the white marble floor, which was cold and hard under my knees.

"Please," I said beseechingly, though the words nearly choked me. "Let me go see my husband!"

"First say that you love to suck his Unseelie cock!" Calista demanded.

"I...I love to suck his Unseelie cock," I repeated—which was actually the truth.

"And say that you love to swallow his beastly cum," Asfaloth added.

"I love to swallow my husband's beastly cum," I repeated—another truth, though I doubted these two knew it. I gave a little sob and let the tears run down my cheeks. "Please—now will you let me see him?"

"She's always such a little bawl-baby," Calista said disdainfully. "You might as well let her visit him—it's not like she can do anything. She has no magic and he's in one of the iron cages."

"I suppose you're right. Guard!" Asfaloth called.

The guard who had escorted me into the Throne Room stepped forward. His cheeks and ears were still burning—probably from what we had seen Asfaloth and Calista doing together earlier.

"Yes, Your Majesty," he said, bowing respectfully to Asfaloth.

"Take this sad little bitch down to the dungeons and let her visit with her husband," Asfaloth told him. "Now, get her out of my sight," he added, unfastening his breeches again. "And don't bring anyone else in here—my sister and I are busy."

"Indeed we are," Calista purred. Bending down, she took his cock in her mouth once more and began sucking vigorously.

Neither of them paid any more attention to me, which was just how I liked it. Wordlessly, the blushing guard nodded at me to precede him and we left the Throne Room.

My plan was going well—exactly as I had hoped.

30

But once we reached the dungeons below the Summer Palace, I found my plan had hit a snag.

I didn't know it at once, of course. At first, things seemed to be going well. The guard led me deeper and deeper into the dank recesses of the lower Palace. There were no other prisoners that I could see, but most of the cells had wooden doors with only thin slits at waist level, for shoving in a tray at meal times. So I had no way of knowing if they were occupied or not.

Once we got to the back of the dungeon, my guard began to be uneasy.

"Please, Princess—are you certain you wish to go further?" he asked. "The prisoner you wish to see is being kept in an iron cell. The touch of it could mean sickness or death for one as delicate as you."

Little did he know that the iron didn't bother me. I could feel it getting closer—it felt like a heavy weight in the air. All Fae hate and fear iron but, just like that night I had spent with Liath in the Mortal Realm, I found that the presence of the deadly metal didn't affect me.

Still, it wouldn't do to let the guard know that.

"I wish to see my husband—no matter what the risk or danger," I said firmly. "Please be so kind as to take me to him."

"Very well…" The guard stopped at the end of the row of wooden doors set into the stone wall. This door had no slit in it at all which worried me—had they even been feeding Liath or giving him anything to drink?

The guard took out a key ring and unlocked the door. He pulled it open and winced back, like a man wincing from the heat of an immense furnace. I tried to look weak and worried but my whole attention was on my husband.

Inside the cell was another cell—a three-sided one made of iron bars. I wondered who had been gotten to do the work—it must have been mortals since Fae cannot touch the stuff—or stand to be around it for very long. The bars must have been made long ago, for they were rusty and flaking.

And there, lying half propped against the stone wall at the very back of the cell, as far from the bars as he could get, was Liath.

"Please, my Lady—you do not *really* wish to enter, do you?" the guard asked desperately.

"Yes, I do," I said firmly. "If your courage fails you, feel free to wait outside while I visit my husband."

This seemed to sting the guard for he lifted his chin and stepped into the room. Donning a pair of heavy cloth gloves which had been hung on a hook on the wall, he unlocked the door of the three-sided iron cage and swung it wide for me.

"You may go in, Princess," he said in a slightly strangled voice. "But I don't know how long you will be able to stand it in there."

"I'll be here until I'm certain my husband is well," I told him. "Please, give us some privacy."

I could see the guard was more than happy to grant my request. He didn't even relock the cage door—he simply stripped off the cloth gloves and nearly ran from the room, banging the door closed behind him.

Good—now I could concentrate on Liath.

"Liath? My love?" I asked, entering the iron cage to be with him.

Though it didn't hurt me, I could feel the weight of the deadly metal pressing down on me from all sides. How much worse would it be for someone who was truly affected by it, I wondered? It must be like being trapped at the bottom of the ocean with the enormous weight and pressure of the water all around you. Or possibly like being forced to stand near a fiery furnace that was scorching you every minute, but you couldn't get away from it.

Whichever the case, I could see that it had taken a toll on my husband. Liath's face was gray—not his normal color of gray, but the ashen shade of pure fatigue. There were dark circles under his bronze eyes and he was half sitting, half leaning against the stone wall, a look of sheer exhaustion on his face. He was no longer wearing his armor—someone had removed it. He had only his breeches and boots on and his chest was bare.

"Oh, Liath—my love!" I repeated, going to him and stroking his scarred cheek. "Are you all right? Please tell me you're not wounded!"

"Wounded?" He spoke slowly, like a man in the middle of a dream. "No...not...wounded. Just tired and ill...all this iron..."

"Yes, I know—it's awful," I said quickly. "But I'm going to get you out of here and take you home! Come on!"

I tried to pull him to his feet—but I might as well have been trying to lift a horse—Liath was simply too big for me to budge.

"Come on," I urged him again. "Try and help me!"

"Can't move," he muttered and nodded down at his right ankle. "Can't...go anywhere. Sorry."

I looked where he was nodding...and that was when I saw that my escape plot had hit a snag. I had been planning to simply cut a hole in the Great Divide and take him directly home to the Winter Court the moment we were alone together. However, there was a problem.

Not content to surround him on three sides with the iron bars, my cruel cousin had also had an iron manacle placed around Liath's ankle. Thank goodness it was around his boot and not placed against his bare flesh, but even the tough leather could only mitigate the closeness of the deadly metal a little.

I had to get the manacle off of him!

Running out of the cell, I picked up the thick cloth gloves and put them on. The presence of the iron might not bother me, but I still wasn't willing to touch it bare-handed.

I put on the gloves and came back to tug at the manacle around Liath's booted ankle. But it was no good—there wasn't even a keyhole or a lock on it—it appeared to have been welded on. It was also connected to a chain that was locked around one of the iron bars.

Asfaloth hadn't been joking when he'd said that he intended for Liath to rot down here. There was no getting him out of this cell while he was manacled in iron and connected to the iron bars.

What was I going to do?

I took a deep breath. I was going to have to raise some power, I told myself—much more power than I'd been planning on. But I could do it…and I would start with reviving my husband so he could help me.

31

The idea of reviving Liath to full health was easier said than done, however. He had been surrounded by iron for more than a week—such an ordeal would have sapped the strength of any Fae—except for me.

I thanked my Mortal ancestor—whoever he might have been—for my immunity to the deadly metal. My ancestress Talandra who had been bred by so many Unseelie must have had a human lover too, who contributed his seed to the child that was started in her belly during her ordeal. Otherwise I would never be able to do what I was about to attempt.

Taking a deep breath, I reached into yet another hidden pocket. I pulled out a tiny, stoppered flask, no bigger than my pinky. It was full of a special potion I'd had Stableforth help me to concoct before I left.

I looked at the bright red potion which seemed to glow in the dim cell. It was a lust potion—considerably weaker than the poisonous one Great Aunt Acosta had tricked me into drinking—but potent nonetheless. It also contained some of the fertility herbs that her potion had used. I was hoping it would help me now. My magic was based in pleasure and sex—I knew that for certain. I just had to use the knowledge to my advantage.

Pulling out the cork, I downed the bright red stuff in a single gulp. I could feel it working on me at once. My nipples were suddenly tight and sensitive and my breasts became even fuller as they began to make nectar—a side effect of the fertility herbs. My pussy tingled with need and began to get wet.

I could see the sparks of my own lust coming from my body. I gathered them and pushed them at Liath, creating a bubble of protection around him. As it settled in place, he lifted his head and his bronze eyes—which had been so dull a moment ago—began to glow.

"Alira?" he muttered hoarsely. "What...why did you come here?"

"I'm here to take you home," I told him again. "No, don't talk about the iron—we're going to find a way around it," I added, when he opened his mouth. "But first, we've got to get you healthy."

"Don't see how you're going to manage that, little bird," he rumbled weakly. "I've been fucking surrounded by iron for over a week—don't even know why I'm not dead yet."

"You're *not* going to die," I told him. "I'm going to heal you."

But how?

As I contemplated this, I felt a tightness in my chest. I frowned. Possibly Stableforth and I had overdone it with the fertility herbs. My breasts were so filled with nectar that they felt tight and achy.

Thinking of that made me remember how Liath had helped me get over the effects of Great Aunt Acosta's lust potion. He had told me that the nectar my breasts were making was good for healing and nourishment before he sucked it out of me.

Healing and nourishment—exactly what he needs, whispered a little voice in my head.

Exactly!

"So you're going to heal me, little bird?" Liath asked, interrupting my thoughts. "How are you going to do that?"

"Like this," I told him. Straddling his lap, I pulled at the red silk gown, lowering it to bare my breasts for him. I had asked Shellya to make the fabric stretchy, and now I was glad I had.

Despite his desperate situation, Liath's bronze eyes still blazed when he saw me half naked.

"Mmm, little bird—love your beautiful big breasts," he murmured.

"Good, because you're going to suck them," I told him. "I'm going to give you my nectar and heal you."

His eyes grew wide but before he could say anything, I was pressing one tight, aching nipple to his lips. Liath opened his mouth automatically and sucked my peak in deep. He took a mouthful of nectar and swallowed and I saw his eyes go half-lidded. Then he sucked even harder, taking more.

I moaned softly as he suckled me, emptying my breasts of their healing nectar. I could feel the strength pouring into him with each swallow he took and I stroked his hair and horns, urging him to take more—to take as much as he needed.

At the same time, my body couldn't help reacting to the hot suction of his mouth on my tender tips. Each time he drew on my breast, I felt an answering jolt of pleasure which seemed to travel directly to my aching pussy, where I was getting wetter and wetter.

The sparks of pleasure—both his and mine—were beginning to build up in the air around us. But I knew we needed more—much more—if we were going to circumvent the iron that bound and surrounded him.

"I think that's all, little bird," he murmured at last, after letting my nipple slip from his lips. "Gods, I love to suck your tits. But surely you didn't come just to feed me your nectar."

"No, I didn't," I told him firmly—if a little breathlessly. "I still intend to take you home, but we have to overcome the iron—have to find a way to break the chain that binds you." I nodded at the iron chain and manacle.

Liath's face was grave.

"I don't think that can be done."

"Yes, it *can*," I insisted. "With enough power—I can see the sparks flying all around us—we just need more of them."

His bronze eyes went half-lidded.

"I think I know what to do—remember how we raised enough power for you to turn our bedchamber into a jungle?"

I bit my lip.

"Yes, I remember. But...you want to taste me? Here?"

"You can't be surprised—you came prepared didn't you?" His eyes traveled over the thin white silk panel at the center of my dress. "You're not wearing any panties under that, are you?"

He was right—I had come prepared to raise power by sexual means—though I hadn't known how far we would have to go. Still, I was more than willing—if still just a little shy when it came to this act.

"Don't be shy, little bird," Liath rumbled. "You know you have the most delicious pussy in the entire Fae Realm, don't you?"

I was glad that he could apparently read my thoughts again—he really must be regaining his strength.

"Yes, I am," he said, answering my thought. "Your nectar healed me, little bird. But now I need your honey. Can you give it to me?"

Feeling my heart pound, I nodded.

"How...how do you want to do it?"

Liath's bronze eyes went half-lidded.

"Want you to ride my face," he growled hoarsely. "Ride me and suck me at the same time—that way we can both raise power for your magic."

As he spoke, he slid down to lay full-length on the floor. Then he beckoned to me.

"Come here and feed me that sweet, wet pussy," he growled.

His hot words and the look of pure lust on his face made me feel positively molten from the waist down. By the Shining Throne, how I wanted him! My breasts were still out and now I moved the silk panel of my dress aside as I went to straddle him.

I was a little uncertain as to my position, but Liath reached up and guided and supported me with his big hands. It was clear that the nectar I had fed him had helped him regain his strength, for he held my weight easily and lowered me down so that my pussy was right over his mouth.

"Gods, little bird—love to lick your sweet little cunt," I heard him growl. And then his hot, wet tongue was invading me—sweeping up and down my slit with ever-deepening strokes as he lapped me for my honey.

I moaned and reached forward to steady myself on his rock-hard abdomen. I was straddling his head and facing his feet so it was impossible to miss the thick bulge rising in his trousers.

Remembering what he had suggested, I bent down and unfastened his fly. His thick shaft with its mushroom shaped head came out at once and I grasped it in one hand and bent to give the broad crown a soft, open-mouthed kiss. There was a bead of precum on it already, which I licked up eagerly.

I both heard and felt Liath groan as I began exploring him with my tongue. His own tongue was buried deep in my pussy, eagerly lapping my honey. The vibrations of his groan seemed to tickle my clit and made me gasp and buck my hips.

"Easy now, little bird." Liath tightened his hold on me, his big hands keeping me in place. "Don't go all over the fucking place—stay where I can get to you," I heard him growl. "Can't lick your pussy unless you're a good girl and hold still."

"I...I'll try," I whispered breathlessly. "You know I always want to be your good girl, Liath."

"You'll be my *very* good girl if you lower your pussy down further," he instructed. "Don't be afraid, little bird—press that hot little cunt to my mouth—let me *really* fucking taste you."

He was right that I had been holding back a bit—I was afraid I might crush him. But feeling his big, warm hands on my hips and ass and the heat of his breath against my wet, open pussy decided me. With a moan, I lowered myself completely, pressing my wet slit to his lips and letting him have complete access to my pussy.

"Gods, little bird—*yes,*" Liath growled and began lapping me hungrily again.

I moaned and went back to licking and sucking his thick cock. We were making progress—the pleasure sparks rising from both of us were filling the air. I only hoped that the guard didn't choose this moment to come back or he would see something even more graphic than the scene in the Throne Room.

But I couldn't think of him for long. I could feel myself reaching the peak and knew I would be coming soon—only I didn't want to come this way. I needed something deeper—something *more* to build my power to the absolute maximum.

So after a moment, I stopped licking Liath's shaft and wiggled my hips.

My answer was a muffled groan and then I heard him rumble,

"What's wrong, little bird? Doesn't it feel good?"

"It feels *wonderful.*" As I spoke, I lifted myself and turned to face him. "But it's not what I need."

Liath frowned.

"And what do you need, sweetheart?"

I took a deep breath.

"You told me on our wedding night that you wouldn't take me until I begged you to. Well, now I'm begging. Liath—I *need* you to take me. It's the only way to raise enough power to break the iron chain and get you out of here."

He frowned but nodded.

"This is certainly not the place I'd planned to take you—I wanted your first time to be special, baby. But…I can see your point."

"It *will* be special," I promised him. "Because it will be you taking me—I'm begging you, just as you said I would."

He gave me a rueful grin.

"Unfortunately, with this iron still so near, I'm afraid it's going to have to be the other way around. *You* must take *me*."

"What?" I frowned at him. "How?"

"You'll mount me," Liath said simply. "Just pretend you're mounting a horse and sitting in the saddle. Only in this case, part of the saddle goes deep in your sweet little pussy."

He nodded down at his cock, which was still hard and sticking out of his trousers.

I felt my heart pound as I considered this idea. I had always thought the only way for a man and a woman to be together was for the man to be on top of the woman as she lay on her back. Well, I had thought that until I saw my cousins rutting together in the Pool of Seeing, anyway. But I hadn't ever thought there could be a third way —had never dreamed of mounting my husband like a horse.

Liath rumbled laughter and I knew he had caught my thoughts again.

"That's right, little bird—you must mount me. But take your time about it—you still have your maiden barrier, so the first time won't be easy," he warned me.

"I know," I said, turning myself so I was facing him and throwing a leg over his lean lips. "I'm counting on it."

In point of fact, I was. Liath had showed me how pain and pleasure could mix to make my power even stronger and of course, there would be elements of Blood Magic in play as well. If this didn't raise enough power to sever the iron manacle around his ankle, I didn't know what would.

Still, it took some nerve to position myself with the broad head of his cock against the mouth of my pussy.

"Slowly, little bird," he murmured, holding me by the hips. "And touch yourself—give yourself pleasure before you come down on me."

I thought that was an excellent idea. With a little moan, I slipped my fingers into my wet pussy and began sliding them lightly across my aching clit. This wouldn't have worked if I was still supporting myself, but Liath had me by the hips, holding my weight as I lowered myself onto his shaft.

"Gods, baby—love to watch you touch yourself. Be a good girl for me and pet that pussy," he ordered in a hoarse growl.

I was more than willing to obey.

"Yes, Liath!" I gasped as I stroked my pussy. And then I felt the thick head of his cock breach my entrance and press against my maiden barrier.

For a moment my fingers stilled, but Liath shook his head.

"No, little bird—keep petting your pussy," he ordered. "Give yourself pleasure to offset the pain—this is going to hurt a bit."

I bit my lip and kept going. I could feel him sliding deeper into me. My pussy was so wet and hot that he was moving easily, despite my tight virgin channel and his own thick girth.

Then there was a bright-white moment of pain. I cried out and felt a gush of wetness down my thighs. Looking down, I saw some blood on Liath's flat abdomen.

"It's all right, little bird," he murmured soothingly, holding me in place. "It's just your virgin blood. Once this pain is over, it will all be pleasure—I promise you."

My first impulse had been to try and get off of him, but I squashed it ruthlessly. Blood magic and pain magic and pleasure magic—they were all building inside me. I could feel the forces swirling inside and I could see them dancing in the sparks of power coalescing over our heads. Golden and blood red and black, they moved in patterns too complicated to understand and every moment there were more of them.

"Keep touching yourself, little bird," Liath reminded me. "And let me know when you're ready to go on."

I twitched my hips and flexed my inner muscles experimentally. I felt stretched wide open since Liath's shaft was very large, but the pain was gone. At last I nodded.

"I...I think I'm ready to go on," I told him.

"Good." He nodded. "Then I'll lower you down some more until I'm all the way inside you."

I bit back a moan as I felt his thick shaft sliding deeper into my tight but no longer virginal pussy. Finally, we were consummating our marriage—finally we were really becoming one!

At last I felt the broad head of his shaft pressing hard against the mouth of my womb and knew he could go no further. He was all the way in me now and I had never felt so full.

"Do you feel that, little bird?" Liath rumbled. "Feel me filling your soft little cunt with my cock? Gods, you're so tight and wet around me!"

"It feels *good*," I moaned. "*Really* good. And I feel so full—you're *really* big."

He rumbled laughter.

"I'm on the large side but you'll get used to me. Are you ready for me to move yet? Ready to let me fuck you and fill you, little bird?"

I lifted an eyebrow at him.

"I thought *I* was the one taking *you*."

Liath nodded.

"You have a point. All right—you do the taking. Move yourself up and down so my shaft slides in and out of you."

I braced myself on his hard abs and began to do exactly that. With a little gasp, I slid up until only the broad crown was still lodged inside me. Then I came down so that his thickness stretched my inner walls again and the head of his cock gave the mouth of my womb a rough kiss.

An involuntary moan was drawn from my lips. Oh, that felt *good!* I lifted myself and lowered myself again—then again and again, faster and faster.

"That's right, little bird." Liath's bronze eyes were burning with lust as he held me loosely by the hips. "That's right—fuck yourself on me. Be my good girl and fuck that soft little pussy on my hard cock!"

I moaned again, loving the way his hot talk made me feel inside. It was almost as arousing as feeling him pierce me.

"Liath, this feels...feels so good!" I told him, panting as I spoke. "But it would feel even better if...if you thrust up into me!"

"Ah—so *now* you want *me* to do the taking," he growled, his eyes flashing. "Hang on, little bird—I'm more than willing."

His grip on my hips tightened and he pulled me down hard onto him, making me gasp with pleasure.

"Oh, Liath!" I moaned. "Oh, it feels so *good.*"

"Don't forget to rub your little button," he growled. "I want to feel you coming all over my shaft, little bird. Want to feel your tight little pussy squeezing me until I shoot my cream deep inside you."

I did as he told me, keeping up the outer stimulation while Liath managed the inner with his deep, delicious thrusts inside me. He gripped my hips with his big hands and my breasts bounced every time he entered me.

My whole body felt as though it was made of sparks by now. I could feel my peak getting closer and closer and I wanted to give myself completely as I came for him. But at the same time, I didn't want to lose track of the plans I had for my magic.

I had three things I needed to do with the immense power I was building. First, I wanted to free Liath from the iron that was imprisoning him. Second, I wanted to heal him completely and utterly of the ravages of the deadly metal he had been surrounded by so long. And third, I needed to rip a hole in the Great Divide to make a portal back to the Winter Court. My hands were busy so I couldn't use my knife this time. I would have to use my mind—which I was confident I could do. With this much power, I felt I could do *anything*.

Of course, this was all a lot to concentrate on while I was simultaneously being driven wild with pleasure as I rode my husband for the very first time. But I set my intentions firmly—told my magic, "*This is what you have to do*"—and then allowed the pleasure to take me.

"That's right, little bird," Liath was growling as he pounded up into me. "Take it nice and deep. Take my cock deep in your soft little pussy and come for me!"

"Oh...oh, *Liath!*" I moaned, and suddenly I felt the pleasure peaking inside me. It rushed out of me in a cloud of sparks more numerous than the stars in the sky. My inner walls were quaking, trembling and squeezing Liath's shaft, which seemed to be too much for him.

"Gods, baby—can't hold back," he groaned. "Need to fill you with my cum!"

I felt a hot, wet spurt deep in my pussy, bathing the mouth of my womb and then showers of pleasure sparks were shooting out of Liath too—with every spurt inside me there were more and more of them.

I gathered them all—the pleasure, the pain, and the blood sparks —(there were more pleasure than anything else)—and I threw them outwards. I sent them into the iron all around us and I sent them into Liath himself.

Lastly, I felt for the Great Divide—the magical curtain which separated the Summer Court from the Winter Court and all of the Seelie Fae from the Unseelie Fae and I gripped it with my mind. Imagining a blade with moonstones in the hilt, just like Liath's long dagger or my little knife, I stabbed it into the fabric that divided our two realities.

Power poured out of me as my pleasure exploded outward and I lifted my head and cried my husband's name over and over. The sparks were flying everywhere and dimly I felt the fabric of the Great Divide ripping—tearing as it never had before. This was no small rip, easily mended after a hasty trip from one Realm to another. It felt as though I had grabbed the entire curtain and was tearing it down!

But I didn't have long to think about the strange sensation. The power and the pleasure were too much...too, *too* much. I felt myself losing hold of reality. Grimly, I tried to stay conscious—I needed to keep control of my magic, I told myself. But the combination of overwhelming sensations was simply too much.

With a gasp, I collapsed on Liath's broad chest and knew no more.

32

"Alira? Little bird? Gods, are you all right? Wake up—please, wake up!"

Liath's deep voice and his hand patting my cheek brought me back from the deep darkness I had somehow fallen into.

"Wh-what?" I blinked, opening my eyes at once. "What...what happened?"

"You lost consciousness when you came again. Gods, it scares the fucking hell out of me when you do that!" He stroked my cheek, his bronze eyes worried. "How do you feel? Are you all right?"

"I...think so." I realized I was still laying on his chest and made myself sit up. Liath was no longer inside me but there was blood on both our thighs. My virgin blood.

Blood magic. Pleasure magic...pain magic, whispered a little voice in my head. What was going on?

"What did I do?" I asked, because I knew I had done something, even if it wouldn't come to me right away.

"See for yourself," Liath growled. He nodded around us and I looked and saw...

"By the Shining Throne!" I exclaimed.

For every single iron bar had been turned into a rose vine and all of them were blooming—filling the small cell with their rich, sweet scent. The iron manacle around Liath's ankle was now a circlet of flowers and the chain was nothing but a blooming vine, which he stripped easily off his leg.

But that wasn't the only change.

"Liath!" I exclaimed, reaching up for him, since we were both on our feet by now and straightening our clothes. "Oh, dear..."

"What is it, little bird?" He took my hand and pressed my palm to his lips for a kiss. "Is there a problem? Did you turn my nose to a rose too, while you were at it?"

I had to smile at his remark, but I wasn't so sure if he would be laughing once he found out what I had done.

"Your scar," I murmured, stroking his cheek, which was now perfectly clear. "The one you told me not to heal because you got it trying to save Quill..."

"Yes?" He frowned and put his own hand to his cheek. "Fuck—it's gone!" he exclaimed, looking surprised.

"I'm sorry," I said contritely. "I didn't mean to do it—I just wanted to heal you completely so that was what I told my magic to do."

Liath rumbled with laughter.

"It's all right, little bird—I forgive you. And I hope that wherever he is, Quill forgives me," he added more soberly. "The Gods know I tried to get to him on time."

"I'm sure he would forgive you—especially if he knew what good care you've been taking of his little sister," I said gently. "Come on, Liath—let's go home."

"I'll be more than happy to come home with you, but I don't have my dagger," he growled.

"That's all right, I've got my knife," I said. I frowned. "I *thought* I tore a portal for us, though—back when I was getting rid of the iron and healing you."

Liath looked impressed.

"That's a hell of a lot to do all at the same time while you're coming so hard, little bird."

I blushed.

"Well, I just told my magic to do it and then just kind of…let it go when I, er, came. But I don't know why the portal didn't work. I was sure I felt the Great Divide tearing."

In fact, it had felt like it was *more* that tearing—but I must have been mistaken for there was no dark opening leading into the Winter Court.

"Two out of three isn't bad," Liath said practically. "You said you had your knife, right? Give it to me."

I took the little knife out of my secret pocket and handed it to him. It looked like a toy in his huge hand but he gripped it confidently and reached above his head to open a portal.

But though he spoke words of power and made the ripping motion with the knife, no portal appeared.

"What the fuck?" Liath muttered. He frowned at the knife and tried again—and then again. "What in the hell is happening?" he asked at last.

I shook my head.

"I don't know. Maybe we need to get out of the Palace to make a portal to the Winter Court?"

"It's never worked that way before," Liath rumbled, frowning. "But I guess it's worth a try. Come on, little bird and stay behind me," he added. "If anyone tries to stop us, I'm going to make them fucking sorry."

I saw the gleam in his eyes and knew he was deadly serious. We were both sick of the Summer Court and we just wanted to go home.

"All right," I said. "I'll be right behind you but be careful—there was a guard out there who let me in to see you in the first place."

"He won't bother us if he knows what the fuck is good for him," Liath growled. "Come on."

We went.

33

There was no guard in attendance when we exited the cell, for which I was grateful. He had seemed like a decent male and I didn't like the idea of Liath having to hurt him.

The dungeons looked the same as they had before—well, other than the fact that any iron had been turned to rose vines. There were several cell doors that looked like they had sprouted gardens.

I stayed behind Liath as we mounted the long, winding stairs to the main floor of the Palace. But when we got there, I noticed something strange.

"Liath," I said, tugging his elbow. "The floors!"

"What about them, little bird?" He was still scanning around us, making sure the coast was clear and we weren't about to run into a group of Seelie soldiers.

"The floors," I repeated. "They're *gray*. Gray marble."

"So?" He frowned at me.

"So—they were *white* before. All the floors in the Summer Palace are white marble," I pointed out. "Just as all the flagstones in the Winter Palace are made of black marble. So how are they gray now?"

Liath took a moment to study the floor.

"Fuck if I know," he muttered at last. "Come on—let's just get out of here!"

We went quickly down a long corridor and were making for the courtyard where I had come in—and where we had been married—when I heard a familiar sound—the clip-clopping of hooves.

I frowned. How could it be? That sound didn't belong here—not unless someone had decided to ride their horse down the hallway, which didn't make sense.

"What the fuck is that?" Liath asked, as both of us came to a halt. "It sounds like—"

Just then the owner of the hooves came around the corner and a familiar voice exclaimed,

"Your Majesties!"

"Stableforth?" Liath and I both said at the same time.

"What are you doing here, Master Stableforth?" Liath asked him. "How did you get to the Summer Court?"

"But this *isn't* the Summer Court—it's the Winter Court!" the centaur protested. "Or...it was just a little while ago," he added, looking confused. "But that was before everything got all shaken around."

"Shaken around? What do you mean?" I asked.

The centaur shook his head.

"It is difficult to explain, my Princess," he said. "It was as though a great disturbance ran through all the magic in the Realm and then suddenly the floors of the Palace turned gray—which is quite wrong. For the floors of the Palace have not been gray since the Winter Court and the Summer Court were one and the same. It was when the Great Divide was put into place that they separated and the Winter Court was left with black floors while the Summer Court was left with white ones."

"The Great Divide…" I put a hand to my mouth. "By the Shining Throne…"

"What? What is it, little bird?" Liath demanded.

But I shook my head.

"No—surely not," I muttered to myself. "It can't be true."

"Tell us what you're thinking, Princess, and we will tell you if it might be true or not," Stableforth said.

"Well…" I hesitated. "Remember all those prophesies you two told me about? About how someone was supposed to unite the two Realms—the two Courts?"

"Not just someone—*you*," Stableforth said firmly. He frowned. "But I thought it wouldn't be possible for many years. Not after the Shadow Throne rejected your first attempt to sit upon it."

"Wait a minute—you tried to sit the Shadow Throne?" Liath's eyes went wide and he seized me by the shoulders. "Tell me you didn't!"

"I *had* to," I said, frowning. "I didn't think I had enough power to get you out on my own." I shrugged. "It turns out I did though."

"Alira, that was so fucking dangerous!" He gathered me into his arms, giving me a hug so tight I could barely breathe. "Gods, little bird—I had no idea you'd do something so foolish!"

"I would do *anything* to bring you home again," I whispered. "Now, could you loosen your grip? I can't…breathe!"

He loosened his grip but didn't let go of me entirely. His face was still filled with concern as he kept me in his arms.

"You need not worry, my Prince," Stableforth said to him. "The Shadow Throne simply said, 'Not Yet.'"

"And then it told me I had to prove myself," I told Liath. "Which I guess maybe I did? I'm not sure—but at least you're free of your iron cell and we can go home." I frowned. "*If* we can figure out where home is."

"Home is here," Stableforth asserted. He frowned. "Well, except the floors are wrong. Your Majesty," he added, turning to me. "You were saying something about the Great Divide?"

"Oh, yes." I nodded. "Well, I was trying to rip a portal in it just a while ago while Liath and I were...well, while we were *together*..." I could feel my cheeks getting hot but I made myself go on. "But when I pulled on it, it didn't just feel like I was ripping it. It felt like..." I frowned. "Like I had pulled the whole thing down. Which I know, doesn't make sense."

"Actually, it might. If the prophesies are true..." Stableforth shook his head. "No, we cannot guess. We must verify. We need to go to the Throne room—that is the only place we'll be able to tell for sure."

"Tell what?" Liath growled. "I just want to get out of this fucking place and go home, Stableforth. I've been stuck in an iron cell for over a fucking week."

"How horrid for you, my Prince!" Stableforth shuttered. "But if what I am thinking is correct, our home—the Winter Court—no longer exists. At least, not as we know it."

"What?" Liath and I exclaimed at once.

"What the fuck are you talking about?" Liath growled.

"As I said, we must go to the Throne Room to be sure," Stableforth repeated stubbornly. "If your Majesty will not come with me, I must go alone."

"Of course you're not fucking going alone," Liath exclaimed. "Come on—we'll go together. Alira—"

"I know," I said. "I'll stay behind you—don't worry."

"Good. Come on."

And the three of us made our way down the long hallway, to find out what had become of our home.

34

The Throne Room doors were open but no one was guarding them. We had seen several Seelie couriers and nobles on the way there—but we saw several Unseelie ones as well. They were wandering around as though lost—all of them disorientated by the sudden change that seemed to have happened. They didn't bother us and we didn't bother them—it was as though everyone was walking in a dream.

Liath stepped warily through the golden doors and I saw my cousins at once. The two of them were sitting on the stone steps of the dais where the throne sat. Asfaloth was rubbing his head, where the Sun crown sat askew and both of them were looking confused.

It was the Shining Throne itself which drew my eye, however. It had…changed.

No longer was it a low golden couch—it looked more like the Shadow Throne, I thought. That was, it had grown taller and narrower, though there was still room for two to sit. It wasn't gold anymore either—neither was it black, like the Shadow Throne. It was silver but the cushion on it was blood red, like the one on the Shadow Throne.

There was another similarity as well—I saw a fist-sized diamond embedded on the back of it, at the crest, just where a ruler's head might be if he or she sat directly in the middle of the throne. It was just where the deadly ruby had been in the Shadow Throne, I thought.

"I was right!" Stableforth exclaimed, stamping a hoof and surprising me so much I jumped. I had been studying the new throne, which I felt drawn to for some reason.

"Right about what?" Liath growled. He was keeping a wary eye on Asfaloth and Calista.

"Right in thinking that the two Realms of Fae have merged!" the centaur said. His eyes were wide with excitement and he gestured as he spoke. "Princess Alira has torn down the Great Divide, allowing the Winter Court and the Summer Court to become one again, as they have not been for a thousand years. Look!" He pointed at the throne. "The pictures in all the history books show that it looked just like that. The Throne of Worthiness and Merit, it was called. Or often just the Shining-Shadow."

"I don't understand," I said, frowning. "How can you put the Shining Throne and the Shadow Throne back together?"

"What I really want to know is if this new throne—this Shining-Shadow—denies those who try to take it unlawfully in the same way the Shadow Throne did," Liath rumbled. I was sure that Great Aunt Acosta's gruesome death was uppermost in his mind as he asked.

"As to that, I *do* know that the Shining-Shadow will punish any it deems unworthy if they attempt to sit it and use its power," Stableforth said thoughtfully. "Though I am not certain if the punishment is as cruel and deadly as that of the Shadow Throne. I would think that being merged with the Shining Throne would temper it with mercy."

"What's that you're saying?" Asfaloth snapped, finally taking notice of us. He rose to his feet and sauntered over, rubbing his head and further knocking the Sun Crown askew. "What are you even doing here?" he asked, glaring rudely at Stableforth. "Who let an Unseelie half-breed like you into the Summer Court?"

"No one *let* him in," I snapped. "And Master Stableforth is a *centaur*."

"I know what the fuck he is, but he doesn't belong here—not in *my* kingdom, you little whore," Asfaloth snarled.

"Watch how you speak to my wife!" Liath stepped forward, his eyes blazing as he glowered down at my cousin.

Asfaloth glared back.

"What are *you* doing here?"

"We banished you to the dungeon!" Calista snapped, coming to stand beside her brother.

"I released my husband since you would not," I said, lifting my chin. "I freed him from the iron."

"You? You couldn't free a frog from a pond," Asfaloth sneered.

"I have magic now," I told them. "Enough to tear down the Great Divide—which is why all the floors have changed colors and the throne is not the same."

"*You're* the one who broke the throne?" Asfaloth demanded.

"Broke it? What the fuck do you mean?" Liath said.

"He *means* that we were just sitting in it when it suddenly shoved us out and we wound up on the floor!" Calista complained. She narrowed her eyes at me. "Are you telling us *you* had something to do with that, you little freak?"

"I'll only say it one more time—keep a civil tongue in your mouth when you speak to my wife!" Liath growled at her.

Calista turned pale and took a step behind her brother.

"I don't have to listen to you! I am Queen of the Summer Court and my brother is the King!" she snapped, from the safety of Asfaloth's shadow.

"Not anymore, I think," Stableforth said, frowning. "Not now that the two Realms have merged. The Shining-Shadow Throne will choose its own ruler or rulers," he added, glancing at me and Liath.

Asfaloth saw the look the centaur gave us and his face twisted into an ugly sneer.

"If the Realms have merged as you say, then my sister and I will be *twice* as powerful!" he exclaimed. Taking Calista's hand, he pulled her towards the dais where the new throne sat. "Come—we must take our rightful places!"

"I would not do that if I were you," Stableforth called to them. "While the Shining Throne had no mechanism for rejecting an unworthy candidate, the Shining-Shadow most certainly *does*."

"What is he blathering about?" Calista demanded, as she and Asfaloth climbed the steps to the throne together.

"Nothing that needs to concern us, dear sister," Asfaloth said smugly. "Come—sit with me and we shall rule over both the Seelie and the Unseelie Reams together!"

"I really don't think—" Stableforth began, but it was too late—the two of them were sitting side by side on the new, silver throne with smug looks on their perfect faces.

But a moment later, their faces began to change.

"Brother—I am stuck!" Calista cried.

"So am I—why can't I move?" Asfaloth exclaimed. He seemed to be twitching in his seat, though he could make no large movements, and so was Calista. I remembered how it had felt to be judged by the Shadow Throne—how it seemed as though invisible bonds held me in place. Was that what was happening now?

Suddenly, a brilliant beam of rainbow light shot from the diamond in the back of the new throne. It bifurcated into two beams which passed directly into the back of both Asfaloth and Calista's heads.

I winced and squeezed my eyes nearly shut, waiting for the inevitable carnage. But to my surprise, it didn't come. Instead, a voice began to speak. It sounded a little like the Shadow Throne, but it was higher and more melodious.

"Denied" it declared. *"On the grounds of narcissism, selfishness, cruelty, pettiness, and the dreadful misuse of your magic."*

"What...what are you saying?" Asfaloth croaked. "My sister and I...never misused our magic."

"Never—we never did!" Calista squealed, agreeing with her brother.

"You have both been weighed in the balance and found wanting," the throne informed them. *"Your punishment is the removal of your magic and a sentence of Mortality."*

"What? What are you saying?" Asfaloth gasped. But as he spoke, the beam of light that was coming from the fist-sized diamond at the back of the throne seemed to somehow reverse itself. Instead of pouring into him and Calista, it appeared to be sucking something *out* of them. Don't ask me how I knew that, but it was very clear to me somehow.

Asfaloth and Calista wiggled and squirmed, but they were unable to break free. After a moment, the beam stopped and the diamond went dark. However, the Shining-Shadow Throne wasn't quite done with them. It spoke again.

"You shall both be cast into the Mortal Realm," it informed my cousins. *"You may not enter the Realm of the Fae again until you repent of your evil deeds. But you will never regain your magic."*

Then it was as though invisible hands were lifting Asfaloth and Calista roughly to their feet. The Sun Crown flew off Asfaloth's head and landed with a *clink* at his feet. A portal suddenly appeared in front of them—a shining silver oval. When I looked through it, I saw the Mortal Realm with all the people dressed in their strange blue trousers.

"You cannot do this to us!" Asfaloth howled. "I am the King of the Summer Court!"

"And I am the Queen!" Calista shrieked.

The throne paid no attention. The invisible hands shoved my cousins forward and together they stumbled into the Mortal Realm. As soon as they did, the portal closed with a final sounding *pop!*

I stared at where they had been, scarcely able to believe it. My cousins, who had tormented me all my life—who had killed my brother and most likely my father—were gone forever. Stripped of their magic and banished to the Mortal Realm.

I burst into tears.

35

"Alira? Little bird? What's wrong, baby? What's wrong?" Liath gathered me into his arms at once, stroking my hair gently as I wept.

"I don't...don't know," I finally choked out through sobs. "I hated them—they were so cruel to me! And they killed Quill and probably my father, too. I don't know *why* I'm crying."

"Maybe you're crying with relief, little bird," Liath said gently. "They can never hurt you again. They're gone and they're not coming back."

"Not unless they repent completely—which I rather doubt," Stableforth put in.

"You're probably right." I sniffed and swiped at my eyes with the long sleeves of my gown but I made no move to leave my husband's strong arms. His warm scent comforted me.

"And even if they do come back, the Shining-Shadow Throne has taken their magic from them and probably added it to its own considerable supply," the centaur went on. "What it needs now is a ruler—

or rulers," he added. Bending low, he picked up the Sun Crown which had fallen off of Asfaloth's head.

"Stableforth, what are you suggesting?" Liath growled. "Are you saying that Alira should try to sit the new throne? Because she barely escaped the Shadow Throne—I don't want to risk losing her!"

"I am saying that you *both* should try the throne," Stableforth told us. "After all—there is room for two and you and the Princess are the last ones left of both the Seelie and Unseelie Royal bloodlines."

I had a sudden thought.

"What about Asfaloth and Calista's mother—my Aunt Lyrah?" I asked.

"Ahem..."

I turned and saw to my joy that it was Tansy standing there. My Brownie maid was looking uncomfortable but anxious to see me.

"Oh, Tansy!" I wiggled out of Liath's arms and ran to hug her tight.

"Princess." She hugged me back. "What are you doing here?"

"That's a very long story," I told her. "But I promise I'll tell you once I figure it all out myself."

"That's fine then." She nodded her head. "But I thought I heard you ask about Her Ladyship Lyrah."

"Yes—where is she?" I asked. I had never been fond of my Aunt but it was undeniable that she was next in the line of succession, since she was my mother's sister and she was older than me.

"Ah, I'm sorry to be the bearer of bad news, Princess Alira," Tansy said. "But I'm afraid that Lady Lyrah passed the very night as Good King Euberon." She tapped one cheekbone, right under her eye. "Very suspicious it was, if you take my meaning."

I took it all right. Had Asfaloth and Calista killed their own mother as well as my father and brother? Maybe the Shining-Shadow Throne had let them off too easily! They ought to *die* for their awful crimes.

"Death is easy and far too quick. Their punishment will be long and difficult," a voice said in my head.

I jumped and looked at Liath.

"Did you say something?"

He frowned and shook his head.

"No, why? Did you hear something?"

"I thought..." I looked at the silver throne, glimmering at the top of the dais.

"You thought what, my Princess?" Stableforth said.

"I just..." I shook my head as I walked slowly back to where Liath was standing. "I thought I heard the Throne *talk* to me—in my head. It said that Asfaloth and Calista's punishment was going to be long and difficult. It was the same way the Shadow Throne talked to me and told me to prove myself."

"And you *have* proved yourself," Stableforth said gravely. "You and Prince Liath should come and sit upon the Shining-Shadow Throne. The two of you have earned it."

"I don't know, Stableforth..." Liath looked at the silver throne askance and I couldn't say I blamed him. He'd seen both his Great Aunt and his sister killed by the Shadow Throne and we had all just watched as Asfaloth and Calista were stripped of their magic and kicked out of the Fae Ream, probably forever—since I couldn't see those two *ever* feeling sorry for their crimes.

Was it any wonder that Liath was reluctant to try his own luck? I thought not. In fact, after all I had seen, I was scared too. Except I felt something else as well—for some reason I was *drawn* to the massive silver throne sitting on the dais.

Without knowing what I was doing, I took a step towards it.

Liath seized my hand and squeezed so hard it hurt. I yelped and turned towards him only to see his face filled with anxiety for me.

"Alira, don't do this," he murmured. "We can rule without taking the throne. We're still a Prince and Princess, after all. We don't *have* to be King and Queen."

"I would not be so quick to discard this opportunity to sit the Shining-Shadow Throne, my Prince," Stableforth said, before I could answer. "According to all the texts I have ever read, this chance comes once and never again. And I believe the throne is meant for you—the two of you."

"But…" Liath stopped, a look of indecision on his face.

"Please, Liath…" I tugged on his hand. "For me—let's try it. I think it *wants* us to sit on it."

"You think so, huh?" he growled, but allowed himself to be pulled up the steps of the dais where the throne sat waiting.

But before I could be seated, he took me by the shoulders and peered anxiously down into my eyes.

"What are we going to do if it decides we're un-fucking-worthy and strips us of our magic and ejects us into the Mortal World? What then, little bird?" he demanded.

I looked up at him calmly.

"I don't care."

"What?" Liath demanded. "What are you talking about?"

"What I just said—*I don't care,*" I told him. "As long as the two of us are together, I don't care where we end up or even if we have magic or not." I shrugged. "I've done without it most of my life, anyway. But I *can't* do without *you*. So please, Liath—sit with me. Please?"

He sighed and raked a hand through his long white mane.

"Gods, little bird—why can't I say no to you?"

"Maybe because you don't want to." I gave him a little smile. "Come on, Liath—either we're the rightful rulers of the newly united Realm or we're regulars at Harry's Bar. Either way, as long as we're together, it will be all right."

Liath sighed again and nodded.

"All right. On the count of three then… One…two…three!"

And we sat down on the Shining-Shadow Throne together.

36

I felt the invisible bands again, clamping around my wrists and ankles, holding me in place. So did Liath because he gritted his teeth and I heard him mutter,

"Fuck!"

I tensed all over. Any moment I expected to either be killed by a blast of light or told by the throne that we were unworthy and ejected into the Mortal Realm.

To my surprise, neither of those things happened. Though it seemed to take forever for the throne to make up its mind about us, at last it spoke.

"You have been weighed in the scales and deemed worthy. Welcome, New King and Queen of the Fae Realm. Long may you reign!"

I let out the breath I'd been holding and beside me, I heard Liath doing the same thing. We dared to look at each other and I saw hope and love and joy shining in his bronze eyes.

"Liath?" I whispered.

"Don't you mean *King* Liath?" Stableforth trotted carefully up the steps and held out the Sun Crown to Liath.

But my husband shook his head.

"No—the Sun Crown has always gone with the Shining Throne. And though the throne is no more—or, er, it's *changed*—the crown should still go to the rightful heir. Only Alira should wear it."

"But...but..." I looked up uncertainly. "*You're* the King—don't you want to wear the crown?"

He shook his head.

"Why, because the King always wears the crown? No. You proved in the dungeons that you're the most powerful Fae in the Realm. You fucking tore down the Great Divide! *You* should wear the crown." He motioned to Stableforth. "Put it on her head."

Uncertainly, I leaned forward and allowed the Centaur to crown me. The Sun Crown adjusted itself at once, fitting around my temples like a gleaming band of light. I looked up at Liath.

"Thank you," I whispered.

His eyes were glowing with pride.

"Didn't I tell you on our wedding night that you'd be the most powerful Fae in either Realm? I'm so damn proud of you, little bird."

He cupped my cheek and bent down for a long, sweet kiss, which I was glad to return. When the kiss finally broke, I felt the by-now familiar symptoms. My nipples were tight and my breasts were filled with nectar—not to mention the way my pussy was throbbing. I was flushed and needy all over again—as though I had only just swallowed the lust potion.

Well, Stableforth *had* said there might be delayed effects when we made it, I remembered.

"Er, Liath?" I said, raising my eyebrows at him and shifted on the throne. I wanted my husband badly but I wasn't going to be as crass as my cousins and commit sexual acts in a sacred place.

Thankfully, Liath picked up my thoughts—and my needs.

"Well, little bird," he rumbled. "Now that we're King and Queen of the Realm, what do you say we go see if our Royal bedchamber has changed at all?"

"Oh, do you think we should?" I asked, rather breathlessly.

A lazy smile creased his sensual mouth.

"I would say so. I bet no matter what it looks like, it can always use a few more plants. Maybe some climbing roses might be nice."

I could feel myself blushing but I returned his knowing smile with one of my own. Together, we rose from the Shining-Shadow throne and strolled down the steps of the dais in a leisurely fashion.

"Stableforth, keep an eye on things," Liath threw over his shoulder. "The Queen and I might be gone for a little while."

The centaur bowed low and stamped his hoof.

"You honor me, your Majesty."

I waved at Tansy and she bowed and shot me a secret smile which I returned—she knew I was happy with my husband and I could tell she was pleased for me.

As we left the Throne Room, I saw both Seelie and Unseelie Court members in the halls. They were talking to each other—hesitantly, but talking nonetheless. And when we passed by the open door of the courtyard I looked out and saw something I had never seen before.

"Oh, Liath!" I said, tugging on his hand. "Look—the snow is all melted and little green buds and shoots are coming out everywhere." I pointed at the courtyard. "What do they call that?"

He smiled and put an arm around me.

"I believe, little bird, that is called 'Spring,'" he rumbled. "I think we'll be seeing it regularly from now on. Autumn too."

I realized what he meant—now that the Realms were one, time and the seasons could flow once more. There was no more Summer Court or Winter Court, for we were all one big Court and Realm now and Liath and I were tasked with leading it.

I felt my heart overflow at the thought and I hoped that I was up to the challenge.

I was sure that other problems would arise in the future. After all, Calista and Asfaloth weren't dead—they were still out there in the Mortal Realm and no doubt they still had murder in their dark hearts. Also Lily, the human girl who had seemed so special, was there as well. I wondered if I would ever see her again. Was she really a Changeling with fairy blood flowing in her veins?

But then Liath pulled me into our bedchamber and my worries for the future faded in the urgency of the present. We had some redecorating to do, as my husband had pointed out.

I planned to add some roses to our room before the night was through.

THE END?
HONESTLY, I'M NOT SURE.

This might be a stand alone novel or it might be the start of a new series. I think that Alira and Liath's story is pretty neatly wrapped up, but there might be more to tell. I'm kind of fascinated with Asfaloth and Calista—they're so awful, I think they'd make good villains for another story. And what about Lily? I have a sneaking suspicion she might be a Changeling, left by the fairies, and I'm sure she has no idea that she has magic in her blood. So who knows what might happen?

As always, if you've enjoyed this book, please leave a review or a rating. Good reviews are like gold for an author—especially in this crazy crowded book market. They let other readers know it's okay to take a chance on a new author or series. And if you have friends that read, please spread the word. I would really appreciate it, since good word of mouth is the best way to find new readers.

If you want to contact me, you can find me onFacebook[1], Instagram[2], TikTok[3] or Twitter[4]. (Though honestly, I don't tweet a lot, so FB is probably your best bet.) I love to hear from readers, so if you

THE END?

have any further fantasy ideas you'd like to see written, drop me a line and feed my muse. You never can tell what might come of it!

Hugs and Happy Reading
Evangeline

---

1. https://facebook.com/evangelineandersonauthorpage
2. https://instagram.com/evangeline_anderson_author
3. https://tiktok.com/@evangelineanderson
4. https://twitter.com/EvangelineA

Give a Hot Kindred Warrior to a Friend!

Do you love the Kindred? Do you want to talk about wishing you could go live on the Mother Ship without your friends thinking you're crazy? Well, now it's super easy to get them into the Kindred universe.

Just share this link, **https://bookhip.com/HLNPTP**, with them to download *Claimed*, the first book in my Brides of the Kindred series for FREE.

No strings attached—I don't even want to collect their email for my newsletter. I just want you to be able to share the Kindred world with your besties and have fun doing it.

Hugs and Happy Reading!

Evangeline

SIGN UP FOR MY NEWSLETTER!

Sign up for my newsletter and you'll be the first to know when a new book comes out or I have some cool stuff to give away.

www.evangelineanderson.com/newsletter

Don't worry—I won't share your email with anyone else, I'll never spam you (way too busy writing books) and you can unsubscribe at any time.

As a thank-you gift you'll get a free copy of BONDING WITH THE BEAST delivered to your inbox right away. In the next days I'll also send you free copies of CLAIMED, book 1 in the Brides of Kindred series, and ABDUCTED, the first book in my Alien Mate Index series.

DO YOU LOVE AUDIOBOOKS?

You've read the book, now listen to the audiobook.

My Kindred series is coming to audio one book at a time. Sign up for my audiobook newsletter below.

www.evangelineanderson.com/audio-newsletter

Besides notifications about new audio releases you may also get an email if I'm running a contest with an audio-book prize. Otherwise I will leave you alone. :).

BECOME A VIP!

The Aliens & Alphas Bookstore offers you exclusive (pre-)releases, special box sets, and reissues of old favorites that you can't find anywhere else.

www.shop.evangelineanderson.com

Sign up for the Aliens & Alphas VIP list to never miss a release, get exclusive sneak peeks, discounts and so much more.

www.shop.evangelineanderson.com/vip-list

Also by Evangeline Anderson

Below you'll find a list of available and upcoming titles. But depending on when you read this list, new books will have come out by then that are not listed here. Make sure to check my website, www.evangelineanderson.com, for the latest releases and better yet, sign up for my newsletter (www.evangelineanderson.com/newsletter) to never miss a new book again.

∼

Brides of the Kindred series

(Sci-Fi / Action-Adventure Romance)

CLAIMED*

HUNTED*

SOUGHT*

FOUND*

REVEALED*

PURSUED*

EXILED*

SHADOWED*

CHAINED*

DIVIDED*

DEVOURED*

ENHANCED*

CURSED*

ENSLAVED*

TARGETED*

FORGOTTEN*

SWITCHED*

UNCHARTED*

UNBOUND*

SURRENDERED*

VANISHED*

IMPRISONED*

TWISTED*

DECEIVED*

STOLEN*

COMMITTED*

PUNISHED

PIERCED

TRAPPED

BRIDES OF THE KINDRED VOLUME ONE

Contains *Claimed, Hunted, Sought* and *Found*

BRIDES OF THE KINDRED VOLUME TWO

Contains *Revealed, Pursued* and *Exiled*

BRIDES OF THE KINDRED VOLUME THREE

Contains *Shadowed, Chained* and *Divided*

BRIDES OF THE KINDRED VOLUME FOUR

Contains *Devoured, Enhanced* and *Cursed*

BRIDES OF THE KINDRED VOLUME FIVE

Contains *Enslaved, Targeted* and *Forgotten*

BRIDES OF THE KINDRED VOLUME SIX

Contains *Switched, Uncharted* and *Unbound*

BRIDES OF THE KINDRED VOLUME SEVEN

Contains *Surrendered*, *Vanished*, and *Imprisoned*

BRIDES OF THE KINDRED VOLUME EIGHT

Contains *Twisted*, *Deceived*, and *Stolen*

Also Available in Audio

All Kindred novels are now available in PRINT.

Also, all Kindred novels are on their way to Audio, join my Audiobook Newsletter (www.evangelineanderson.com/audio-newsletter) to be notified when they come out.

~

Kindred Tales

The Kindred Tales are side stories in the Brides of the Kindred series which stand alone outside the main story arc.

These can be read as STAND ALONE novels.

MASTERING THE MISTRESS*

BONDING WITH THE BEAST*

SEEING WITH THE HEART*

FREEING THE PRISONER*

HEALING THE BROKEN* *(a Kindred Christmas novel)*

TAMING THE GIANT*

BRIDGING THE DISTANCE*

LOVING A STRANGER*

FINDING THE JEWEL*

BONDED BY ACCIDENT*

RELEASING THE DRAGON*
SHARING A MATE*
INSTRUCTING THE NOVICE*
AWAKENED BY THE GIANT*
HITTING THE TARGET*
HANDLING THE HYBRID*
TRAPPED IN TIME*
TIME TO HEAL*
PAIRING WITH THE PROTECTOR*
FALLING FOR KINDRED CLAUS*
GUARDING THE GODDESS*
STEALING HER HEART*
TAMING TWO WARRIORS*
THE KINDRED WARRIOR'S CAPTIVE BRIDE*
DARK AND LIGHT*
PROTECTING HIS MISTRESS*
UNLEASHED BY THE DEFENDER*
SUBMITTING TO THE SHADOW*
SECRET SANTA SURPRISE*
THE PRIESTESS AND THE THIEF*
PLAYING THEIR PARTS*
RAISED TO KILL*
HEALING HER PATIENT*
DELIVERED BY THE DEFENDER*
ACCIDENTAL ACQUISITION*
BURNING FOR LOVE*

HIDDEN RAGE*

ENTICED BY THE SATYR*

SAVED BY THE BEAST*

LOVED BY THE LION*

BONDED BY TWO*

TAMING THE TIGER*

DRAGON IN THE DARK*

GUARDED BY THE HYBRID*

QUEEN OF THEIR COLONY

FINDING HIS GODDESS

FAKING IT WITH THE HYBRID

TIED TO THE WULVEN

SHARED BY THE MONSTRUM

KINDRED TALES VOLUME 1

Contains *Mastering the Mistress, Bonding with the Beast* and *Seeing with the Heart*

KINDRED TALES VOLUME 2

Contains *Freeing the Prisoner, Healing the Broken* and *Taming the Giant*

KINDRED TALES VOLUME 3

Contains *Bridging the Distance, Loving a Stranger* and *Finding the Jewel*

KINDRED TALES VOLUME 4

Contains *Bonded by Accident, Releasing the Dragon,* and *Sharing a Mate*

KINDRED TALES VOLUME 5

Contains *Instructing the Novice, Awakened by the Giant,* and *Hitting the Target*

KINDRED TALES VOLUME 6

Contains *Handling the Hybrid, Trapped in Time,* and *Time to Heal*

KINDRED TALES VOLUME 7

Contains *Pairing with the Protector, Falling for Kindred Claus,* and *Guarding the Goddess*

*Also Available in Audio

~

Kindle Birthright series

(Sci-Fi / Action-Adventure Romance)

The Children of the Kindred series

UNBONDABLE*

~

Born to Darkness series

(Paranormal / Action-Adventure Romance)

CRIMSON DEBT*

SCARLET HEAT*

RUBY SHADOWS*

CARDINAL SINS (coming soon)

DESSERT* (short novella following *Scarlet Heat*)

BORN TO DARKNESS BOX SET

Contains *Crimson Debt, Scarlet Heat,* and *Ruby Shadows* all in one volume

*Also Available in Audio

~

Alien Mate Index series

(Sci-Fi / Action-Adventure Romance)

ABDUCTED*

PROTECTED*

DESCENDED*

SEVERED*

THE OVERLORD'S PET

ALIEN MATE INDEX VOLUME ONE

Contains *Abducted*, *Protected*, *Descended* and *Severed* all in one volume

*Also Available in Audio

All Alien Mate novels are now available in PRINT.

∾

The Cougarville series

(Paranormal / Action-Adventure Romance)

(Older Woman / Younger Man

BUCK NAKED*

COUGAR BAIT*

STONE COLD FOX*

BIG, BAD WOLF

*Also Available in Audio

∾

The CyBRG Files with Mina Carter

(Sci-Fi / Action-Adventure Romance)

UNIT 77: BROKEN*

UNIT 78: RESCUED*

*Also Available in Audio

~

The Institute series

(Daddy-Dom / Age Play Romance)

THE INSTITUTE: DADDY ISSUES*

THE INSTITUTE: MISHKA'S SPANKING

*Also Available in Audio

~

The Swann Sister Chronicles

(Contemporary Fairy / Funny / Fantasy Romance)

WISHFUL THINKING*

BE CAREFUL WHAT YOU WISH FOR*

*Also Available in Audio

~

Nocturne Academy

(Young Adult Paranormal/Action-Adventure/Romance)

LOCK AND KEY*

FANG AND CLAW*

STONE AND SECRET*

*Also Available in Audio

~

Detectives Valenti and O'Brian

(1980s M/M Romance)

THE ASSIGNMENT

I'LL BE HOT FOR CHRISTMAS

FIREWORKS

THE ASSIGNMENT: HEART AND SOUL

∽

Forbidden Omegaverse Series

(Paranormal Romance

Step-Brother / Foster Brother Romance)

HIS OMEGA'S KEEPER*

THE BRAND THAT BINDS

Also Available in Audio

∽

Compendiums and Box Sets

ALIEN MATE INDEX VOLUME ONE

Contains *Abducted, Protected, Descended* and *Severed* all in one volume

BORN TO DARKNESS BOX SET

Contains *Crimson Debt, Scarlet Heat,* and *Ruby Shadows* all in one volume

BRIDES OF THE KINDRED VOLUME ONE

Contains *Claimed, Hunted, Sought* and *Found*

BRIDES OF THE KINDRED VOLUME TWO

Contains *Revealed, Pursued* and *Exiled*

BRIDES OF THE KINDRED VOLUME THREE

Contains *Shadowed*, *Chained* and *Divided*

BRIDES OF THE KINDRED VOLUME FOUR

Contains *Devoured*, *Enhanced* and *Cursed*

BRIDES OF THE KINDRED VOLUME FIVE

Contains *Enslaved*, *Targeted* and *Forgotten*

BRIDES OF THE KINDRED VOLUME SIX

Contains *Switched*, *Uncharted* and *Unbound*

BRIDES OF THE KINDRED VOLUME SEVEN

Contains *Surrendered*, *Vanished*, and *Imprisoned*

BRIDES OF THE KINDRED VOLUME EIGHT

Contains *Twisted*, *Deceived*, and *Stolen*

HAVE YOURSELF A SEXY LITTLE CHRISTMAS

Contains *Kidnapped for Christmas*, *Cougar Christmas* and *Season's Spankings*

KINDRED TALES VOLUME 1

Contains *Mastering the Mistress*, *Bonding with the Beast* and *Seeing with the Heart*

KINDRED TALES VOLUME 2

Contains *Freeing the Prisoner*, *Healing the Broken* and *Taming the Giant*

KINDRED TALES VOLUME 3

Contains *Bridging the Distance*, *Loving a Stranger* and *Finding the Jewel*

KINDRED TALES VOLUME 4

Contains *Bonded by Accident*, *Releasing the Dragon*, and *Sharing a Mate*

KINDRED TALES VOLUME 5

Contains *Instructing the Novice*, *Awakened by the Giant*, and *Hitting the Target*

KINDRED TALES VOLUME 6

Contains *Handling the Hybrid, Trapped in Time,* and *Time to Heal*

KINDRED TALES VOLUME 7

Contains *Pairing with the Protector, Falling for Kindred Claus,* and *Guarding the Goddess*

NAUGHTY TALES: THE COLLECTION— Volume One

Contains *Putting on a Show, Willing Submission, The Institute: Daddy Issues, The Institute: Mishka's Spanking, Confessions of a Lingerie Model, Sin Eater, Speeding Ticket, Stress Relief* and *When Mr. Black Comes Home.*

ONE HOT HALLOWEEN

Contains *Red and the Wolf, Gypsy Moon* and *Taming the Beast*

ONE HOT HALLOWEEN Vol.2

Contains *The Covenant, Secret Thirst,* and *Kristen's Addiction* + BONUS: *Madeline's Mates*

∽

Stand Alone Titles

(Sci-Fi OR Paranormal Action-Adventure Romance)

ANYONE U WANT

BEST KEPT SECRETS (Step-Brother romance)

BLIND DATE WITH A VAMPIRE

BLOOD KISS

BROKEN BOUNDARIES (M/M romance)

CEREMONY OF THREE

COMPANION 3000[*]

DEAL WITH THE DEVIL[*]

DEFILED

EYES LIKE A WOLF (Foster Brother romance)

FOREVER BROKEN (M/M romance)

GYPSY MOON

HIS OMEGA'S KEEPER* (Step-Brother romance)

HUNGER MOON RISING

MADELINE'S MATES

MARKED

OUTCAST

PLANET X*

PLEASURE PLANET

PLEDGE SLAVE (M/M romance)

PUNISHING TABITHA

PURITY*

RED AND THE WOLF*

SECRET THIRST

SEX WITH STRANGERS

SHADOW DREAMS

SLAVE BOY (M/M romance)

STRESS RELIEF

SWEET DREAMS

TAMING THE BEAST

TANDEM UNIT

THE BARGAIN*

THE COVENANT*

THE LAST BITE (M/M romance)

THE LAST MAN ON EARTH*

THE LOST BOOKS (M/M romance)

THE PLEASURE PALACE

THE SACRIFICE*

THE THRONE OF SHADOWS

'TIL KINGDOM COME (M/M romance)

*Also Available in Audio

∼

Stand Alone Titles

(Contemporay Romance)

A SPANKING FOR VALENTINE (BDSM)

BOUND AND DETERMINED, anthology with Lena Matthews, includes *The Punishment of Nicollett*

COUGAR CHRISTMAS (Older Woman / Younger Man)

DANGEROUS CRAVINGS* (BDSM)

DIRTY GIRL

FULL EXPOSURE (with Lena Matthews)

KIDNAPPED FOR CHRISTMAS (BDSM)

MASKS* (BDSM)

MORE THAN FRIENDS (BDSM)

PICTURE PERFECT* (Step-Brother romance)

STR8TE BOYS (M/M romance)

'TIL KINGDOM COME (M/M romance)

*Also Available in Audio

∼

Naughty Tales

(Short Reads to Get You Hot and Bothered)

CONFESSIONS OF A LINGERIE MODEL

PUTTING ON A SHOW (Step-Brother romance)

SIN EATER

SPEEDING TICKET

THE SWITCH (An erotic interlude with the characters of DANGEROUS CRAVINGS)

SEASON'S SPANKINGS

WHEN MR. BLACK COMES HOME

WILLING SUBMISSION

NAUGHTY TALES: THE COLLECTION— Volume One

Contains *Putting on a Show*, *Willing Submission*, *The Institute: Daddy Issues*, *The Institute: Mishka's Spanking*, *Confessions of a Lingerie Model*, *Sin Eater*, *Speeding Ticket*, *Stress Relief* and *When Mr. Black Comes Home*.

∽

YA Novels

THE ACADEMY[*]

[*]*Also Available in Audio*

About the Author

Evangeline Anderson is the *New York Times* and *USA Today* bestselling author of the *Brides of the Kindred*, *Alien Mate Index*, *Cougarville*, and *Born to Darkness* series. She lives in Florida with a husband, a son, and the voices in her head. (Mostly characters who won't shut up.) She has been writing sci-fi and paranormal romance for years and she welcomes reader comments and suggestions at **www.evangelineanderson.com**.

Or, to be the first to find out about new books, join her newsletter:
www.evangelineanderson.com/newsletter

For updates on Young Adult releases only sign up here instead:
www.evangelineanderson.com/young-adult-newsletter

She's also got a mailing list for updates on audio books:
www.evangelineanderson.com/audio-newsletter

- facebook.com/evangelineandersonauthorpage
- twitter.com/EvangelineA
- instagram.com/evangeline_anderson_author
- pinterest.com/vangiekitty
- goodreads.com/evangelineanderson
- bookbub.com/authors/evangeline-anderson
- tiktok.com/@evangelineanderson

Made in United States
Orlando, FL
23 June 2023